Rituals

Books by Mary Anna Evans

Rituals

A Faye Longchamp Mystery

Mary Anna Evans

Poisoned Pen Press

Copyright © 2014 by Mary Anna Evans

First Edition 2014

10 9 8 7 6 5 4 3 2 1

Library of Congress Catalog Card Number: 2013933208

ISBN: 9781464201677   Hardcover
      9781464201691   Trade Paperback

Poisoned Pen Press
6962 E. First Ave., Ste. 103
Scottsdale, AZ 85251
www.poisonedpenpress.com
info@poisonedpenpress.com

Printed in the United States of America

For little Adam

Acknowledgments

I'd like to thank all the people who helped make *Rituals* happen. Michael Garmon, Erin Garmon, Rachel Broughten, Amanda Evans, Robert Connolly, and Matt Hinnant read it in manuscript and provided their customary astute observations. Suzanne Quin, Nadia Lombardero, and Kelly Bergdoll were my analytical chemistry and pharmacology consultants. They are responsible for the passages in which I got things right, and they are innocent of wrongdoing on any occasions when I did not.

As always, I am grateful for the team of people who help me get my work out into the world where readers can find it. My agent, Anne Hawkins, has been looking out for my interests for a very long time now. Because I can trust that my editor, Barbara Peters, and the rest of the hardworking Poisoned Pen Press staff will ensure that my work is at its best when it reaches the public, I am free to focus on creating an interesting world for Faye. Special thanks go out to Suzan Baroni at Poisoned Pen Press. She was doubly efficient in getting *Plunder* to the Florida Book Awards judges, making me doubly fortunate in winning two bronze medals for Faye's seventh adventure. Much gratitude goes out to my publicist, Maryglenn McCombs, for letting people know that Faye and her stories are out there, ready for the reading.

And, of course, I am grateful for you, my readers.

Working notes for Pulling the Wool Over Our Eyes:
An Unauthorized History of Spiritualism
in Rosebower, New York

by Antonia Caruso

They call me Toni the Astonisher.

I never hit the big-time but, for a while, I was the most successful small-time magician in America. I played Vegas, but never The Strip. I played the biggest halls in the most mid-sized Midwestern towns. I opened for aging rock bands whose careers had descended to the point where headlining a state fair was a good gig.

I have an abiding passion for overblown, overwrought 1970s progressive rock, and my agent knew that I would take as much as twenty percent off my minimum fee if one of my idols was on the playbill. It was always my position that since one does not get rich as America's biggest small-time magician, one might as well have some fun. There is not much money to be made on the state fair circuit, but the rock gods and I sometimes amused ourselves by demanding that our M&Ms all be green. Or, later, blue.

I am a pragmatic person, and I have a pragmatic person's need for security. Therefore, I never tried to earn my living solely as a magician. I taught high school physics,

*which means that my booking agent was adept at maxi-
mizing all those school holidays. During the school year,
I was only available to be a magician between three p.m.
on Friday and eight a.m. on Monday, so he knew every
venue within a semi-reasonable drive of my Syracuse,
New York, home. The man made a nice living taking care
of people like me, and he earned it.*

*In the summers and over the Christmas break? I would
go anywhere he sent me. One fine New Year's Eve in the
early 1990s, I played a third-rate casino so close to the Las
Vegas strip that I could see its neon glow from my hotel
room window. This was the apex of my showbiz career.*

*Now? After thirty-five years of faithful service, I
recently snatched a generous retirement from the hot
little hands of the New York state pension system. Let's
do the math, folks. (You can see that I will always be a
teacher at my core.) I finished college at twenty-one,
thanks to the December birthday that graced me with
many years spent as the youngest, smallest, and smartest
kid in the class. (Social ostracism is such a special way
to spend one's childhood.) That makes me fifty-six now.*

*I may eventually go back to doing magic at two-bit
venues, but for now I think I've earned some time to
enjoy my pension and the booking fees that I squirreled
away for decades. I'm probably out of my mind, but
I'm spending my first months of decadent leisure here
in Rosebower, writing this book about the weirdest little
town in New York.*

*Why Rosebower, the touristy epicenter of the faux-
metaphysical world? Because there is something about
a physics education that makes a person a crusader for
truth. There are people in this world who take the money
of lonely people, desperate for an answer to the riddle
of life. These lost souls flock to fakers—psychics, faith
healers, astral projectionists, mediums, palm readers,
and all their cheating kin—and they come away with*

no answer to life's riddle and without a chunk of their hard-earned money.

This is the kind of thievery that will make a mild-mannered physicist mad. More to the point, it will make a flamboyant and strong-minded physicist/magician ready to go to war. Hence, this book.

Here in Rosebower, where psychics have fleeced the faithful since the days of Houdini and before, I am on a mission. I am writing a history of this little town and its roots in the early days of table-floating, Ouija-board-loving, nineteenth-century Spiritualism. Between the covers of this book, I will reveal all the ways that Rosebower's fakers have convinced their victims to believe in magic. I doubt it will stop the tourists from coming here looking for ghosts but, if I don't speak up, vulnerable people will keep paying to see expensive wonders that can be explained away by simple physics and sleight-of-hand. The fakers will have won.

I would never expose the illusions of an honest magician running an honest show. But "psychics" who fleece people by faking the ghosts of their loved ones? They are profiting from real pain. There is no code of honor to protect con artists.

When the spiritual mediums of Rosebower see my book, they will wonder why, with all their extrasensory powers, they failed to foresee the coming apocalypse.

Chapter One

The dark liquid rose in the syringe. Experience had proven that injecting more than its full volume of three cubic centimeters was impractical under these circumstances. This was unfortunate. A higher dose would have served the purpose better.

Caution for patient safety would ordinarily require certain safeguards. Injecting an air bubble into someone's bloodstream could have...consequences...but only if the person wielding the hypodermic needle cared whether the patient lived or died.

The hollow needle encountered only slight resistance before emptying itself into the softness beneath. That was its job, puncturing. The job of the syringe was to deliver its secret cargo.

Soon, it would do so again.

◇◇◇

"Hey, Mom?"

Ignoring her impulse to do a victory dance every time Amande called her "Mom," Faye Longchamp-Mantooth turned to her adopted daughter and said, "Hmm?"

"I'm *exhausted*. How come I'm so tired when all I did was sit at a desk all day? And it's only Monday."

"Well, we did work six days straight last week."

Faye stopped walking. She grabbed her hips with both hands to stabilize them while she twisted her torso hard to the left, then to the right. It was the only way she knew to stretch out the little twinge in her lower back that had lingered since she was pregnant with Michael. He was two now, so she guessed the little twinge would be with her for life.

Amande grabbed Faye's shoulder and rubbed her fist hard over those sore back muscles. It helped.

"You're good at that. I'm glad I keep you around." Faye didn't tell her that her neck hurt, too. Otherwise, she'd soon be enjoying a full body massage on a public sidewalk in downtown Rosebower, New York. "My grandmother was a secretary, so all her workdays were like the one we just spent. Every night, she walked in the house and announced, 'I feel like I've been beat with a stick.'"

"That's exactly what it feels like!" Amande gave Faye's lower back a final punch. It felt good, but it almost sent Faye face down onto the concrete. Her new daughter was a big, beautiful six-footer and Faye was a flyweight. "It feels like I've been beat with a stick."

Since Faye and Amande had a contract to do cultural resources management for a tiny historical museum that had been run by amateurs for a century, they'd spent the past week hunched over piles of unfiled papers and undocumented artifacts. There was no end in sight.

"Welcome to the world of the small-time consulting archaeologist, Sweetheart. Sometimes you get to work outside, digging up cool stuff. And sometimes you spend your time indoors with old, dusty junk. It all pays the bills."

"Then we'll sit inside and try not to sniff too much dust. It could be a lot worse," said Amande, who had lived most of her life in a world where the bills didn't always get paid.

Faye wasn't sure there was another teenager alive who brought such a sunny disposition to a summer spent working for her mom. Her own disposition swung daily from sunny to dark. She loved having this chance to be alone with her daughter, but she missed her husband Joe and their son Michael so fiercely that it kept her awake some nights. Knowing her as he did, there had been nights when she'd picked up the phone and it had rung in her hand before she'd even poked in Joe's number.

"Oh, my dears, I am so glad I caught you before you went back to that dingy hotel room."

Myrna Armistead's voice approached from behind, but slowly. She didn't look as perky as usual but, at Myrna's age, she was lucky to be traipsing the sidewalks at any speed. Faye had enjoyed watching this aging spinster's awkward overtures for Amande's friendship. Even past eighty, the mothering instinct is powerful, and Myrna wasn't choosy. She'd barely known forty-two-year-old Faye a week, but she had already tried to mother her a few times. Faye had let her.

"Tilda and I would be honored if you'd both join us for dinner. And a spiritual reading afterward, if you like. My sister tells me the spirits are thick around the two of you. Good spirits," she added quickly, when she saw the alarm on Amande's face. "They are the essences of all the people who have loved you. Tilda has the sense that you both have many loved ones who have passed over, maybe more than you have left on this side of The Great Divide. Let her help them talk to you."

Welcome to Rosebower, Faye thought, *where hearing voices did not result in heavy medication and a quick trip to an in-patient unit.*

The little Victorian-era town was located smack-dab in the western New York cradle of Spiritualism, and it was full of people who were certain they could talk to the dead. To Tilda's credit, she had a reputation for utter honesty. Her psychic readings involved no faked floating tables or Ouija boards or mysterious rappings. Tilda's reputation seemed to be based on the fact that people believed her when she talked.

Why shouldn't they? Faye liked the woman's lined, honest face. If Tilda were to give Faye a message from her great-great-grandmother Cally Stanton, she would be inclined to believe it, despite the fact that Cally had been dead for nearly eighty years. Faye was a scientist, which made it hard for her to believe that Tilda could really talk to the dead, but she had seen some strange things in her life. She didn't want to have dinner with Tilda and Myrna and her long-dead kin tonight, but not because she didn't believe. Faye was just dog-tired.

Amande, too, had been dog-tired thirty seconds before, but there was now a light in her eyes that told Faye it would be hours before she saw her bed. "A spiritual reading? That's like a séance, right?"

◇◇◇

Because Faye had lacked the energy to say no to a teenager who smelled adventure, she was now using a fresh-baked honey-yeast roll to wipe up the puddled juices of Tilda's succulent pot roast. Scooping up the last bites of home-grown beets and tiny green peas, Faye leaned back in her chair, unable to do anything but sigh. She was way past dog-tired now, but she was happy. Myrna, whose pudgy face was as warm and sweet as the honeyed bread, sat beside Faye, rubbing her own round belly.

"I'm sure that meal was tastier than you would have gotten at the old Vandorn house where you're staying. Remember it, Tilda? Father's friend lived there and we used to visit when we were little. Somebody has made it into a hotel. Imagine! So many people who touched our lives have passed over. But when you cook, Sister," she said, "I feel like Mama has come back from the dead."

"She has, Dear. She's here now."

Tilda's barely perceptible smile lit a face so narrow that it called to mind Faye's mother's old-timey criticism of the looks of a too-thin woman: "That woman's hatchet-faced."

There was a softness to Tilda's eyes and her short white hair that made up for her straight-edged face and whip-thin body. Faye respected her, for sure, and she thought she'd like her as much as she liked Myrna, once she got to know her better.

Tilda glanced around the room as if there were friendly spirits sitting in each of the eight extra chairs surrounding her awesomely handcarved mahogany table. If Faye hadn't been so contented and full of beef, she might have rolled her eyes at the idea of spirits who had nothing better to do than watch them eat. This would have made her hate herself for disrespecting the cook who made such an incomparable pot roast.

"Would anybody like some candy?" Myrna handed a box of goodies around the table. "I can't cook like Tilda, but I do like sweets. Here, take all you like."

Faye thanked her and took a big bite of the dark gelatinous thing in her hand. It was licorice. Acrid, medicinal, noxious licorice. Somehow, the fact that the licorice had been dipped in chocolate made the flavor even worse. Could one actually spoil chocolate?

Faye locked eyes with Amande. Her daughter hated licorice, too, but the girl wouldn't want to hurt Myrna's feelings any more than Faye did. Faye responded to her daughter's "Help me!" look by surreptitiously depositing the uneaten portion of her candy into a paper napkin and slipping it into her purse. There was no help for the stomach-turning mess in her mouth, so she swallowed it whole. Amande followed suit.

To distract the ladies from Amande's waste disposal, Faye asked Tilda about the house's antiques. It was stuffed to over-flowing with Victorian rosewood settees and hand-crocheted antimacassars, and its walls were hung with portraits of genera-tions of Armistead ancestors.

As Tilda started to answer her, Myrna interrupted. Faye had the feeling that this happened a lot. "There are things in this house that belong in the museum where you're working. See—"

"Not while there's an Armistead alive," Tilda said flatly, proving that she'd learned long ago the secret to being heard in Myrna's presence: Speak loudly and feel free to interrupt. "Some of these pieces are original to the house, and it was built in 1836. They belong in the family."

As twilight deepened outside the dining room's many-paned windows, Tilda moved around quietly, lighting a collection of spherical antique oil lamps made of all colors of glass. Faye judged that they were all antique and hand-blown. Their flick-ering light suited the old house better than the electric bulbs in the converted gasoliers overhead would have.

"See those chairs? There have been more than family butts in them." Myrna was whispering in Amande's ear, but the whispers of a woman with failing ears don't conceal much. "See that swivel-seat chair made out of cast iron? The one in front of the secretary desk?"

Amande did, and so did everybody else in the room.

"Elizabeth Cady Stanton sat there, not long after she delivered the keynote address at the convention for women's rights in Seneca Falls, not far from here. Lucretia Mott visited on another occasion. She sat there." Myrna pointed at a slender chair with original horsehair upholstery.

Myrna had a rapt audience. Amande scampered across the room and fondled the horsehair. "Mom's taking me to Seneca Falls while we're here. She says we have to make a pilgrimage to the place where women put their demands in writing, just like men. After that, I'm supposed to vote every chance I get, as soon as I turn eighteen. Next year." The last two words were delivered with an emphasis that said, "And I can't wait."

"I like your mom," Tilda declared. "It's good to exercise our rights. And to remember the people who got them for us. Shall we spend some time with their spirits? Would you still like a reading?"

Faye had to admit she was curious. Also, Myrna was muttering, "Where's that candy? The little girl and her mother may want some more," and Faye was in all-out licorice-avoidance mode. She would have endured the most cringe-inducing fake séance if doing so would have spared her a second dose of that candy.

"Yes," Faye said. "We'd be honored if you would do a reading for us, Tilda."

Myrna led them into a room tucked under the stairs while Tilda took a private moment to prepare. Since the builders of grand old homes like this one took their stately staircases seriously, there was room for a large square area under the second floor landing, with a narrow, sloping extension beneath the steps. The underside of each stair could be seen, rising stepwise one-by-one. For an odd moment, Faye felt trapped inside the surrealist art of M.C. Escher with its impossible staircases to nowhere.

A chair, old and threadbare, was tucked under the stairs. Behind it was a dark area where an adult would have to stoop and then crawl. The square portion of the room was almost completely occupied by a round table. In its center sat a crystal ball, not large but utterly clear, glinting atop an ornate stand of tarnished goldtone metal.

Myrna busied herself with a pile of folding chairs stacked in the depths of the slant-roofed space. She could barely carry a single chair, so Faye and Amande rushed to help. Once they were in place, Myrna beckoned them to sit, chatting like someone who hadn't met anybody new in years.

"We do this every night, just the two of us. It's important to tend our bonds with family members who have passed over. Mother. Father. Tilda's dear husband Edwin. Not to mention all the family we never met on this plane at all. There are so few of us Armisteads left. Just the two of us, really, and Tilda's daughter Dara. We have some distant cousins-by-marriage in Texas—not Armisteads, but kin on Mother's side—but we could never ever go there."

"Why not?" Faye asked. "Airplanes fly back and forth to Texas every day." Tilda and Myrna seemed to have financial means to make the trip, if they really wanted to go.

"I could go, but I don't like to leave Tilda. She doesn't travel."

Myrna leaned so close that Faye could see her reflection curving across the surface of the crystal ball. For some reason, the distorted image made Faye look up at the uncomfortably low ceiling. It seemed to be sinking even lower.

"Tilda *really* doesn't travel," Myrna went on. "She hasn't left Rosebower since Edwin died. I think there are even parts of Rosebower that are too far from home for Tilda."

Rosebower was a postage stamp-sized town built long before cars came along. It was physically impossible for two places in Rosebower to be far apart. Tilda must have a fearsome case of agoraphobia.

Myrna was still spilling her sister's secrets. "The only reason we have a car is to make it easier for Tilda to get her groceries home."

"The grocery store's only three blocks away," Amande pointed out. "She could walk over there every morning and bring home enough food for the day. Cars are expensive. There's no reason to pay for insurance on a car you don't need."

Amande knew what she was talking about. She had lived most of her childhood with no motorized transportation but a boat. She was such a reasonable girl, but the human mind is not always reasonable.

"Tilda thought it over and decided that it scared her to think about driving a car to the store once a week, but it scared her more to think about being forced to walk there every single day. Even after all these years, that car wouldn't have two thousand miles on it, except for the fact that Tilda let her daughter Dara drive it a little when she was a teenager. I think maybe the odometer reads about five thousand now."

"The chrome-yellow '72 Monte Carlo out front? It's only got five thousand original miles?" Life without a car had given Amande a motorhead's heart.

"I bet Tilda would let you take it for a spin. She leaves the keys in it."

Amande looked ready to forget the séance, so she could sprint outside and ogle the classic car before dark. She kept her seat, though, because Tilda had entered the room. An air of stillness entered with her, but Myrna couldn't let the stillness settle without sneaking in a little more family lore.

"Tilda was…is…the most gifted medium of her age, just as Father was before her. She still takes the occasional client, but she must really like you girls. She doesn't do this for everybody."

Windowless and claustrophobic, the tiny room made Faye feel disoriented even before Tilda, still silent, lit a low oil lamp and placed its open flame under the crystal ball. Faye grew curious, despite her skeptical nature. The ball, lit from below in a way she'd never seen in the movies, glowed as if from within. At the risk of ruining the spiritual tone of the evening, Faye indulged her own geekiness, leaning in to examine it. When she tried to look through the crystal, images of objects on the other side were inverted.

Faye understood the optical principle at work, but its effect was hypnotic and unfamiliar. When Tilda daubed her palms with scented oil and rubbed them over the crystal ball, warmed by flame, Faye thought, *This is interesting. None of the fortune-telling gypsies on* Scooby-Doo *ever did that.*

The fragrance of the heated oil was already rising on warm air when Tilda lit a misshapen lump of incense. She placed it on a ceramic tray that was painted with intricate geometric patterns, holding the burning incense in front of her face with both hands and drawing the aroma in through her nose. Combined with the perfumed oil, it filled the room with a fragrance that was too strong to be pleasant, yet wasn't oppressive.

"Join hands, please," Tilda said in a commanding voice. After three deep breaths, she said, "You were not always mother and daughter."

Faye's mental fraud detector gave Tilda demerits. She was certain that Myrna knew she'd adopted Amande recently, and it was obvious that Tilda immediately heard any gossipy tidbit that Myrna discovered.

"Amande's mother sent you to her. She knew that you would care for her child."

The curmudgeon inside Faye who bore a grudge against Justine snorted. If Amande's mother had cared so much, why had she walked away from a toddler and never come home?

Then Faye's internal fact checker reminded her that Justine had died only a few days before Faye got the job that took her to Amande. From a Spiritualist's perspective, death had finally given Justine the chance to manipulate events in her daughter's favor. She'd never had a shot when she was alive. Justine's life had been hard from birth to grave.

Faye's fraud detector, always fair, removed one demerit from Tilda's side of the ledger.

Tilda closed her eyes and took more easy breaths. "The two of you are bound by more than blood. Your ancestors are happy that you found one another. Your mothers have found each other on the other side, and they share your joy."

Well, that was an unprovable bit of feel-good psychobabble. Faye was about to issue another skeptic's demerit when she noticed an uncountable number of orbs of light flickering in her peripheral vision. The orbs were all colors, pure and beautiful, without a tone of gray in any of them. The lights danced. They passed through objects and human bodies. They couldn't possibly be real, not in a physical sense, but she couldn't stop looking. Could anyone else see them?

Myrna and Tilda were looking only at the uplit crystal ball, but Amande's eyes were darting from the lamplight to the room's dark corners and back again. The girl wasn't just confused by what she saw. She was scared.

Faye gave her daughter's hand a squeeze. Then Tilda mentioned their mothers again and a shadow fell over Amande's face. "Your mothers are both here. They have not let go of the pain of living. You should know that your fathers left of their own accord. Your mothers did not send them away."

Tilda had nailed that one, almost. Faye wasn't sure she'd say her father had left of his own accord. More accurately, the draft board had said, "Here's a one-way ticket to Vietnam," but Tilda was right that her mother hadn't sent him away.

About Amande's father, she knew exactly nothing, because Justine had never told anyone who he was. Justine had abandoned her daughter after a year of single motherhood and she was dead now, so there was no one to ask. There never would be. If Faye were to ever muster a grain of sympathy for Justine, it would be because she could imagine being a lonely teenaged mother with no help in sight.

The glowing lights flitted around the room, reflecting in Tilda's glasses and throwing a luminous glow on Amande's dark curls and her honeyed-brown skin. Faye wanted to ask Tilda whether the orbs were supposed to be the souls of dead people, but she was too relaxed to make the effort.

Even if they were ghosts, they didn't scare her. They hovered near the four women at the table, flirting with the idea of touching them, then passing right through their bodies, always at the heart.

Faye tried to decide what color her mother's orb would be, or her grandmother's, or her father's. What about Douglass? What color was his soul? He had been a rock for her, almost a father, someone she could trust to protect her when needed and to let her go when the time came. Two glowing orbs, cool green and deep blue, flew in tandem past her cheek, and she heard Douglass' voice rumble in her ear. "He sent me, you know. Your father sent me to take care of you. And now we're both here."

Then she felt herself enfolded by woman-arms, more than two of them. Her mother and her grandmother were there, both of them, but they were silent, because there was nothing about their love for her that she didn't already know. She wanted to stay there with them, but she looked at her daughter's face and saw a tear streaking down her cheek. The tear brought Faye back to herself.

"Stop it." She half-rose from her chair, breaking her hold on Myrna's hand. "Stop it now. We've had enough."

Stupid. How stupid could she be?

Amande didn't have Faye's memories of being a cherished child. There had been only one stable force in Amande's life before Faye and Joe came along, and that was Miranda, the step-grandmother who had raised her. Hardly a year had passed since Amande learned that her runaway mother had succumbed to cancer. Days after receiving that tragic news, Miranda had been knifed to death.

It was too soon for Amande to be reminded of the grandmother she'd lost and the birth mother she'd never known. It was simply too soon.

There were arms around Amande now, real ones, as Myrna reached out for the shaken girl, who was already cradled against Faye's chest.

"I'm so sorry, Dear," Myrna said. "Sometimes this happens. Sometimes, it hurts to touch the ones we miss so terribly. The pain will get better. You'll be glad later, I promise. These experiences freshen the bonds and bring our loved ones closer. But there's no need to rush things, now that you know what's possible. Any time you feel like talking to your mother…or anybody, really…you come back here. Tilda can help you."

Tilda hadn't spoken yet. While they talked, she'd turned her drooping eyes from one face to another, as if hoping someone would tell her what had happened. If Tilda were to ask Faye that question out loud, the only answer she'd get would be, "Hell if I know."

Faye wished for Joe. Every last gram of her was a scientist, so she would never stop looking for rational explanations for even the strangest events. Her husband, on the other hand, was sometimes content to let things be. He also possessed a comfort with the power of nature that was rooted in his Creek heritage, and his intuition was so keen that he often seemed psychic when he'd done nothing more than pay attention.

Faye's own Creek heritage was so diluted by her African and European blood that she rarely felt a connection like Joe's to her American roots. Joe was her spiritual touchstone.

Joe would be able to help her make sense of this experience under Tilda's staircase. If Faye had thought Tilda possessed psy-chokinetic powers that could magically snatch Joe out of Florida and bring him to her, Faye would have willingly braved another session around the crystal ball. But not with Amande. Faye knew she was wishing for the impossible, but she didn't ever want to see another tear on that vulnerable cheek.

Chapter Two

Myrna was gathering up the leftover licorice. From the number of pieces left in the box, Faye judged that even Tilda didn't like it. Faye became very intent on looking for her purse, hoping to avoid eye contact that would prompt Myrna to offer her another piece.

Tilda stepped between Faye and Myrna's foul candy. Faye was deeply relieved.

There was an ache in the psychic's sharp blue eyes. "I grieve for your daughter's pain. If I'd known about her mother, I wouldn't have...well, it's done now. And to have lost her grandmother as she did. It was brave of her to open up to you and your husband. Very brave."

She looked over her shoulder to be sure that Amande was out of earshot in the next room, trying out Lucretia Mott's chair.

"One day, when she's ready—and she *will* be ready—tell her that her mother came back to her when she died. Everywhere Amande goes, Justine is there. She couldn't help her daughter when she was alive, but now she can."

Faye wanted to be jealous. *She* was Amande's mother now. Justine had forfeited everything when she abandoned her. In her heart, though, she knew it would be better for Amande to feel that her mother cared, even if she had no evidence beyond the word of an octogenarian who believed she could talk to dead people. One day, she would tell her daughter what Tilda had said.

Myrna walked them to their car, hugged them both and made sure they used their seat belts, then she walked toward the sidewalk, purse in hand. Where in Rosebower could she be going? Everything was closed.

Faye didn't like to see Myrna walking alone after dark. Her vision was bad. She was gasping before she even reached the sidewalk. Her short-term memory left a little to be desired. Sometimes old people wandered away and never came home, and moments like this made those tragedies possible.

Faye rolled down her window. "Do you need a ride some-where, Myrna? I thought I heard you say you were ready for bed. Let me take you back inside."

"I *am* going to bed. My bed's over there." Myrna gestured at another early nineteenth-century house across the street, just as impressive as Tilda's. In fact, it was utterly identical to Tilda's. "Our great-great-great-grandfather built hers, and his brother built mine."

Amande poked her head out her own window. "Do you have a secret room under the staircase, too?"

Myrna hobbled over to be close to the girl. "I *do*. The ban-isters on my staircase are carved of the same pretty wood, and my brass chandeliers are just as brassy. And I have the other half of the family antiques. You have to see it all. Say you'll come soon."

Amande promised she would, and Faye pulled the car out of Tilda's driveway. If she'd been dog-tired before, she didn't know how to describe her status now. Double-dog-tired?

The rental car gave a polite ding. She might be double-dog-tired, but now she was going to have to find the energy to feed this car another tank of expensive gasoline.

◇◇◇

Amande hadn't spoken while Faye pumped the gas. She hadn't said more than two words since they drove away from Myrna. At first, Faye's judgment had been that it was better to leave her alone. Right now, she was doubting her judgment.

Finally, Amande spoke. "I saw her. I saw my mother. In the crystal ball. I wanted to bust it open and let her out, because she looked like she was trapped in there."

"I saw some weird things, too. How do you feel about seeing Justine?"

"I feel like I've had some questions answered, except I don't know what my questions were."

Faye pulled out of the gas station parking lot and turned onto the narrow northbound lane of Rosebower's Main Street. She felt like she needed to maneuver carefully through this conversation.

"How did you know which one was your mother?"

Amande cocked her head in Faye's direction. "She looked like the picture I have of her, the one taken when she was my age. Only she was older. But why do you say 'which one'?" My mother was the only…um…visitor I saw. Who did you see?"

"I didn't see anybody I recognized. I didn't see anything but lights…pretty lights. It was better than it sounds. My mother was there, and my grandmother. I think my father was there, right next to Douglass."

"You've told me about Douglass. He came to you tonight? And you were with your father for the first time that you remember? How cool is that?"

It was cooler than Faye could say, so she didn't try. Instead, she said, "Look. The diner's still open. I happen to know that they have banana splits on the menu."

Faye could hardly have been less hungry, not after their gargantuan meal. Also, the flavor of licorice might have put her off her food forever. Amande, however, was a growing girl and she'd had no dessert that she was willing to swallow.

Within minutes, they were giving their order to Julie, the waitress.

"I'm not very hungry," Faye said. "Let's split one."

"That's not why they call it a banana split."

"You're going to make your old mother eat a whole banana split? She'll get fat."

"You're not old and you have the metabolism of a hummingbird."

Faye rewarded Amande for this flattery with an entire banana split, and she couldn't say she didn't intend to eat every bite of her own.

She eyeballed the solemn girl. "You okay?"

"I'm always okay."

"Yes, you are."

"We're alike that way." Amande used her napkin to wipe a stray spot of chocolate syrup off the table. "Other people have had it easy so far, but maybe they'll fall apart when things get bad. You and me…we already know what bad is, and we already know we can take it."

Faye wished she'd been the one offering the sage observations.

Six scoops of ice cream, two bananas, and four bad jokes later, Faye saw her daughter smile. Her work was done.

◇◇◇

Joe woke suddenly. It took a moment to come back from the dream and realize where he was.

Faye wasn't here, and that felt wrong. He was still wearing his clothes, and he felt like he'd just finished running a marathon.

Oh, yeah. He'd spent the day chasing a two-year-old. He *had* just finished running a marathon.

This revelation also explained why there was a crushing weight on his chest. He'd gone to sleep with Michael on top of him. This beat the other explanation for that crushing weight, a heart attack at the tender age of thirty-three.

The dream was still reaching for him. Now he remembered what woke him.

Douglass. Douglass didn't come to him often. When he did, it meant Faye needed him. He put the boy to bed and picked up the phone.

Later tonight, he'd build a fire in the fireplace. Just a little one, because it was hot outside. When Joe needed to commune with the dead, he didn't need much. A little fire and a fistful of sacred herbs would do.

◇◇◇

A stop for gas. A stop for ice cream. Faye's bed didn't feel any closer than it had when she'd left Rosebower.

She had picked their quaint bed and breakfast at the Vandorn House on the outskirts of Buffalo for several reasons—some of them rational. It was cheaper than Rosebower's one and only inn, and it was even quainter. Faye had totally gotten into planning this mother-daughter trip, so when it came to choosing their lodgings, she'd decided that girlier was better. Their bedroom dripped with chintz, ruffles, and lace, and the thought of its million-thread-count sheets made Faye long for bed even more.

From the comfort of home, she'd figured that this place's quaintness-to-cheapness ratio made the thirty-minute drive to Rosebower worthwhile. It was also situated near several major highways, and Faye had big plans for this trip that didn't all involve work. The time they lost on their daily drives to Rosebower would be made up on the weekends, when she planned to take Amande on road trips in all directions to look at potential colleges. And, of course, there would be the very girly pilgrimage to Seneca Falls.

When it came to travel-planning, Faye was uncommonly astute at figuring out how to get the most experiences per dollar spent, but she sometimes neglected the limits of human endurance. She was exhausted, and Amande looked like she could hardly hold her head up. A more convenient hotel might have been better, but they were locked into their current lodgings because she had negotiated a sweet monthly rate with the proprietor.

Her phone rang and she saw that it was Joe. Damn her self-imposed rule against talking on the phone while driving. She believed in the good example mode of parenting, and she didn't ever want Amande careening down a highway with her phone in her hand and her mind a million miles away. Faye needed to talk to Joe even more than usual, and that was saying a lot, but rules were rules. She let the call go to voice mail.

Amande rested her head against the passenger window. Faye hoped she was sleeping instead of seeing her dead mother trapped in a crystal ball.

◇◇◇

The parking situation at the B&B was almost as quaint as its pocket-sized bathroom. Faye took care navigating the narrow lane to the parking lot around back. This was good, because as she rounded the sharp curve, she found her way blocked by a lemon-colored car. It had missed the final curve, then skidded sideways into three parked cars. The echoes of those three impacts, one after the other, must have been still reverberating when Faye and Amande arrived, because a crowd was only beginning to gather.

Faye stopped her car and got out. Various versions of "What in the hell just happened?" were sounding as she pushed her way through the onlookers. She didn't know what in the hell had just happened, but she certainly knew who owned that car. How many mint-condition yellow 1972 Monte Carlos could there be in western New York? Amande was at her side, helping her get through the crowd. Faye wished she'd had the presence of mind to tell the girl to wait in the car.

Faye recognized the B&B's owner, who was leaning in the window of the old Monte Carlo, and she recognized the woman at the wheel. It was Tilda, who looked uninjured but terribly upset.

"Faye!" Tilda called out. Her voice was weak and harsh.

The hotel manager stepped aside. Faye had to lean in close to hear Tilda. A strong odor of smoke from her clothes and hair and breath signaled that all was not as it seemed. Tilda's wheezing breaths scared Faye enough to make her ask if someone had called 911.

Three people pointed to the cell phones at their ears. Help was on its way. Faye sensed that this was a good thing.

Tilda had a lot to say, most of it unintelligible. Exhausted from trying to speak, she sank back, her head lolling against the driver's seat. Faye hadn't understood much, but she'd caught a few troubling phrases. "Needed to be safe," and "No place to go," and "Nobody to trust." Still more troubling was this: "Myrna... she wouldn't wake up. I couldn't...Faye, can you help?"

By the time the paramedics arrived, Tilda was dead, and Faye was left to wonder why a dying agoraphobic who had traveled only a couple thousand miles since 1972 had driven thirty miles to ask a relative stranger for help.

Chapter Three

Faye didn't know Myrna's number or address, but she was able to give the emergency personnel enough information to find her. Then she told the story of Tilda's final moments several times to various people in uniform. Finally, they left her alone while they examined the Monte Carlo and its owner, trying to figure out what had really happened to Tilda.

Faye had long since sent Amande to their room, over the girl's protests that she wanted to be where the action was. One of the prerogatives of parenthood was the occasional ability to separate a child from "the action."

Now, she was alone in the parking lot, still too upset to let her daughter see her in this condition. She wanted…needed… more information, and she had a bad feeling about the sooty stench of Tilda's dying breaths. There was only one Rosebower number stored in Faye's phone, so she called her client, Samuel Langley. He'd lived his entire life in Rosebower, so he surely knew the Armistead sisters. And, though she'd told the emergency personnel how important it was to find Myrna, maybe somebody local could find her quicker than an outsider wearing a uniform.

When Samuel answered his phone, Faye could tell by the background noise that he wasn't sitting alone at home. She heard voices and a siren and the engines of more vehicles than had any right to be on the streets of nighttime Rosebower. "What's happening down there?"

His response was overpowered by the sound of another siren.

Faye tried again. "Samuel, something's happened to Tilda Armistead. I need to find Myrna."

"We've got Myrna. Nobody could get her to answer the phone—the woman's half-deaf—so several of us who live nearby took matters in hand. We got a ladder, broke a window, and went looking for her. She's fine. But did you say you knew where Tilda was?"

Faye could hear shouting and the quiet wailing of a woman's voice. She thought of her call to 911. It would have triggered a call to Tilda's next of kin, but Samuel was telling her that Myrna wasn't home. Faye doubted she had a cell phone, so she couldn't know of Tilda's death. The noise of sirens said that *something* was going on in Rosebower, in terms of emergency personnel, but Faye could feel a disconnect between what she knew and what Samuel knew. Even twenty-first-century technology can't be instantaneous. Tonight, that time lag had a deadly feel.

All Faye could do was tell Samuel what she knew and ask him to do the same. "Tilda was here at my hotel with me until… Samuel, she's dead. Some kind of respiratory failure, I think. It sounds like something just as awful may be happening where you are."

Now Samuel was yelling outright. "I'll call you back, Faye. I can see firefighters suiting up to look for Tilda right now. I can't let them go into a burning house for no reason."

The line went dead.

◇◇◇

Faye watched the last marked car pull out of the parking lot. Tilda's body had long since been taken away, but Faye could already guess the result of the autopsy. The cause of death would be smoke inhalation.

Samuel had called back, telling her that he'd been enjoying a nightcap on his back porch swing when he smelled smoke. The ground floor of Tilda's house had been fully engulfed in flames when firefighters arrived, but they'd been able to quench the fire quickly. The exterior walls were still standing and the roof was mostly intact, but the flames had been impressive while they raged. Samuel was the youngest resident on Walnut Street. His neighbors had reached the time in life when they sometimes had trouble waiting for sundown to make it socially acceptable to go to bed. If he'd gone to bed even minutes sooner, the whole house would have been gone.

And if Tilda had escaped even minutes sooner, she might not be dead. No matter how hard she tried, Faye couldn't shake the image of a woman in her eighties, alone, fighting her way out of a burning house.

Faye thanked Samuel for the information, saying, "It's late and neither Amande nor I have had any sleep. We may not be at work on time tomorrow."

"Take your time. Tell me, Faye. Were you and Tilda close? I don't mean to be rude, but she wasn't big on leaving town. What on earth possessed her to drive to your hotel?"

"I knew her well enough to know that she was agoraphobic, but I don't have any idea why she came to me for help tonight. It sounds like she lived on a street full of people she knew much better, and they would have wanted to help."

"Of course, we would've wanted to help, but I wouldn't say any of us knew her any better than you did. Tilda has always kept to herself. I'm sorry you're mixed up in this terrible thing. Take your time getting to work tomorrow."

Faye thanked him and broke the connection. Then she dialed home. Joe answered so quickly that she imagined he'd been sleeping with the phone on his pillow.

Working notes for Pulling the Wool Over Our Eyes:
An Unauthorized History of Spiritualism
in Rosebower, New York

by Antonia Caruso

*There are people who think I'm a killjoy. Those people
enjoy the antics of fakers. They say that séances and communing with the dead are, at worst, harmless entertainment. We pay our entertainers. Why shouldn't we pay
our fortune-tellers, even if they are fake?*

*I think my idol, The Amazing Randi, explains it best
when he says there is a real danger in believing people
who claim that they can solve real problems—like, for
instance, the energy crisis and environmental decline—
by magic. For example, there are common illusions that
give the impression of matter or energy springing into
being from nothingness. One of them looks like a large
faucet, suspended in mid-air, from which water flows
unceasingly. To the eye, water is being made out of nothing and the illusionist responsible deserves a citation from
the Reality Police for violating the Law of Conservation
of Matter.*

*If the illusionist is enterprising, a small water wheel
is part of the apparatus, merrily turning in the flow of
water being created from nothing. Thus, the illusionist*

is creating energy from nothing, and the Reality Police exact very high fines from people who build perpetual motion machines violating the Law of Conservation of Energy. Even worse, the size of the punishment dealt to those who defy entropy, the relentless killjoy that will eventually make motionless atomic particles of us all, is incalculable.

So is it true? Can anyone build a faucet that creates water and energy? Of course not.

In reality, there is a pipe running upward, hidden by the gushing flow of water that supports the faucet. Attached to this pipe is a submersible pump that recirculates the water so that it can flow out again. This pump requires electricity to do its magical work.

Voila! Energy has not been created out of nothing, and neither has matter. Entropy continues uninterrupted in its quest to destroy us. The Reality Police can rest easy.

There is no harm in an illusion that makes the audience laugh and say, "Wow! How did he do that?" But if that audience is in the thrall of someone unethical enough to suggest that such violations of the laws of physics are possible for people with magical powers, then a very real harm has been done. People who believe in impossible things may lack an understanding of the need to conserve water and energy, and they may feel no pressing need to vote for people who are willing to deal with reality.

A society consisting of people who believe in the irrational could find itself in a condition where only magic can save them. I don't know about you, but that's not a society I ever want to see. Consider this book my contribution to the rationality of the world.

You can thank me any time.

Chapter Four

The ruins of the old house reminded Faye of Tilda's body. The northern summer sky hanging over it was a bright clear blue, without the brassy gleam of the morning sky over her Florida home. Traveling down the rural highway to Rosebower would have been a pleasant morning's drive if Faye hadn't known she'd find this at the other end.

The building looked almost as it had looked the night before, weathered siding freshly painted in period-appropriate shades of ochre, but the scalding smoke that had ruined Tilda's lungs showed itself in dark smudges over the house's broken windows. A house was a much smaller loss than a human being, but Faye grieved for it anyway. She'd come to believe that old homes grew souls over time, soaking up the happiness and sorrow of their human occupants. Her own home, Joyeuse, had stood as long as this one, plus a little more, and it had its own spiritual presence. Tilda's house was dead now.

Faye saw Samuel standing on the sidewalk nearby, so she parked and joined him there, with Amande at her side. He was watching a woman move around within the yellow crime-scene tape bounding Tilda's property. She carried a camera in one hand and a cell phone in the other.

"The fire inspector," Samuel said, nodding in the woman's direction. "She's already said that she wants to talk to you. You two—and Myrna and poor Tilda, of course—were the last people in the house before it burned."

"How's Myrna?"

Samuel spoke like a man who was choosing his words carefully. "About as well as you could expect. She was up all night, pacing and crying. There were a few of us with her, including her niece Dara. I thought we should call a doctor, but the others vetoed that idea. They called Sister Mama and she sent something over that knocked Myrna right out. She's still sleeping."

Faye looked at Amande. "Have we met Sister Mama?" The girl shook her head.

Samuel smiled for the first time that day, maybe for the first time since Faye had laid eyes on him. He was a very serious soul. Fortunately for Faye, he was serious about local history, and he had enough spare cash to front the money for the historical society to hire her. For this reason, Faye was inclined to overlook his funereal air.

Samuel's skin was unlined and his dark hair was only lightly streaked with gray. Now that she'd seen him smile, she realized that he might actually be in his early forties, about her age. One would think that independent wealth would have made him a bit more lighthearted.

The fire investigator approached, slipping her phone in a pocket to free her right hand. Extending it first to Amande, then to Faye, she said, "I'm Avery Stein. You must be the Longchamp-Mantooth women. Can I ask you a few questions?"

Faye nodded, and Avery beckoned for them to step over the crime-scene tape. As they walked toward the house, she asked, "Do you remember anything unusual about your time in Ms. Armistead's house last night?"

"You mean, other than the séance and the crystal ball and the fact that Tilda was pretty sure she could talk to dead people?" Amande asked.

Avery nodded, giving a quick, shy smile. Faye thought she might be almost as close to Amande's age as her own. She was also almost as sturdily built as Faye's strapping daughter.

The open flame under Tilda's crystal ball had haunted Faye all night, so she described it to the investigator.

"Do either of you remember where she stored the lamp oil? Was it in the room with you?"

Faye and Amande both shook their heads.

Faye said, "I don't know about the fuel. The lamp under the crystal ball was full when Myrna lit it, but there must have been a good-sized jug of fuel somewhere nearby. Tilda seemed to like oil lamps better than electricity. I remember that she had a collection of glass lamps on the dining room sideboard and on a secretary in the living room. She lit them all as the sun went down."

A crease appeared between the eyebrows of Avery's freckled forehead. "I...didn't know about the other lamps."

From this Faye inferred that Avery had found the séance room and the oil lamp inside it. She also inferred that Avery was trying not to let them know what she'd already discovered about the fire, and that she was probably a very poor poker player.

A stepladder stood beside the house's dining room window. Avery indicated that she'd like Faye to climb up and look in the house. "I've been inside, and all indications are that it's structurally stable, but I won't put you at risk till I know more. Just tell me if you can see anything through the window that might be important. Does anything look different than it did when you left last night?"

Faye climbed the ladder. Unbidden, Amande clambered up behind her. Even standing a step below Faye, Amande could easily see over her mother's shoulder. Faye saw Avery consider stopping the girl. Instead, the arson investigator grabbed the ladder's legs to steady it under the weight of two people.

Faye could see through the dining room and into the parlor, so the entire space where she and Amande had visited with the Armistead sisters the night before was visible—except, obviously, for the interior of the séance room. She was surprised to see how much of the area was still recognizable. The firefighters had quenched the fire before the roof caved in, so the rooms were littered with bits of fallen ceiling material, but they weren't filled with debris. The wood floor was scorched, but still in place.

Faye could see footprints in the ashes where Avery, and probably some technicians, had already done a full inspection. She could also see scars on the floors and walls that she knew from experience were sites where samples for the arson lab were collected.

"Lucretia Mott's chair." Amande sighed. Its horsehair upholstery had surely burned like an acetylene torch.

Near the window, Faye could see that Tilda's china cabinet, though scorched, had withstood the fire, except for its shattered glass doors and the broken glassware inside. The sideboard across the room was in similar condition. But where were the oil lamps that had been scattered across its surface? A house fire wasn't hot enough to melt and consume glass, was it? She should at least be able to see shards of the lamps' colorful glass in the ash atop the sideboard.

And what about the lamps that had been on the secretary in the parlor? Faye squinted in that direction, but her eyes weren't up to the task.

"Amande, do you see the lamps that were on Tilda's secretary desk?"

The answer was quick and sure. "Nope. Nothing but a little bit of ash." Amande started to scan the room again, but her seventeen-year-old eyes whipped back to the secretary. "Where's the chair? Remember? That's where Elizabeth Cady Stanton's chair was. In front of the secretary."

Faye did remember, and she remembered the chair's impressive cast-iron construction. The chair's upholstery was probably history, but there was no way that a house fire would have burned its base beyond recognition. Where was it now?

They both saw it at the same time, while Avery stood below, fidgeting as if she wished the ladder would hold all three of them.

Amande pointed so enthusiastically that Avery had trouble keeping the ladder upright. Faye held on as best she could. "The Stanton chair—why is it in the hallway? It wasn't there last night. It couldn't have been. It's sitting smack in front of the entrance to the séance room, blocking the door."

Amande was right. Faye could see the ornate cast-iron base of the old swivel chair lying on its side on the hallway floor. The upholstery had burned away, but the metal portions were almost unscathed.

"That's one reason why I asked you two to take a look," Avery says. "I couldn't think of any reason for that chair to be there. Nor the broken glass."

That's when Faye noticed the colorful bits of glass sprinkled through the ashes on the hallway floor, like ceramic tiles in one of Pompeii's ancient mosaics. They were all within a few feet of the séance room's door. Its stout oak had been almost totally consumed, and chunks of its half-burned wood lay on the floor.

Coal-dark marks as tall as Amande marked the walls around the door. Faye was chilled to think of Tilda trapped in the house, struggling to escape, banging fruitlessly on Myrna's door, driving to Buffalo while choking to death from smoke inhalation. Then she saw something that drove those disturbing images from her brain.

A stout length of wood dangled from a nail that had been hammered into the jamb of the door to the secret room. A second nail still protruded from the other end of the piece of wood. It had been hammered into something, probably the door, but that portion of the door had been consumed by the fire. Had the wood been nailed there the night before?

Of course not. It would have held the door closed. They could never have gotten into the room with that board barring the entrance. Faye pointed it out to Avery, whose very poor poker face told her that she'd already seen it.

Faye did her best to think of a good reason, or even a neutral reason, for that board and its nails to be nailed to a door that was used daily. "Someone might have nailed that board there to try to keep another person out of the room, but it would only work for the amount of time it took the other person to find a crowbar and pry the board off."

Avery nodded, but she kept her mouth shut. She was poker player enough to wait and see what Faye did with the exact same data she'd already had time to consider.

"Here's another scenario." Faye was moving inexorably toward a mental picture she didn't want to conjure. "It's more disturbing, but it's also more logical, since it can't be undone with a simple crowbar. Maybe somebody was in the room, and another person was trying to keep that person in there by using the board as a makeshift lock. The trapped person would be on the wrong side of the door to pry it off. This would be a big problem if the house were on fire."

The scorched iron chair lay on the hallway floor in silent support of this scenario.

It takes time to nail a door closed. A heavy iron chair, jammed under the doorknob, can deliver that time. If someone's intent had been to trap a person—Tilda, perhaps—behind that door, then the chair, the strip of wood, a hammer, and two nails would have done the trick.

If the person willing to do such a thing was also an arsonist, then Tilda's cherished oil lamps would have been the last necessary element. The colorful pattern of broken glass on the hallway floor took a different shape when Faye considered that a burning oil lamp crafted of handblown glass would have been the Victorian equivalent of a Molotov cocktail. Shattering Tilda's burning lamps against a door crafted of long-seasoned hardwood would have been a particularly artful way to commit murder.

Amande was just as capable of following the broken glass clues as Faye. "Do you think somebody did that to…to Tilda?"

Faye had the urge to fling her hands over her daughter's eyes.

"Do you think Tilda was murdered?" Faye asked Avery. "Do you?"

"You're looking at the same evidence I did. Yes, I think that evidence points to murder. What do you think?"

Faye didn't want to say.

"I can track your whereabouts last night," Avery said. "Mostly with witnesses, plus there was a lucky shot of you on a convenience store video. I know you didn't do this to Mrs. Armistead, but it is very important that you don't tell anybody else about what you see here. I needed you to confirm the condition of the door and the location of the chair when you left last night. You've done that. And you've also done me a favor by telling me what all that broken glass was about. From this point on, all I need is your silence."

Since Faye was too horrified to speak, that might not be a problem.

"You understand why, don't you?"

Faye found her voice. "Of course I do. If anybody other than you, me, or Amande suggests that this was anything other than an ordinary house fire, then that person has been talking to the killer. Or, more likely, that person *is* the killer."

Chapter Five

Faye was a borderline workaholic. She knew how to have fun, and she did so on a regular basis, but few things could prompt her to avoid a job that needed doing. Time at the museum, breathing dust instead of soot, seemed to hard-driving Faye to be exactly what her daughter needed to recover from the shock of Tilda's death.

They passed through the museum's main display area, heading for the inadequate workroom that served as both repository and laboratory but addressed neither function well. Faye was in a hurry, but Amande lingered among the displays, asking, "When are we going to tackle *this* stuff?"

Faye's very intellectual response was, "Um…hmmm…maybe we'll work on it next week."

This job had come with an unexpected problem. The museum's existing displays weren't remotely interesting to the casual tourists the museum was intended to reach. Well, Faye was making a presumption when she inferred that the historical society was reaching out to tourists. It wasn't like anyone had ever written a mission statement or done any planning whatsoever. It looked to Faye like someone, or a lot of someones, had piled a bunch of old stuff in this old building and called it a museum.

Faye was such a history nerd that it was a marvel she hadn't married a ninety-year-old. If it was old, she was interested. Rosebower was a fascinating little town, with a history full of Spiritualists, religious reformers, and radical feminists. Faye had expected to find a cute little museum, amateurish but fun, needing only her professionalism and organizational flair. Nope.

She looked around the cluttered room, hoping to find a historical jewel that she had somehow missed. Nope again.

Faye had done this kind of work before, helping her friend Douglass bring his Museum of American Slavery up to professional standards. Douglass' generous salary had made a hungry grad student's life easier, and she'd taken extra coursework because she'd wanted to do a good job of curating and archiving his collection. Douglass and his museum had given Faye plenty of experience in sifting through random stuff acquired by an enthusiastic rich person, but his happy morass of uncatalogued minutiae couldn't hold a candle to Samuel Langley's museum—if one could even call it a museum.

Some of the storage cases looked like they'd been purchased and filled when the town was founded in 1830, then ignored. Samuel was apparently not a devotee of Spiritualism, because there wasn't a single crystal ball or photograph of Houdini in sight. There was nothing related to women's rights, either, so he was missing his chance to engage feminists after their pilgrimage to Seneca Falls. In fact, Samuel didn't seem interested in the nineteenth century at all, so he'd also overlooked things like the abolition movement and the religious ferment of the Second Great Awakening.

Instead, his displays were full of flint tools and dusty potsherds, poorly labeled and ill-displayed. This focus explained why he'd advertised for an archaeologist rather than an archivist. Faye had spent her first hour on the job perusing the pottery fragments that Samuel had chosen for display, hoping for something that fulfilled the mission she'd like this facility to have—connecting the fascinating history of Rosebower with its community and the world at large. She'd sent photos of the lithics to Joe, hoping for the same thing. Nope, yet again.

Early on, Faye had approached Samuel with the idea of starting a dialogue with the Seneca Indians and other nearby Nations that could be used to enhance the museum's interpretation of their ancestors' culture. No luck. The man wasn't interested.

It had been a long time since museums existed only to display pretty and interesting stuff, transmitting information rather than inviting people to participate. Worse, even if this room had been the King Tut's tomb of amateur museums, Samuel and his predecessors hadn't kept records of who the donors were, or when the donations occurred, or…well…anything. And, just to put a cherry on top of all those problematic displays, they were also boring.

"What about that stuff?" Amande pointed to a huge display in the center of the room. "It *looks* cool."

This "cool" stuff was the crux of Faye's problem. She already hated the sight of the Rosebower spear, the runestone, and the Langley Object.

According to the museum's exhibit labels, the Rosebower Sspear and the runestone proved that Scandinavian explorers didn't just beat Columbus to the New World by centuries. They'd beaten him by millennia, founding all the great precolumbian American civilizations. The Scandinavian explorers were the real Aztecs, Incas, Mississippians, Clovis people, and Mayans, all rolled into one. This was crazy talk, and incredibly disrespectful to the people who actually did live in precolumbian America, but Samuel believed it.

In an even more outrageous bit of crazy talk, Samuel believed that his Langley Object proved that aliens from other planets had visited thousands of years before the Scandinavians brought civilization to the New World.

Aliens. Faye was still trying to wrap her mind around Samuel's crackpot notions about Europeans and Toltecs. What on earth was she going to do with this so-called alien artifact?

Helpful displays explained this imaginary alien invasion, suggesting that more traditional scholarship was a conspiracy of Biblical proportions. In one last slap at orthodoxy, the exhibit labels claimed that the writers of the Holy Bible itself, not to mention the writers of every holy text on Earth, had started this conspiracy.

Charming.

Faye had already launched two abortive strikes on these theories. Samuel had responded pleasantly, but his mind was made up. Aliens had come to Rosebower. And also ancient Scandinavians. He believed in these things very deeply.

Faye felt that her best hope to salvage this job was to find something in the museum's archives that was much better than its supposed treasures. And by "better," she meant "real." This real treasure could take center-stage in the museum, and Samuel's conspiracy artifacts could go into deep storage. She would have had more faith in this plan if one of the conspiracy artifacts had not been named for her client's family.

For the time being, the best Faye could do was to walk past the spear, the runestone, and the object, pretending they weren't there. She flapped a casual hand in their direction, saying, "We'll deal with those later," and led her daughter into the museum's workroom.

◇◇◇

Toni the Astonisher had developed a comfortable routine. She worked on her book for a couple of hours in the early morning, then she took a long walk, ending at the diner for a late breakfast. After eating, she asked Julie to make her a to-go cup of coffee that would see her through a few more hours at the keyboard. Those quiet hours of focused concentration couldn't have been more different from teaching school.

Running a physics classroom had been an awful lot like performing a magic act. She'd had to be absolutely prepared, and her lesson plans couldn't just lay out the laws of physics. They had to entertain, too, because she was working with the fragmented attention spans of modern adolescents. Improvisation had been a way of life. Adolescents don't follow scripts and they don't behave as expected.

Toni had been in Rosebower for weeks, much longer than the usual one-day-and-gone tourist, so she knew that people were watching her and wondering. Going against her naturally gregarious nature, she'd kept to herself. She'd mentioned to Samuel that she was writing a book, therefore the whole town knew it, but she didn't want anybody to probe any deeper than that. As far as the citizens of Rosebower were concerned, she was the quiet lady who seemed to have come here to get away from…something.

She'd watched and listened enough to know who was who. She'd even come to like some of the targets of her espionage. Myrna Armistead, for instance. As Toni made her morning trek for breakfast and a coffee to-go cup, she could see Ms. Armistead walking down the sidewalk across the street, leaning heavily on the arm of an elder from her church.

Aging was a funny thing. Ms. Armistead seemed to have good days when she hurried around town, visiting friends and shopping, but there were bad days, too. More of them, recently. This looked like a bad one, and it made Toni sad. It was impossible to breathe the same air as Myrna Armistead without liking her. She moved through the world in a hazy loving glow.

Toni had seen much less of Myrna's sister Tilda, who wasn't the glowing type. Tilda kept to herself, seeing her clients at home and avoiding the social scene at the diner and the town's lakeside park. Toni knew her only by her reputation, which was sterling. Tilda Armistead was a town councilor, and she was reputedly the most gifted spiritual practitioner in living memory. Myrna might have been universally loved, but Tilda was universally admired. Toni harbored a trace of hero worship when it came to Tilda Armistead, which was silly for a woman who didn't believe anybody had the powers Tilda claimed to have. Nevertheless, it was true.

A bright yellow flash of crime-scene tape at the corner of Walnut and Main caught her eye. The tape surrounded Tilda Armistead's grand old house, moving gently in the early summer breeze. Only when she saw the sooty stains rising above all the house's windows did she realize that she'd been smelling smoke for at least a block.

The odor was spreading over Rosebower, announcing the wreck of Tilda's house, but Toni had paid no attention. She looked over her shoulder and saw Myrna's back as she walked away. The woman held the church elder's elbow with one hand and used the other to dab her eyes with a handkerchief. Oh, this didn't look good.

Someone at the diner would be able to tell her what had happened. The smell of smoke and the sight of Myrna's delicate hankie warned Toni to brace herself.

◇◇◇

The museum's workroom was full of sagging cardboard boxes holding things that bereaved adult children couldn't part with, but didn't want to store. Everyone thinks their family heirlooms belong in a museum. In very few cases is this true.

Smart museum curators find a way to politely refuse family keepsakes. Rosebower didn't appear to have ever had a smart museum curator.

Still, archaeologists are treasure-hunters at heart, so every time Faye opened a box, she hoped for a miracle. Instead, she usually got early-twentieth-century family photographs that someone had donated because it seemed a shame to throw them away. She liked looking at the black-and-white images of serious people in hand-sewn clothes and quaint hats, but the photos were unlabeled. There wasn't much Faye could do with these mystery pictures.

Faye had given a big box of photos to Amande, asking her to sort out the ones with an identifiable background. She'd thought it might be interesting to compile an exhibit showing how Rosebower landmarks—Main Street or the lakeside picnic area, for instance—had changed over time. Most of the other photos were probably worthless for her purpose, which was telling the story of Rosebower in four rooms or less.

Maybe Samuel would enjoy having a museum open house where residents could have a chance to identify Great-great-aunt Maud among all those trapped-in-time faces. In most cases, Faye would be perfectly happy for Great-great-aunt Maud to go home with her descendants, thus decreasing the load of paper in this room by one piece.

With no donation records, she wasn't sure she could ethically go even that far. Depending on New York's abandoned property laws, ridding the museum of this stuff might be more trouble than it was worth. She didn't have the budget to jump through the legal hoops. She didn't even have the budget to find out exactly what those hoops were in New York.

Her work plan, which Samuel had approved, was to identify and catalog materials that should definitely be retained. Everything else would be stored properly—and by "properly," Faye meant "for God's sake, not in cardboard boxes"—then deferred for later re-evaluation. In a world-class museum, some of the deferred items would have been destroyed. In Rosebower, the new archival boxes would probably just sit, forever. Part of her job would be to train Samuel to say no the next time someone offered him the contents of his parents' attic.

Amande stuck a photo in front of Faye's nose. "Retain or defer?"

The cars and their sherbet-colored paint jobs dated from the 1950s. Faye thought the faded shades of old color photos were pretty, so she was going to have trouble weeding them out, but some things had to go. She was pretty sure this photo was one of them, until she noticed the town's one-and-only diner in the background. A spherical sign, adorned with neon tubes and metal spikes, rose from the parking lot. It was just so…so…tacky and Sputnik-fearing and atomic, and this might be its only surviving photo.

She sighed. "Keep it for the Main Street exhibit. But don't stop asking me. We've gotta do something about those overstuffed displays or the floor's gonna cave in. Samuel won't like paying for a new one."

"Let's get him to pay us instead," Amande said.

"I like the way you think."

◇◇◇

Faye's cell phone beeped. She had told it to let her know when noon rolled around, because checking the time every five minutes wouldn't bring lunch any faster.

"Let's go see if we can find the hole in the diner's parking lot, the one where that futuristic neon sign used to be," she said, grabbing her purse and rising in a single motion.

Amande quickly darkened the screen on her tablet. Faye felt her brows lower into her own mother's what-have-you-been-doing? face.

"Don't worry. I've been off the clock for ten minutes. I'm keeping track of my hours. My timesheet will be accurate."

Faye wished she didn't look so much like her mother, because she knew what a charming face she was showing her daughter.

"I was talking to Dad. Really."

Faye didn't think her eyebrows could go any lower.

"It's a surprise. Let's go eat. You look like your blood sugar's hanging down around your knees."

Faye hated it when her daughter was right. No, that wasn't quite true. Faye hated it when she, herself, was wrong.

◇◇◇

It was only a few blocks to the diner, past the blackened hulk that had been Tilda's house and the house of mourning that was Myrna's. The sooty smell in the air made Faye walk faster. If Tilda Armistead had been killed by a resident of Rosebower, then the murderer was likely within a half-mile radius of Faye. The stench of smoke probably reached that far.

The sidewalk took them past two quaint tea rooms, both opened within the past year. They served lunch to the increasing numbers of tourists who came to Rosebower for spiritual readings and, on Sundays and selected evenings, to spend an hour in a real live Spiritualist church service. Faye hoped the tourists put some money in the collection plate, because it didn't seem right to use a church as a tourist attraction.

Samuel wasn't paying Faye and Amande enough to eat at the tea rooms. Besides, when Faye traveled, she liked to eat where the locals ate. The Rosebower Diner, which she now knew had once been called The Jetstar, was more her style.

The diner was still furnished in 1950s chrome, vinyl, and linoleum. The air was savory with roast chicken. Faye doubted that this place was going to offer her a side of okra or turnip greens—she was in New York, after all—but it did what it did very well.

An elderly African-American woman sat in a wheelchair pulled up to the table next to theirs. A slight young man with ebony skin and close-cropped hair sat with her, methodically shoveling her meal into her mouth. Rather, he was trying to do it methodically, but she kept shaking her head from side to side. Faye could see that he didn't like it when she messed up his rhythm.

Trying not to watch their battle of wills, she listened to Amande order fried chicken without warning her that it probably wouldn't taste like it did at home. Neither would the gravy on her mashed potatoes.

One of the benefits of travel was learning that people in different places did things differently. Making gravy without a roux was different, but it wasn't wrong. Well, okay, maybe Faye's grandmother wouldn't have considered it actual gravy, and maybe Faye didn't intend to eat any of it, but that didn't mean it was wrong.

The waitress left their table, paused at the next one and asked, "Would you like some more Pepsi, Ennis?" Now that Faye knew the man's name, she had a focus for her rising discomfort. Ennis wasn't raising his voice at his companion. He wasn't speaking to her at all, but Faye could see his frustration in every motion of the spoon.

Her own frustration crept up another notch when the old woman began trying to speak. "Ous. I…"

Ennis took the opportunity to slip in a bite of potatoes when she opened her mouth to speak. Faye watched closely, worried that he was going to choke her with such antics, but the woman seemed fine.

Again, "Ous…I!"

Was she saying "ouch"? The words didn't seem to match his actions, not in a way that would suggest he was hurting her. As for the word, "I," maybe she was just asserting herself. Or maybe she was asserting her dignity.

Faye couldn't decide whether she should intervene, nor what she would say if she did. If she intended to make a scene, then

"I think you should feed the lady nicer," seemed inadequate. She was on the point of doing it anyway, when a tall blur blotted out her view of the wordless little drama.

Amande had shoved her chair back, leapt to her feet, and positioned herself behind the wheelchair before the woman's companion could scoop up more of the potatoes that he was letting drip off her chin.

Seizing a wheelchair handle with one hand, Amande said, "Come on, Ma'am. If you want to go outdoors to eat, I'll take you."

Then she looked Ennis in the eye and said, "Do you not understand the word 'outside' when someone says it to you? I wish my grandmother were still here. I'd feed her potatoes all day long."

With her other hand, she plunked the woman's plate onto the tray fastened across the arms of her wheelchair. Then she snatched the spoon from Ennis and pushed the chair out of the diner at top speed.

Feeling like the incompetent assistant of an avenging angel, Faye picked up the old lady's napkin and her glass with its bendy straw. Giving Ennis a withering look, she followed her daughter's sweeping exit.

◇◇◇

Ennis LeBecque was startled to see his gravy train roll out the diner door. His Great-aunt Sylvia Marie, known to all of Rosebower as Sister Mama, had kept him on a short leash ever since his mother went into rehab, then disappeared immediately upon release. He had other relatives, some much closer in blood than Great-aunt Sister Mama, but they were all worthless and she had known it. Sister Mama was only semi-sane, even before the stroke, but she had the financial clout that came with being the first root doctor to recognize the potential income to be made from Internet sales. She also had an unswerving devotion to one high-flying ideal: "Family first."

This devotion did not make the old lady a pushover. Sister Mama's family devotion had precise gradations. Grown adults were expected to fend for themselves. On those occasions when they failed, Sister Mama dependably paid her relatives' bail or sent their landlords a check for the rent, but she never ever gave them money. Unless it was a full-out emergency, grown-ups were on their own.

Old people were different. When Ennis' grandmother broke her hip, Sister Mama had helped her find a nursing home that Medicaid would cover. After she'd plunked her sister-in-law into this government-funded prison, she had dependably sent her presents and letters and nice little checks to cover all the things that Medicaid didn't, but Ennis' grandmother had never breathed free air again. Ennis wasn't sure that Great-aunt Sister Mama should get to decide where people lived, just because she was the only family member with an operational checking account.

If Sister Mama could be said to consider old people as different from all those other people with their hands out, she considered children to be different still. When Ennis was thirteen, his mother had gotten into so much trouble with her dealer that Sister Mama's physical presence had been required to keep her from being found shot dead in an alley. Once she arrived in Atlanta, Sister Mama had dug around until she found out that beds in rehab centers were not nearly so non-existent as she had been told on the phone.

Perhaps they were non-existent for regular people, but not so for root doctors who knew how to sway bureaucrats with the proper midnight conjuring and the proper herbal incenses and incantations. Once the recalcitrant bureaucrats had seen the errors in their thinking, Sister Mama had plunked Ennis' mother in a magically available rehab-center bed. Then she had left her niece to fend for herself after treatment, because adults are supposed to be able to do that.

Ennis, however, was no adult. He remembered the way Sister Mama used to talk to herself, back when she could talk. That's what she had done on the day she put his mama where he couldn't see her. She had talked to herself.

"So what am I gonna do 'bout you?" She'd been looking at Ennis, but talking to the air. "I can only spend so much on any one relative that's flat-broke, because I got so many of 'em. But there's times when it helps a body to be flat-broke. Let's see what can be done for a boy without two pennies to rub together."

By then, she was already the hoodoo queen of the World Wide Web, so her Internet skills were inarguable. A few hours of web-crawling, a few more hours of phone work, and a few nights of midnight conjuring had resulted in a few days spent hauling Ennis from one boarding school to another. Once more, Sister Mama's persistence and arcane talents had paid off. An elite boys' school had agreed to take Ennis as a scholarship student.

Her duty done, Sister Mama had plunked him in an institution full of rich classmates who knew he was a charity case and never let him forget it. For all his years there, she dependably sent him cards and presents and enough money to buy occasional sodas and candy bars, but not enough money to buy drugs.

Yes, Sister Mama was even smart enough to do the math on addiction. Sometimes he had been able to hoard his money and work out a deal to get just a little taste of the stuff that had ruined his mother's life, but the options of an impoverished social pariah were limited. Mostly, Ennis had drunk root beer and counted the days until he was a grown adult, able to fend for himself.

Any reasonable person would have told him to be grateful to Sister Mama for yanking him out of the slums, but Ennis was, and possibly always would be, a self-centered adolescent. He blamed Sister Mama for his mother's absence, instead of thanking her for keeping his mother alive. He blamed her for his loneliness and, in his mind, he painted her as a woman who stored troublesome people in places where they wouldn't be troublesome any more.

When Sister Mama had her stroke, Ennis had been the obvious person to come help her. He'd just collected his associate's degree, with the kind assistance of the Pell Grant people and Sister Mama, and he'd had time to assess just how horrifying the job prospects for a community college graduate truly were. He'd had no possessions that wouldn't fit into the asthmatic old car that his great-aunt had bought him for graduation.

Sister Mama's body might have been wrecked, but that first stroke had left her mind sharper than a green persimmon. She had seen that Ennis needed a job. She had known that he was educated enough and smart enough to take over her empire. She had also known that she would eventually need the kind of hands-on care that was unpleasant but necessary. Ennis was physically strong, in a slender and wiry sort of way. She had presumed he was grateful to her.

It was entirely possible that she had presumed wrong.

Chapter Six

As Faye and Amande parked the wheelchair at a picnic table behind the diner, Julie brought out their meals.

"Thank you so much for helping her," she said, gesturing toward the silent woman, sitting contented in the pale northern sunshine. "Ennis has been behaving uglier to his aunt by the day. He never hits her or does anything to call the sheriff about, but the whole town's upset about how he treats Sister Mama. God knows what's happening with her business and her money. He's probably got power of attorney."

As she left, she said, "Dwight—that's my boss—he says there's no charge for your meals today. He's been so upset about Ennis that I imagine you'll be getting free desserts every time you come in here, forever."

So this was Sister Mama, the town's famed root doctor. Faye had called around after she heard that Myrna was taking the woman's herbal potions, and she couldn't find a soul who was willing to say anything against Sister Mama. She was reputed to have cured cancer and made barren women into happy mothers. If the stories were all true, this wizened old woman had conquered the common cold. She could probably cure a rainy day.

Samuel, who had a rich man's appreciation of business savvy, had told Faye that Sister Mama was quick to see the business potential in Internet sales of hoodoo paraphernalia. Her wares ranged from mojo bags to hex-cleansing floor washes to graveyard dirt. Unfortunately, it seemed that even Sister Mama couldn't cure old age nor, unless Faye missed her guess, a serious stroke.

Faye didn't like the idea of Myrna taking anything prescribed by a woman in this condition. It seemed impossible that Sister Mama was capable of prescribing anything these days. Did that mean Myrna was taking whatever Ennis wanted to sell her? Faye wouldn't trust the man to give her an aspirin, much less an unknown number and quantity of unnamed herbs. She mentally penciled an end-of-the-day visit to Myrna into her schedule. Faye wanted to check out Myrna's health with her own eyes, and the bereaved woman would be needing her friends today.

Faye and Amande took turns helping Sister Mama with her meal, and the disabled root doctor ate very competently when she wasn't angry with Ennis. She still couldn't speak, but Faye was struck by the way she studied Amande's features. The girl was lovely, yes, but Faye thought Sister Mama saw something else. She wondered what it was.

After they'd all eaten their fill, they took a moment to enjoy the mild air. Faye couldn't say she blamed Sister Mama for wanting to eat outside.

Faye looked up and saw Ennis pausing self-consciously outside the diner's side door. When he saw that she'd noticed him, he walked over.

"I apologize for my behavior. Thank you for helping my aunt with her lunch. It's been…hard…lately. I'll try to do better." After he'd said his piece, he'd wheeled Sister Mama away.

Faye remembered her mother's and grandmother's last years. Being needed around the clock was hard and lonely. She had a notion of what Ennis' life was like, but that didn't mean she could excuse his behavior.

◇◇◇

The clock crawled toward quitting time. There was a reason Faye was here, doing work so tedious that her competitors hadn't bothered to bid on it. Her firm couldn't afford to be picky, and Samuel had approved a budget that would pay her salary for six weeks. Even better, it would cover clerical help that Amande was well-capable of doing. In this economy, a paying summer job for a seventeen-year-old was no small thing.

Best of all, the project budget included travel expenses for them both, providentially paying for a trip that she had so wanted to give Amande. She didn't know where the child would go to college but, as long as Faye had breath in her body, she would go. While they were in New York, they would drive around and look at college campuses, just to get an idea of what they were like. Just to feed her daughter's dreams.

When Faye and Joe had first met Amande, the girl had been frantically brainstorming ways to fund a longed-for college education. Recently, Faye had stumbled across some of those plans. At the top of the list was "Earn as much free college credit as the school system will give me," a strategy Faye applauded. At the bottom of the list were "Sell my blood," and "Sell my plasma," along with Internet-generated information on how often she could do that and how much income each sale would generate.

Faye had torn this piece of paper into itty-bitty pieces. Her daughter was going to college, and she would be keeping all her blood while she did it.

Opening another unlabeled box, Faye found dozens of stone tools that looked an awful lot like the ones already on display. Amande was staring out the window, but Faye merely cleared her throat without comment. If her daughter could tolerate this level of boredom for weeks, while weathering a seventeen-year-old's mood swings, then the two of them just might enjoy this trip.

Without bringing her eyes back from the window, Amande held up another photo. "Display or defer?"

Amazing. The child could work while she daydreamed.

The photo was an unremarkable shot of somebody's brand-new Chevy. "Defer," Faye said victoriously. She handed Amande the box of stone tools. "Now, put the freakin' photos away. I want you to take pictures of these things and zap 'em to your father."

Amande fondled the chipped stone tools. "Oooooooh... Dad's gonna love this part of the job."

"Yup. He's gonna be able to tell me who made all this stuff and how long ago. Then he's gonna tell me whether they rate a big shiny display case or whether they should be properly stored someplace where they will never again see the light of day."

"Dad comes in handy sometimes."

Yes, he did. The only reason Faye and Amande could be in New York, breathing museum dust, was because Joe was watching little Michael. In theory, Joe would be catching up on the company's accounting while Michael napped. In actuality, Faye expected to go home to a mud-covered child who had learned to track deer, and a grown man sheepishly admitting that he had no idea of the state of their accounts receivable.

Faye figured there were worse things than being married to a man who could hear a quail breathe, then put an arrow in its eye. Even if their accounts receivable always fell short of proper recordkeeping standards, Joe's family would never starve.

Working notes for Pulling the Wool Over Our Eyes:
An Unauthorized History of Spiritualism
in Rosebower, New York

by Antonia Caruso

*I'm having some trouble getting motivated today. Some-
one unique lost her life last night.*

*Most of the charlatans of Rosebower trigger every last
one of my crusader impulses, but I genuinely admired
Tilda Armistead. Did I think she could work magic? Did
I believe she could deliver messages from the dead?*

Of course not.

*If I believed that, I'd have been camped on her front
lawn, begging her to put me in touch with the parents
I loved so well. I did believe, however, in Tilda's honor.
In all my efforts to dig up dirt on these people, I found
no evidence that she ever cheated anybody. No one
remembers a lie crossing her lips, not once.*

*Until lately, I had the time and opportunity to dig up
all the dirt I pleased on Tilda Armistead and on everybody
else in town. Until Dr. Faye Longchamp-Mantooth and
her daughter arrived to straighten up Samuel's museum,
I had free run of the place. Samuel Langley is putty in
the hands of anybody who shows a little interest in the
history of his goofy hometown.*

Until the Longchamp-Mantooth ladies talked Samuel into closing the museum while they worked, I pored over decades of Rosebower's weekly newspaper. I never found a single advertisement touting Tilda Armistead's services. Nor her father's nor her grandparents' nor their parents'. The Armisteads never needed to debase themselves with tawdry ads in commercial publications. Everybody with an interest in Spiritualism knew who the Armisteads were, and they came here to see them.

It took me a while to notice one of the most telling things about Tilda. The woman was born in the early 1930s. She married in 1960, late for that day and age. She stayed married until her husband died twelve years later. To all accounts, the marriage was solid. Yet her name was always Armistead.

Tilda kept her maiden name. In 1960. How often do you think that happened?

I wish I'd known Tilda better. All I can do is guess, but I'm thinking that a woman who kept her own name in 1960 had a strong personality and an unshakeable family pride. The Armisteads founded Rosebower and, along with the folks in nearby Lily Dale, they had a hand in founding Spiritualism itself, back in the nineteenth century when it was so much easier to believe in ghosts.

Sir Arthur Conan Doyle, the father of the ever-logical Sherlock Holmes himself, believed in the original fakers, the Fox sisters, who lived quite near here. Something about western New York makes people go irrational over ghosts or religious reform or seemingly unattainable things like woman's suffrage. Sometimes they talk to angels and dig up golden tablets. Maybe when people are snowed in for most of the winter, something inside them ferments.

Sir Arthur believed that the Fox sisters were genuine mediums who could communicate with spirits through unearthly knockings and rappings. He continued to believe, even after one of the girls confessed to fakery and proved that she could duplicate the ghostly noises by cracking her toes. (Cracking her toes! How would you like to be famous for a century or two because you could crack your toes really loudly?) The good sir refused to believe her confession. He also publicly believed in fairies.

Tilda Armistead was born into a family of people who had actually met Sir Arthur Conan Doyle, as well as his doubting adversary, Harry Houdini. Her mother was born to a woman whose grandmother knew the feminist leaders who caused so much trouble at Seneca Falls. No wonder an heiress to such a heritage wished to keep her own name. Tilda was an Armistead through and through.

If Tilda had lived to see my book published, she would have never spoken to me afterward. In it, I will expose her family as dupes, used by the fakers in their midst who were only out for a quick buck. But until that day, I would have liked to have been her friend.

I don't feel much like writing today.

Chapter Seven

Ennis LeBecque didn't take well to public humiliation. Nobody likes humiliation, and the free-pumping testosterone of a twenty-year-old man made Ennis like it even less. Testosterone whispered things in his ear, violent things. It made him want to wipe the smug victory off the face of the girl who had embarrassed him in the diner. It made him want to hurt somebody. It made him want to see the victorious girl's pretty face again.

A brain that takes a daily bath in hormones is easily confused. Ennis wanted to punch Amande. He wanted to kiss her. He wanted to show her who was boss. He wanted to buy her flowers. He wanted her bitchy-looking mother to be far, far away. Maybe it was the bitchy-looking mother that he wanted to punch. He liked girls, but he didn't like women.

Women were selfish, like his mother. They were controlling, like his Great-aunt Sister Mama. Girls were probably just as cruel, at their core, but they could still be pushed around. Powerless people made Ennis feel better about himself. Of course, the girl in the diner hadn't seemed powerless, but maybe that was because her mother was there. Ennis had a notion that he could show her who was boss, if he could just get her alone.

In the meantime, he would hoe Sister Mama's garden and pick the day's harvest of herbs. He would wash and chop and simmer the roots and leaves, following Sister Mama's recipes to the letter, then Sister Mama would tell him he'd done it all wrong. The woman couldn't even talk, but she could still push him around with grunts and gestures and judicious use of the stink-eye.

Ennis had ambitions, and being the unpaid servant of a hoodoo practitioner was not one of them. He had doubled Sister Mama's online business, and she was still paying him with room, board, and a tiny allowance. He was nearly done here. His exit strategy was in full swing. Sister Mama could find somebody else to feed her strained peaches for the short time that remained to her.

He should be focusing on his plans to get the hell out of Rosebower, but he couldn't keep his mind off the girl. What would she look like when he'd wiped the smug smile off her face?

◇◇◇

Faye's heart sank when Myrna opened her front door. Her friend looked terrible. Myrna's breathing was ragged and the fact that she was weeping uncontrollably didn't help. Sociable to the end, she didn't let these physical constraints keep her from answering her own door, despite the fact that there were several people in the house who could have done it for her.

She led Faye and Amande into the dining room, where the long table, so like Tilda's, was set for tea. A white-haired man hovered at Myrna's elbow, and she introduced him as Elder Johnson, saying that he had been sent by the church to sit with her, though not in grief. According to Spiritualist beliefs, Tilda was not gone. Elder Johnson was here to support Myrna until she established contact with her late sister.

Faye wondered what would happen if Tilda's spirit showed up and told somebody she'd been murdered. If this happened, Faye would be forced to believe in ghosts. Unless, of course, the person contacted by Tilda was also the murderer, the only resident of Rosebower who could know that detail.

Two people in their mid-forties sat across the table from Myrna. They were striking, in a calculated way. The woman had waist-length hair in a very attractive shade of red that was almost natural. She was tall and fair, with long arms, long fingers, and a long neck. Faye thought she looked like medieval royalty.

Amande must have agreed, because she leaned toward her mother and whispered, "It's the Queen of Hearts." A glance at the woman's elaborate dress, low-necked and cinched at the waist to accentuate her full hips, confirmed that Amande's observation was dead-on. It also made Faye want to laugh, which would have been inopportune in a house of mourning.

The man beside the Queen of Hearts was as eye-catching, though not nearly so tall. His shoulder-length white-blond hair matched his blond brows and lashes, so Faye supposed that his dramatic coloring was more God-given than the Queen's.

"He looks like Dad, only not," Amande breathed into her ear, barely audible.

She was right again. Like Joe, he had green eyes, and his strong features were made even more masculine when framed by long hair. Also like Joe, his coloring would turn heads from twenty paces, but while Joe's skin was bronze and his hair was almost black, this man was arrestingly pale. His torso was also notably narrow in comparison to Joe's broad shoulders and barrel chest. Faye gave him a few seconds of study and decided that his androgynous good looks did nothing for her, but she could tell that Amande thought otherwise.

The Queen of Hearts was speaking. "A doctor, Auntie. Let me take you to a doctor."

"Oh, no, no. There hasn't been a doctor in Rosebower for years, not since Samuel's cousin Oscar passed to the other side. I just need some rest and," she paused for breath, "perhaps a time of prayer with Elder Johnson."

The Queen seemed accustomed to steamrolling right over Myrna. "There's a twenty-four-hour clinic twenty miles down the road." She reached across the table and took Myrna's hand between both of hers. She rubbed it reassuringly for a moment, then resumed steamrolling. "We can be back by dark. Come." She stood, presuming that Myrna would rise with her.

But Myrna kept shaking her head and saying, "No, no, no, no, I can't. Dara, I just can't. I need to be here. I need...I just can't."

Apparently, Myrna had her own case of agoraphobia, and it was almost as bad as Tilda's had been. Dara sat back down. Even the Queen could see that her aunt wasn't going anywhere.

"Allow me," said Elder Johnson.

Bowing his head in prayer, he paused a moment, then placed a hand on each of Myrna's temples. Her breathing slowed. Moving his hands to her shoulders, he watched her closely. After a time, he seemed to see something that Faye didn't, because he moved his hands to encircle Myrna's wrists.

Faye knew that Spiritualists practiced "the laying on of hands" as a healing ceremony, and she knew that it wasn't unique to Spiritualism. When her mother and grandmother lay dying, the minister of their Holiness church had visited their bedsides often. Faye had never believed he had supernatural healing skills, but he'd given them comfort and she was grateful.

The relaxation creeping over Myrna's face made Faye wonder whether she should ask Elder Johnson if he could do something about her own sore neck. Still, the bereaved woman's color was terrible. Somebody needed to get Myrna to a doctor, even if it meant drugging her first.

At Faye's left elbow sat the very outgoing Amande, who had already introduced herself to the white-haired man on her other side.

"Mom, this is Willow. Dara is his wife, and she is...was... Tilda's daughter."

"Is. The word is 'is.' Death is not the barrier you perceive it to be."

Faye watched her daughter stare at Willow, goggle-eyed, as he intoned these words of wisdom. The man was working the easiest audience he'd ever have.

Willow seemed to be finished talking, so Amande turned her eyes on Myrna. She looked as relieved as Faye by the woman's improved appearance. Leaning toward Faye but still watching

Myrna, she murmured, "Maybe she'd feel better if somebody gave her a piece of that awful candy."

Myrna didn't hear her, but Willow's younger ears did. Amande looked mortified when he proved it by saying, "I think you're right. Dara and I brought her aunt some of that candy she likes, and this might be just the time to give it to her." He reached into a bag on the floor by his feet and pulled out a box identical to the one Myrna had passed around on the night of the fire.

He offered Amande a piece, then grinned at her confusion. "You don't have to take any. Some people like licorice and some don't, but Dara's aunt sure does. And we do." He offered the candy around the table, but Dara was the only person who accepted. Then he pulled out a piece for himself, took a huge bite, and placed the box on the table where Myrna could see it. Within twenty seconds, she was chewing on a piece and trying to get everyone present to join her. Since they had all tasted the stuff, everyone refused except Willow and Dara, but her duty as a hostess had been fulfilled. Every time Myrna bit into a piece of the candy, the odor of licorice filled the room.

Now Myrna was relaxed and happy, but her face was still grayer than her hair. Faye could tell that Dara was marshaling another argument in favor of a trip to the doctor, but her maneuvering was interrupted by a knock at the door. Dara leapt to her feet and answered it, preventing Myrna from burning the energy to get up and do so herself. Dara returned with Ennis.

Faye could see that the young man had not expected to see his lunchtime nemesis and her mother. He refused to look directly at them, but Faye saw him peek twice out of the corner of his eye.

Good. Let him think that people everywhere were looking out for his aunt.

He addressed Elder Johnson. "I told Sister Mama what you said about Miss Myrna, and she sent this." He held out an unlabeled brown glass vial with an eyedropper lid.

The elder didn't take it at first, scrutinizing Ennis for a long minute. Maybe he'd heard the gossip about Ennis and his treatment of his aunt. "You told her everything I said? Quick shallow breathing? Racing heart? Cyanosis of her nails?"

"I did. She wanted to come herself, but she looks almost as bad as Miss Myrna. I told her to stay put, because I could most certainly bring a bottle over here and tell you that the dose is ten drops every three hours. Sister Mama said you should put them in a cup of hot water with a spoon of sugar and make her drink it down fast." He turned his head toward the ailing woman. "Miss Myrna, she said you can put it in your tea if you want to. She also wanted me to tell you that the sugar don't do nothing, so you can leave it out, but she knows how you like your sweets."

There was a teacup on the table in front of Myrna. In fact, at some point in the proceedings, someone had put full cups in front of Faye and Amande. Either Myrna had summoned the strength, based on eighty years of hospitable urges, or Dara had done it to keep her aunt still.

Myrna seemed perked up by the very idea that Sister Mama was taking care of things. Without asking Ennis what was in the bottle—and would he have known?—she counted ten drops into her teacup. Then she polished off the contents in a single draft.

Dara's eyes were glued to Myrna, but Willow was smiling at the horrified looks on Amande's and Faye's faces.

"What was *in* that stuff?" Amande asked him, quietly, so Myrna wouldn't hear.

"Tinctures of about twelve different roots and herbs, I imagine, probably dissolved in 150-proof home brew," Willow said. His easy laugh made his white hair swing. Faye could see Amande's eyes following it as he talked. "I couldn't begin to tell you which roots she prescribed in this particular situation. Sister Mama has a huge garden and several huger greenhouses and she has the accumulated skills of every gardener since Adam. If, over the past fifty years, Sister Mama decided that she needed to grow a plant that was native to Tasmania or Finland or Ecuador, she figured out how. There could be anything in that bottle, but I'll lay odds that it does Miss Myrna some good. Sister Mama has a lifetime of miracles to her credit."

The conversation circled around meaningless chit-chat, but the chit-chatters' hearts weren't in it. Their eyes flicked toward Myrna, time and again, but the weary woman didn't seem to notice. To pass the time, Dara told a funny story about how her foot once fell asleep while she was onstage. "I was flinging the tarot cards around, jiggling my leg the whole time."

"I couldn't figure out why you were stalling," Willow said. "I started making up stuff to say while I waited for you to stand up."

"Be glad I stalled. Otherwise, I'd have fallen on my face, and you'd have had to scrape me off the stage."

Faye nursed her zero-proof tea for a quarter-hour, watching Dara sparkle for her very small audience. During that time, Myrna's color did improve and Ennis disappeared. She guessed that Sister Mama had told him to come home promptly and report on her patient's condition, though how she was communicating so well with her nephew was anybody's guess. Maybe they'd developed a sign language system, or maybe her speech got better when she wasn't angry.

Faye had spent that quarter-hour honing her own observation skills. She could see Tilda in her daughter's lean form, although Dara must have gotten those hips and that flamboyant personality somewhere else. Her faultless posture, so like her mother's, was a form of physical dignity. Faye could also hear a crisp intelligence in Dara's words that harked back to Tilda.

Faye suspected that Myrna too had inherited the family smarts but, for whatever reason, she chose to hide them. She more than made up for those hidden brains with social acuity. It would be a mistake to underestimate either woman.

Different as they were, Myrna and Dara were blood relatives. Though their approaches to life were different, Faye could see that kinship. After Elder Johnson left, Dara got up and sat in his chair, pulling it close to her aunt. The two women shared an emotional effervescence that bore no resemblance to Tilda's reserve. It was touching to watch them together.

They hugged. They forced tea on everyone present. They gossiped. My, how they gossiped.

"Do you think Ennis could've gotten out of here any faster, Auntie? He knows the whole town has heard about this little girl taking him down a notch or two."

The Armistead women—Faye had already ascertained that Dara clung to the family name as tightly as her mother—had grinned at Amande over her lunchtime victory, and Faye had watched the girl relax into friendship with them both. Willow had sat quietly through the Armistead women's goofy jokes, sipping his tea and watching his wife's every move. Faye had rarely seen a man so smitten after years of marriage.

Other than her own Joe, of course.

When it came to Dara, Willow had plenty to watch. She possessed the gift of quiet drama. Her voice was soft and her gestures were slight, but she had the power to make you watch every movement of those expressive hands. Her tasteful bracelets, one on each wrist, slid gently back and forth as she moved. Her riotous red curls swung softly. Her dress was embroidered with beads and splashed with all the jewel tones there were. She would surely make a memorable picture sitting behind her mother's crystal ball, caressing it with hands so like Tilda's.

Faye felt a pang when she realized that the crystal ball had probably not survived the fire. Dara had lost many things in the fire that were far less important than her mother. Still, for the rest of her life, she would have moments when she woke up and thought, "It's gone. The portrait of my great-grandfather. It's gone."

While Faye was thinking, Dara's conversation with Myrna had taken a turn in the same regretful direction. Tears were rolling down Myrna's cheeks as she said, "If only she hadn't been so stubborn. And you, Dara. You're as stubborn as she was, and now it's too late. The two of you lost years that you'll never get back. Why didn't you go sit on her doorstep and stay there until she forgave you? I told you to do that."

Dara's eyes were glittering, too. "Mama passed her gifts to me. Is it so surprising that I got her bullheadedness, too? You're right. I should have lived on her doorstep, if that's what it took to get her to speak to me. You told me to do that, and I should have. I do have one consolation. She will come to me now. From the other side, she'll see my heart and she'll come."

Now Myrna was weeping openly. "But not to me. Why don't I have the family gifts? I'm just a worn-out old lady who's never talked to anybody that wasn't standing right in front of me, in the flesh."

It was Willow's turn to reach a hand across the table and take hers. "And on the telephone. You've talked to me many times when I wasn't right in front of you, and I was always glad to hear your voice. We all have our gifts, Miss Myrna."

Faye gave Myrna a good hard look. She was weeping, but the tremors were gone and her cheeks were pink. Sister Mama's 150-proof miracle had done its work. Dara no longer needed Faye as an ally in forcing Myrna to see a doctor. It was time for her and Amande to go.

She rose, gave hugs and handshakes where they were appropriate, and took her daughter out the door with her, leaving this family to make its own peace.

Chapter Eight

Ennis closed the door to his bedroom and dropped onto the bed. He was glad to see Miss Myrna respond so well to his great-aunt's root medicine. Sister Mama had tried to teach him her secrets, back when she could talk better, but Ennis hadn't had a lot of patience for lessons that looked a lot like the chemistry homework he'd hated so much.

"Just tell me what root to use for what sickness," he'd said.

"There's more to it than that. That's why you need to listen to me. No. That ain't right. You need to listen to your patients... what they're sayin'...what they ain't. You gotta listen to their chests and you gotta hold your hand on their pulses a long time. Not just till you've counted the beats, no. A body's heart will speak for it. You got to learn to listen."

It was no use. Ennis didn't have her healing gifts, and he didn't really want them. When it came to website-building and search engine-optimization, however, he was hell on wheels. Sister Mama had built quite a respectable online presence before Ennis came to live with her, but he had taken her business to a whole new level. It was an understandable error of youth that he hadn't thought ahead to the day when Sister Mama wouldn't be there.

She'd needed him to help out around the house when he'd first come to live with her, but she could still walk and talk and boss him around. He'd counted on having her on his hands for a long time, fiddling with the roots and herbs while he focused on making money.

How could a twenty-year-old, full of life, have imagined the second stroke that wiped away almost everything his aunt had once been?

She still had her moments. Sometimes she could spit out a few sentences, then finish making her opinion known through sign language. She had a letter board she used, pointing to letters that spelled the words she couldn't say any more. When he'd told her that Myrna Armistead needed her, she'd rallied enough to mix the tinctures herself.

And then there were those other times. He didn't like the town talking about the way he'd treated Sister Mama at the diner, but they didn't have to live his life, now, did they? They didn't have to wipe up after an old lady who drooled about half the time. He didn't want to spend his time with the shell of his aunt. He wanted to be with the pretty young girl who had shamed him in public.

He also wanted to know what he was going to do when Sister Mama could no longer tell him how to do root medicine. He figured he could just shut the local practice down. All the real money came from the Internet, anyway. But how was he going to handle the mail-order business?

He knew the recipes for her various hexing powders and love potions. He also knew that she was adamant that there was more to her work than just mixing a few powders and putting them in a bag. He believed her when she said that Goofer Dust packaged by a nonbeliever wouldn't work. Worse, it might even hurt somebody.

Ennis, who was a nonbeliever most of the time, was seriously considering converting all of Sister Mama's product lines to pure talcum powder and sugar water. Nobody knew what she was selling, anyway. Goofer Dust made out of talcum powder couldn't hurt anybody, and neither could a tincture made of sugar water, flavored with a dash of moonshine.

He had no answer to the question of how he was going to hold on to his biggest income stream, the online private clients. They emailed, they texted, they Skyped, and Sister Mama told them what to do to feel better. Was he going to prescribe talcum powder to all of them? Or maybe these special clients would be happy to buy tiny vials of her very potent homebrew with no herbal tinctures in it, whatsoever. He had a theory that Sister Mama's moonshine alone could cure things that modern medicine wouldn't touch. This probably meant that he needed to hurry up and learn to make homebrew.

Ennis was tired of trying to figure out how to keep the Sister Mama gravy train rolling after she passed, but maybe he wouldn't have to do it much longer. He prided himself on his ability to make deals, and he had the mother of all deals on the hook right now. If he landed it—and he did intend to land it—he could show Sister Mama and everybody in Rosebower his back as he moved on to something bigger. Lots bigger.

Failing to land it might trap him in Rosebower forever, hoeing magical herbs until he himself needed somebody to push his wheelchair around.

All of these problems circled around the one central question that drove Ennis these days. It grated on his peace of mind so much that he did stupid things, like losing his temper with his aunt in public. It disturbed his sleep. This one central question never left his forebrain.

What was he going to do when Sister Mama was gone?

◇◇◇

"I don't like to leave you, Auntie."

Dara brought Myrna's footstool and arranged some magazines, a cup of tea, and a box of candy on the table next to her aunt's favorite chair.

"I'm fine. Those magazines will keep me occupied till bedtime. There's no need for you to stay here with me when you've got work to do."

Dara watched Myrna's eyes droop. Her aunt would be reading no magazines tonight.

"I'll come back after the show and help you get upstairs to bed."

The lids jerked open. "I can climb my own stairs. I did it for thirty-five years before you were born."

Dara thought, *Nothing lasts forever, Auntie. And nobody lasts forever, either.* But she only said, "You'll call me if you change your mind about needing help?"

There was a faint nod. The eyelids were settling again, but Myrna was a talker. She could talk until the instant that sleep took her. "I talked to Elder Johnson about your mother's memorial service."

"We should plan for a crowd. The whole town will want to pay their respects, and we'll need to feed them something afterward."

"Your mother didn't want that. Think, Dara. How did Tilda feel about crowds? She wanted a cremation, then a brief time of remembrance with only family in attendance."

"But Auntie. You, me, and Willow are all the family she has. We might as well have had the service while we sat in your dining room this afternoon."

Myrna was dozing off with her tea, candy, and magazines still untouched. "It's what your mother wanted. She told me when I witnessed her will. Tilda was a private woman of great faith. You couldn't make her into something else when she was alive, and you can't do it now. Go do your show. I'll be fine."

Willow was waiting by the door as Dara shut it behind her. They did the same damn show nine times a week, but she could see that he was taut with nervous energy. In a moment, she would be, too. No performer could engage an audience without that energy. Dara's mother had exuded the same energy, even when she had an audience of one.

There is a knack to being fascinating. Performers have it. Regular people just don't.

Dara was torn between her grieving aunt and the audience that was already gathering. She and Willow made a good living, entertaining Rosebower's tourists with their daily dose of magical shock-and-awe. Willow did a masterful job of working the audience, day in and day out, but Dara was the one who owned the stage. She knew it. He knew it.

She was tired of the daily shows, but she needed them like a drug. She wanted to stay here with Myrna, but she wanted an audience more. Theoretically, she had a partner who could have carried on without her on days when she was sick. She should have been able to take a day or two off after her mother died so horribly, but she couldn't.

She could carry the show without Willow, if need be, but he couldn't carry it without her. And they both knew it.

Working notes for Pulling the Wool Over Our Eyes:
An Unauthorized History of Spiritualism
in Rosebower, New York

by Antonia Caruso

*Dara Armistead is not her mother. She resembles her
mother in no way, beyond the fact that they are both
tall, strong-willed women. I know for a fact that she lacks
her mother's integrity.*

*Any reader of my eventual book will know that I do
not believe Tilda Armistead had psychic powers, because
I do not believe that anyone has them. Still, intellectual
honesty requires me to repeat this mantra daily: "I could
be wrong."*

*It is possible that I am wrong in my belief that the
physical world is all there is. It is possible, though I
think it's highly unlikely, that some people can communicate with our dearly beloved ones who have passed
to the other side. If so, then I admit the possibility that
Tilda Armistead was the real thing. I do not give Dara
Armistead that much credit, because there is no question
that she is a fraud.*

*It is no wonder that the two women didn't speak for
the last fifteen years of Tilda's life. It's more surprising that
their relationship lasted as long as it did, but distance*

can be a precious buffer between incompatible relatives. When Dara went away to college, she married Willow and they lived somewhere down south for a while. My contacts in the illusionists' world remember them faintly. They seem to have made quite a splash in a few of the old Confederate states. I've heard Myrna say that it nearly killed Tilda when her daughter would go for months without even letting her know she was alive.

Eventually, though, the young couple saw the potential for making a killing in the family business. They moved home to Rosebower and, from the moment they hit town, Tilda's relationship with her daughter was doomed.

I have uncovered this much hard evidence in the public record: Dara and Willow applied for a business license to practice as psychics within the city limits of Rosebower, and the town's governing council denied their request. Nothing in the public record tells us why.

Dara Armistead is Rosebower royalty. She is not some upstart Rust Belt retiree who wants to move here and supplement her Social Security check by reading palms and tea leaves. There is a story behind Dara Armistead's rejection by the town her ancestors founded. There has to be. And I think I know what it is.

These people believe in what they are doing. When they deliver a message from dead Cousin Fred and departed Aunt Martha, they believe they are helping their tearful clients. Dara's exhibitionist antics horrify them, and there can be no question that they horrified her mother. After Rosebower rejected Dara, she threw their disapproval right back in their faces, building her business barely outside the town limits on property she inherited from her father. In other words, she and Willow work just out of reach of the town council and its annoying ethics requirements.

I have attended the circus that Dara and her husband call a "Spiritualist event" on several occasions. Once every day, and twice on Saturday and Sunday, they pack the tourists into their small custom-built auditorium. I have to admit that they put on a good show, but it is unadulterated old-fashioned hucksterism.

Willow appears to be very good at cold readings, particularly when his victims are lonely middle-aged women. He takes their faces between his manly hands and stares deeply into their eyes, making bold statements and asking searching questions:

"There is someone special in your past, someone who hurt you."

For how many middle-aged women is this statement not true? I can say honestly that it's true for me.

The poor vulnerable victim sheds tears over her faithless lover, and then Willow is off to the races. When he guesses wrong, he is excused, because he has already been right about the doomed love affair. And when he nails something obvious, like, "Your children have never appreciated the sacrifices you made for them," everyone in the room is on his side.

He doesn't fool around with parlor tricks like stealing the poor sucker's watch and having an accomplice hide it someplace amazing. He does not plant fake suckers in the audience who will agree that his most far-fetched statements are miracles of mind-reading skill. He merely chooses the most vulnerable person in the room—and it's usually a woman—then he manipulates her emotions for the entertainment of a crowd.

It's sad to watch, really.

Dara doesn't bother going out among her guests. She remains on the stage at all times, which is a good use of her theatrical flair. She's really a very talented magician. In particular, she is adept at sleight-of-hand. My, how she can make tarot cards spin and fly and disappear!

I find it intriguing that she uses a camera and overhead monitor to give the audience a close-up view of her impressive card-handling skills, but there comes a point in the show when the lights go down and the viewer is left with Dara inside the centerpiece of her cheap-but-spectacular stage—a mostly transparent cage built of glass and mirrors that harks back to crystal balls like her mother's.

I think her crystal stage is built to hide trickery, but I also think that it is no accident that Dara has made herself the center of her world.

Chapter Nine

Faye should have guessed that Amande had something up her sleeve when she turned down pie. Looking at the heavy-laden dessert cart, Faye couldn't comprehend Amande's attitude. She tried in vain to find one treat that didn't feature chocolate, coconut, cherries, or caramel. What wasn't to like?

But Amande was only interested in fiddling with her phone, which she checked at least six times during dinner. (Faye had counted.) What was the use of girls-night-out in their bed-and-breakfast's fancy restaurant if the girls in question weren't talking?

Faye made a mental correction. Amande was talking. She was just talking with her thumbs and she wasn't talking to her. But maybe mothers expected too much. If she and Amande were going to be working together all day and sleeping in the same room every night, then maybe Faye needed to build a little alone time into the schedule for both of them.

Oh, great. She should never have admitted to herself that it might be problematic to work together all day with someone and then sleep in the same room every night. Because that was an exact description of her life with Joe. She'd felt guilty about leaving him with Michael, but maybe she'd accidentally done a good thing for their relationship.

Obsessing over her marriage rendered the caramel-coconut-cherry tart absolutely irresistible. She ordered it to-go and called after the waiter, "Can you put a little chocolate syrup on that?"

"Mom." Amande looked up from her phone. "We have a bottle of Hershey's syrup in the fridge in our room."

"You're right. I forgot."

"You *are* stressed. Tell you what. I have something important to do. I'll go up to our room and take care of it while you wait for your coconut-cherry gut bomb. Bring it with you and we can play some gin rummy while you eat it."

And off she went, worrying her phone's keyboard with both thumbs, while Faye worried over who was on the other end of all those messages.

◇◇◇

Faye shoved the door open with her hip, so that there was no risk of dropping her luscious pile of coconut, cherries, and goo. She was greeted by three voices yelling, "Surprise!"

One of them was Amande's, obviously, because she was sitting cross-legged on her bed with her computer on her lap. The source of the other two voices was a mystery, until her daughter turned the computer screen to face her. Dead in the center of the screen was Joe's handsome face. In his lap sat a squirming lump of boy, gripping his father's long straight near-black hair with both hands.

Faye looked at the computer, unfettered by any wires whatsoever. She thought of all the miles she had flown on an airplane to get here. Not to mention the boat ride from their home on Joyeuse to shore and the car ride to the airport and the miles in the rental car that had brought her here. Yet there sat Joe and his green eyes. She missed him so much. She missed both of them.

Faye could remember when phones had cords. She remembered when photographs came from film that took time to develop. She hadn't always had a phone in her pocket. And she remembered when long distance calls were luxuries.

Reading her mind, or perhaps reading her frugal facial expression, Amande said, "It's Skype, Mom. It's free! Come over here and talk."

Faye knew it was free. She was just adjusting herself to the rocketing pace of technology and the rollicking passage of time.

She settled herself on the bed, but Amande grabbed her shoulders before she could say much beyond, "Oh, you two look so good!" She felt herself pulled back sixty degrees from vertical, at least, as the girl yanked her out of range of the computer's camera.

The girl put her mouth next to Faye's ear and hissed. "This is a big deal. Act like you're impressed."

"I *am* impressed."

Faye hoped they were out of range of the computer's microphone, as well as its camera. See no evil, hear no evil.

"No, really. You're impressed when he shoots a deer and fills up the freezer with it. For this, you need to make him feel like a rock star. It has taken me all day to get Dad up to speed on a simple little thing like video chatting. Seriously."

"When I met your Dad, he didn't know how to use an ATM. I *am* impressed."

Amande removed her hands so that Faye could sit up straight and show her husband how impressed she was.

"Oh, Sweetheart, it's so good to see your face! How did you and Amande manage this? I can hardly believe it. It's almost like a miracle."

Joe beamed. "It ain't such a big deal, not when you've got a smart girl to help you."

Out of view of the computer's camera, Amande squeezed Faye's knee in approval. It seemed her daughter thought she was doing a good job of being impressed by a video chat, something routinely accomplished by nine-year-olds the world over.

"Michael, you're so big! Come closer to the camera so Mommy can see you."

Amande's elbow caught Faye in the ribs. Tiny Faye sometimes had bruises from her big, sturdy daughter's physical expressiveness, especially after she'd said something that sounded dumb to a teenager. "Mom," she hissed. "It hasn't been two weeks. He cannot possibly be visibly bigger."

Faye ignored her. "He's *huge*. Michael, tell Amande and me what you and Daddy have been doing every day."

He stuck his chubby hands two feet apart and said, "Fish!"

Joe, behind him, held his hands up, too, but he was an honest fisherman. His hands were much closer together than Michael's.

Faye caught his eye and he grinned, first down at their not-too-honest son and then at her.

"I swim, too!" Michael's arms flailed in a big windmill, whapping Joe in the chest with every stroke.

"Is that a new bathing suit you're wearing? Show it to Mommy and Amande."

"Yes. Has fish." He raised the hem of his oversized T-shirt to show off the rainbow-colored fish covering his new swim trunks, then he kept going. Michael had just learned to take off his shirt, so he did so at every opportunity. Come hell or high water, that shirt was coming off, and it was coming off now. This new trick lacked the severe ramifications of his last one, removing his diaper.

Joe smoothed the shirt back down over Michael's brown belly, as if he could stop this striptease, but Michael was a toddler. Frustration was not to be borne. A struggle over the shirt ensued.

Faye was on the brink of saying, "Oh, let him take it off. What will it hurt?" when Michael won his small battle. Faye's chest tightened at the sight of the long bandage running below her child's right collarbone. The words, "What in the hell happened?" spilled out of her mouth.

She knew Joe hated it when she cursed.

Faye would have ached at the look of helpless misery on her husband's face, if she hadn't been so angry. It had been a long time since she saw that look. When they'd met, his self-esteem had been buried under a lifetime of the kind of failures that come with learning disabilities the size of boulders.

Joe had worked for years to make up for lost time, and Faye had helped him. She'd taught him to drive. She'd tutored him for his GED, then bullied the university into giving him the accommodations his disabilities required. He'd learned to recognize his own undeniable intelligence. Then they'd built a business together and a life and a family.

It seemed so long ago, but the misery on his face brought it all back. Until this moment, she hadn't realized how terrified Joe was that he would someday let her down.

She had already asked, 'What in the hell happened?" The best thing to do now would be to hold her tongue and wait for his answer.

"He saw me spear-fishing and—"

"Fish!"

"Yes, son, we caught some fish." He put a hand on Michael's back to quiet him. "I didn't take him out there with me, Faye, and I never let him touch the spear. I gave him some rocks to play with on the beach and I stayed close in, so I could make sure he stayed out of the water. And he did. He stayed on the beach like a good boy."

"Yes. No water. Daddy said!"

Faye could see how much it hurt Joe to tell this story, so she tried to help. "You were a good boy to do what Daddy said."

Michael reached for the computer screen, trying to touch her face. The action jostled his wounded shoulder and he winced a little. The child was tougher than beef jerky, so he must really be hurting.

"I told him he could play in the tide pools. You know the ones."

She did. They were two inches deep, tops. She had let him play there less than a month ago.

"Well, he found a sharp stick, almost as long as he is. He was pretending like he was spear-fishing, too, stabbing make-believe fish in the tide pool. I didn't like the looks of the stick and I thought he was being too rambunctious, so I came up on the beach to take the stick away. Honest, Faye. I was hardly ten feet away when he fell. The stick broke under him, and it jabbed up into his shoulder."

Faye told the truth when she said, "You didn't do anything I wouldn't have done myself." Then she listened to Joe describe a sequence of events she'd imagined a thousand times.

Medical crises assume a new level of significance for island dwellers. Miles of water stand between them and help. Joe had done what she'd always known she might someday have to do: he'd stanched the bleeding and bandaged the wound, while assessing whether this was an ambulance-level situation or a trip-to-the-emergency-room situation. Nixing the ambulance, which would have been a helicopter or boat, he had loaded their son into one of their own boats and headed for shore.

Joe told the story calmly, rationally, but Faye got a sense of his level of terror when he said, "On our way in, I called Sheriff Mike. Magda and him met me at the dock and went with us to the hospital."

Joe only asked for help in matters of life and death. Faye could see that Michael had been in no such danger, so Joe must have been at the end of his emotional rope to have made that call. She said, "Thank God for friends. I'm so glad they were there for you." Then she casually asked the question that had been festering since she saw the bandage. "When did this happen?"

It could be easy to lose track of time on an island, so maybe Joe really wasn't sure. Or maybe he didn't want to be sure. "Four days? Maybe five?"

The fact that Faye didn't start screaming things like "Don't you know?" was proof that she was deeply in love with this man.

The conversation had grown boring from a two-year-old's perspective, so Michael had scaled his father's ribcage and was now standing on one broad shoulder. Joe had both his strong hands around the boy's trunk, lest he fall.

Faye couldn't think of much to say that wouldn't leave her bawling. She went with a question that could be answered with a concrete and unemotional number. "How many stitches?"

"Twelve."

This huge number did not remove the distinct danger that she might start bawling. It was time to get off the phone. Skype. Whatever.

She smiled brightly and said, "Michael, it's your bedtime. Will you try not to be taller than me when we get home? And do you promise to do everything your daddy tells you to do?

He's a smart man and you can learn a lot from him." To Joe, she just said, "I love you so much. We'll be home as soon as we can."

After the men in her life vanished from the screen and after she was dead-sure that the audio link was broken, too, Faye looked at her daughter. "Did he think I'd never notice the scar?"

"Sometimes Dad lives in a dream world. You know that."

"When was he going to tell me?"

Neither of them knew the answer to her question, so they went to bed. Since she hadn't been able to say it to Joe and she probably never would, the words circled through her brain through a sleepless night.

When was he going to tell me?

◇◇◇

Amande knew her mother wasn't sleeping. If she herself were sleeping, she would not know this.

She understood how much Faye hated to think of Michael hurting and far away. She loved her new baby brother, and she wasn't looking forward to seeing the scar on his tiny chest. She did not, however, think that Faye fully understood the flip side of this situation: Michael was so lucky to have a long list of people who cared when he hurt.

In Amande's foggy memories of her toddler years, her Grandmother Miranda hovered…her grandmother and no one else. Miranda wept over little Amande's wounds and tended them, but she was the only one. No mother had stood between Amande and loneliness. No father. No other grandparents, no cousins, no friends.

In Amande's mind, even a two-year-old could grasp the concept of tenuous safety: "This person takes care of me. If she goes away, I have no one."

She still prayed at bedtime, the way Miranda had taught her. Tonight, she told God how thankful she was that Michael would never be just one person away from being alone. Then she prayed for Tilda and for Myrna, the sister who had been left alone.

Chapter Ten

Work isn't always fun. Focus on the money you're earning and the bills you're going to pay with it.

This was the scolding that Faye would have expected to give a teenager. It embarrassed her to admit that she was the one who needed scolding. Amande shifted in her chair now and then, and she sometimes gazed out the window, but her to-be-sorted pile was shrinking just as fast as Faye's. They were giving their client good work. Nobody ever promised that it would be interesting.

As Faye opened yet another storage box, Amande gave a little squeak. Faye hurried to the girl's work table, because something about the squeak was distinctly not bored.

"Look at the date on this letter! It says July 17, 1848."

There were many artifacts in this museum that dated from the 1840s and before, but Faye knew very well what had happened near Rosebower on July 18 and 19, 1848—the Seneca Falls convention for women's rights.

Amande's hand was shaking. "It's signed by a woman named Virginia Armistead. And the return address is from Seneca Falls."

She held the letter out to her mother, but Faye didn't take it. This was Amande's moment. Faye just asked, "Can you read it?"

She watched the girl lay the sheets of the letter over her work surface, smoothing them individually with hands sheathed in white cotton gloves. Despite her desire to see Amande do this herself, Faye couldn't resist doing her own hands-off assessment. The paper looked supple and it wasn't terribly yellowed. The use of wood pulp in paper had already begun at the time this letter was written but, by 1848, the Armisteads were living in grand style in Tilda's and Myrna's beautiful mansions. Virginia Armistead would have had the means to buy high-quality paper. Perhaps she was using stationery bought when she was a bride, possibly many years before. It would be no big trick to find out how long she'd been married in 1848.

Faye could see a monogram on the stationery, centered on an elaborate "A" that might have been a symbol of a bride's pride in her new name. So maybe they would find that they were lucky in Mrs. Armistead's choice of writing paper. But had the ink bled or faded? Was her beautiful but archaic penmanship still legible?

Amande's face gave her that answer. As the girl read, her mouth dropped open.

Still agape, she looked up at Faye with her index finger still pointed at the second paragraph. "She says, 'I haven't yet had the pleasure of seeing dear Mrs. Stanton. I am given to understand that she has been at work with her pen, using words on paper to speak for us all. Forgive me, dear husband, if I have mis-spoken, for perhaps she does not speak for you. For myself and our daughter, however, I wish for the security to know that our property will remain ours to control. And, though I know you disagree on this point, I wish to have a voice in all my affairs, including those of my country. I wish to vote. When we gather tomorrow, I shall take the chance to say so.'"

Amande removed her forefinger from the letter. "Oh, Mom."

The history geek in Faye wanted to snatch the letter up and read it, immediately, but the mother in her stilled her hand. There was only one way impulsive Faye would be able to give Amande the chance to fully appreciate what she had found. She needed to leave the room.

"You transcribe the letter," she said as she hugged the girl and then hurried out the door. "I'll go tell Myrna what you found."

◇◇◇

As Faye pulled the museum door shut behind her, she reminded herself that Amande was completely capable of transcribing the letter safely. It was already spread across her clean workspace. She hardly needed to touch it. There was no food or drink in the room, and Faye couldn't imagine her daughter sloshing a Coke across an irreplaceable letter, anyway. Everything would be fine.

Since she was concentrating on disasters that weren't going to happen, instead of looking where she was going, she walked straight into a defenseless pedestrian.

Mortified, Faye looked the woman over to make sure she wasn't hurt. She was older than Faye, but still far from being one of the octogenarians who seemed so common in Rosebower. "Oh, I'm so sorry. That was stupid of me. Are you okay?"

"I hardly felt anything. You're not big enough to hurt a fly."

Faye reflected that she might have inflicted a little damage on both of them, if she'd been traveling at top speed. Fortunately, her momentum had been low.

"Aren't you the archaeologist working for Samuel? My name is Toni. I love history, and I think your work is just fascinating."

"If you like dusty and dirty old junk."

"I don't just like dusty and dirty old junk. I like Samuel's dusty and dirty excuse for a museum."

"You've got to be kidding me. The whole time I've been working in there, I've been wondering if anybody would ever be looking at this stuff when I got finished. If I were completely evil, I would hide a few outrageous captions in the display cases, just to see if anybody reads them."

"Like this, maybe? 'This small bone, a human index finger, is the only remaining relic of Adam, the first man.'" Toni laughed out loud at her own joke.

Faye was an introvert by nature, filling her human need for sociability by surrounding herself with a few cherished friends and family members. Yet there were those times when she met someone and immediately felt a potential for friendship. Something about the keen mind behind Toni's bright eyes, augmented by her confident friendliness, appealed to Faye.

"When the museum reopens," she said to Toni, "make sure to read all the captions. I may leave a few outrageously non-historical Easter eggs for you to find."

"Well, hurry up with it. Samuel has kicked me out of the museum until you have that grand reopening, and I'd like to finish my book before I'm sixty."

"You're writing a book? About Rosebower? Why?"

After she said it, Faye realized that the "Why?" was probably rude. There was no writer alive who did not believe that his or her topic was completely fascinating.

"You're not surprised, are you? You know better than anybody else what happened around here. The abolition movement. The fight for women's rights. The founding of the Spiritualist movement, hot on the heels of the Second Great Awakening of the Protestant religions. Joseph Smith and his golden Bible. In the 1800s, this part of New York was as busy and alive as an anthill after somebody stirred it with a stick. Of course, I can get a book out of that. *Anybody* could get a book out of all that."

Faye nodded to concede her point. She noticed that Toni had fallen in beside her as she walked.

"Are you planning to hit the bestseller lists with the story of Rosebower?"

Toni laughed and said, "I highly doubt that. Maybe it'll sell a few copies and maybe it won't. I'm doing this for fun."

"I hear that tourist traffic in this town goes up every year. It's been years since New Age stuff got fashionable, but it doesn't seem to be going anywhere, and those people are interested in anything metaphysical. They keep coming here to see the places where Spiritualism got its start. This is like Mecca to them. I think you'll sell a lot of books in the local gift shops."

Toni laughed again. "Yeah, and maybe that'll cover what I'm paying to rent a house for a year. I figure it'll take about ten years of gift-shop sales to do that."

"If you don't think it'll be profitable, then why do it?"

"I'm retired so I can do what I want to do. I want to write this book. If I were motivated by a steady paycheck, I would have stuck to teaching."

"You're writing a book. Does that mean you were an English teacher?"

"Physics."

"I loved physics! I took a few courses in college, just for fun," Faye said, surprised to be so comfortable with this woman that she was willing to be unrepentantly nerdy upon first acquaintance.

"Then meet me at Dara's show tonight at seven. I can tell you how she makes cards disappear and tables fly."

"My daughter will be with me."

"Bring her."

◇◇◇

As Toni the Astonisher watched Faye Longchamp-Mantooth walk toward the front door of Myrna Armistead's house of mourning, she wondered at herself. It was no secret to anyone in Rosebower that she was in town to write a book. Samuel knew she'd burned many hours in his museum. But why had she outed herself as a physicist? And why had she promised to tell Dr. Longchamp-Mantooth the secrets behind Dara Armistead's psychic abilities? It would do her work no good for the inhabitants of Rosebower to be warned about the exposé coming their way. She had acted on instinct, but it was done. There was no sense in second-guessing an action that might prove to be the right one.

A performer, particularly one whose act is based on illusion, must be gifted with intuition. A rapport between a magician and her audience is essential. If the people watching do not follow her into a world where magic might be real, then they cannot willingly be fooled.

In Toni's opinion, the ability to sense an audience's belief or disbelief was not a matter of psychic talent. It was an ability to sense the subtle stirrings that said her audience was bored, so she'd better by God say something funny or she would lose them. The sound of the shifting of human butts on upholstery fabric told her when she should quicken the pace of the next illusion, or maybe even skip it.

Toni did not believe that this special sense was magical. She believed it was a part of human nature. Her sense of Faye Longchamp-Mantooth was that she would be deeply interested in Toni's work. That sense also told her that Faye could be trusted.

◇◇◇

Amande knew her mother had no idea that Ennis LeBecque was stalking them.

Oh, okay, maybe he was just stalking her. This was the first time she'd been out of her mother's sight in the twenty-four hours since Ennis first laid eyes on her, yet here he was, not five minutes after Faye walked out the door. And here he still stood, lingering in the doorway from the museum's display area into the work room and thereby blocking her primary exit. Her logical mother would agree that the timing suggested that he had been lurking outside, waiting for Faye to leave.

Amande didn't look at the closet behind her, but she was glad to know that there was an exterior door in there, intended for deliveries. Maybe Ennis knew about it and maybe he didn't, but the rising hairs on the back of Amande's neck were saying, "Make sure you've always got a safe way out."

Ennis stood there, lean and gawky, wearing a goofy smile. All he said was, "Hey."

God, this man was smooth. She fastened her eyes on him, but gave him no answer.

"Are you gonna be in town long?" he asked, looking so pointedly at her chest that she wanted to say, "The girls and I will be here for another month or so."

But she didn't really want to say that. She was pretty sure she wanted him to go away, almost sure, so she decided to remind him that she didn't like him.

"How's your aunt? Did you leave her strapped in her chair and staring out a window?"

He didn't rise to the bait. "She's taking a nap. And she's got me on speed dial." He held up a cell phone. "There's no place in Rosebower that's more than five minutes from our house. Some people live in houses so big that it'd take that long to find an old lady if she got hurt."

This was true enough. Amande laid her gloved hand flat on the Armistead letter, not because she thought it wasn't safe when Ennis was around, but because she felt the need to touch something old and comforting.

He took a step toward her. "Anybody ever tell you that you're pretty?" Another step. "Real pretty?"

"Yes. My dad. He's twice your size and he makes these for fun." She reached into the box of stone tools on her desk and groped for the wickedest spear-point she could feel. It was longer than her hand, and its finely wrought flint retained an edge that would meet the exacting sharpness standards of an eye surgeon.

She held it up for him to see. Both of its honed edges extended from end to end. Her thin cotton glove would be only the barest protection from those edges, if she tried to use it while gripped in her hand. Still, Ennis was no bigger than she was. Amande was pretty sure she could hurt him bad enough to make up for the lacerations her hands would suffer while she was doing it. If she had to. If he quit taking steps in her direction, then this spear point could remain what it now was. A rock.

"I only want to talk to you."

Maybe this was true. Having spent the first sixteen years of her life as a social outcast, and having spent the past year alone with her family on an island, she didn't know how to talk to men any more than Ennis knew how to talk to women. Maybe those stupid hairs on the back of her neck were standing up because she was attracted to him but, more likely, it was because he creeped her out. She had no idea how to tell the difference.

Since she saw no immediate need to defend herself, she palmed the point and rested her hand in her lap. Then she sat and listened. It seemed that Ennis didn't care much what she had to say, as long as he could stand there and look at her while he talked.

"Don't you ever just want to do something crazy?" He gestured vaguely at the window behind her. "Don't you ever want to run down the road...no car, no suitcase, no nothing...and get away from jobs and grown-ups and laws that say we're too young for a goddamn can of beer? Well, don't you?"

He was standing still, so the hand holding the stone point held still, too.

"From what I've seen of the things goddamned cans of beer do to my worthless relatives, I wish the law would keep them away from everybody. How old are you, Ennis?"

"Twenty. Old enough to fill out a draft card, but not much else."

"I think twenty is too old to be talking about 'grown-ups' like they're somebody else. From where I sit, you *are* a grown-up. I'm seventeen and I'm damn sure not a kid. Twenty is old enough to be grateful to the woman who puts a roof over your head. And it's old enough to get a job that earns you a roof of your own. Speaking of jobs—"

Amande nodded her head at the work spread across her desk, but Ennis didn't take the hint.

"I'm grateful to my aunt. Really, I am. You saw me lose my patience with her once. Just once. How many meals do you think I've fed her? For all you know, that was the only time. If you were in my shoes, maybe you'd crack, too."

Amande had heard the waitress say that it *wasn't* the only time, but she'd also heard her say that no one had ever seen Ennis mistreat his aunt physically. Sister Mama didn't look neglected. In Amande's mind, Ennis had two strikes against him, but not three.

She decided she was willing to listen to what he had to say. Nevertheless, she intended to hang onto the rock in her hand until he was gone.

◇◇◇

Faye found it hard to look at the burnt hulk of Tilda's house, across the street from where she stood on Myrna's doorstep. Virginia Armistead's historic letter, still fresh in her mind, reminded her of the history consumed by flames. When had Elizabeth Cady Stanton visited Tilda's house? Was it before or after she added the right to vote to the list of women's demands that spilled out of Seneca Falls in 1848, then stood her ground against the delegates who thought the notion was too radical?

She could hear Myrna's heavy footsteps approaching the door. How long would Myrna and her memories be here?

Time passes, and people are temporary. Human memory is ephemeral. Even physical remnants of the past eventually succumb to flames and rust. Somebody needed to find out what Myrna knew about her remarkable family, so that her memories could be preserved. It occurred to Faye that this someone was her.

Samuel had contracted her to organize his museum and develop a plan to display its contents. These days, the public expected a museum to entertain as well as educate. A professional approach went further than that, seeking to engage the community in an exchange that went beyond linear transmission of prepackaged facts. Multi-media displays weren't just fashionable. They were expected.

A video display of Myrna Armistead talking about women's rights and Spiritualism would be a killer exhibit. All Faye needed to do was convince Samuel that he wanted to pay a little extra for video production.

And photography. Side-by-side photographs of Tilda's house after the fire and Myrna's house, still standing, would make an arresting display. People would love to look at those photos while listening to a recording of Myrna's voice saying something like, "Frederick A. Douglass slept in the front upstairs bedroom of my sister's house, but he took his meals in the dining room of my house while he was in town. My great-great-grandmother was known far and wide for her cooking and Mr. Douglass was partial to her roasted onions." Myrna could help her bring history back to life.

Myrna's stories of visiting activists could be illustrated by photos of the burned remains of the chairs that had once supported the derrieres of two heroines of women's rights—Lucretia

Mott and Elizabeth Cady Stanton. Faye had no doubt that Myrna owned photos of both chairs before they burned. Finally, she was excited about this project.

The door creaked open slowly and Myrna greeted Faye with an endearing smile. It broke Faye's heart to see that smile light a face sagging with fatigue. She loved the idea of working with Myrna to record her family's stories but, from the looks of things, Myrna might not be around long enough to tell them.

Chapter Eleven

Three cubic centimeters is not a great deal of fluid, not when one considers that there are seven hundred and fifty cubic centimeters in a bottle of wine. Three hundred and fifty-five cubic centimeters fit into a measly can of Coca-Cola. Even a teaspoon will hold three cubic centimeters, with room to spare.

It doesn't take long to draw that much fluid into a syringe, and it doesn't take long to inject it someplace where it can do some good. Neither does it take long to inject it someplace where it can do some harm. And there is no arguing the fact that small quantities of liquid have the potential to do great harm. For example, a half-teaspoon of water, barely noticeable in a cocktail, can kill a cell phone stone cold dead.

A medical syringe might be a tortoise-slow way to deliver a deadly something that is assuredly not water, but it is capable of getting the job done, three cubic centimeters at a time.

The needle jabbed its way home, injecting its dark payload yet again.

◇◇◇

Faye had enjoyed her cup of tea with Myrna, but it was time to get back to work. She had successfully dodged all offers of licorice. Its fragrance followed her out the front door, where the scent of smoke still hovered. A single rainstorm would wash away even the last odor of a house that had stood for nearly two hundred years.

She saw Avery sitting across the street from Faye, in the side yard of Tilda's burned house. The woman sat in a folding chair strategically placed in the shade of a spreading oak, where she looked like someone who was more comfortable being outside than in. Hard at work tapping notes into her tablet computer, the arson investigator started when Faye spoke.

"I'm sorry if I scared you. I just wanted to ask what will happen to what's left of Tilda's house."

Avery looked up at the burned house, squinting like someone who needed a minute to refocus after doing too much up-close work. "It'll have to come down, and soon. Obviously. Myrna's been in touch with Tilda's insurance company."

"It's a shame. Every day, I learn something new about the historical significance of that old house."

Avery nodded, looking up and down a street lined with homes almost as old and fine as Tilda's had been. "I hate to see houses like these go. You should see what goes into them. When they come down, I get a really good look at how they were built. When there are bricks, they're handmade, perfectly laid in beautiful patterns. Masons worked cheap in those days. And the carpentry…"

"Mortise-and-tenon joints? And hand-whittled pegs instead of nails?"

"Yeah. It's really something to see. You sound like you know something about historic buildings. But I guess you would. You're an archaeologist."

"And I live in a house older than this one was. I know quite a bit about leaky roofs and very old plumbing." Faye felt an idea bubble up. "Can I take pictures while the house is coming down? And maybe collect a few bricks and pegs for the museum?"

"It's Dara's house now. The bricks and pegs belong to her, so you can have them if she says so. You'll have to stay a safe distance away during demolition, but there's nothing to keep you from taking pictures."

The notion of being able to display something in Samuel's museum that was actually interesting made Faye ready to go right back to work, but Avery wasn't finished talking.

Avery looked her in the face, and Faye realized that it was the first time she'd seen the investigator's eyes without their customary professional veil. They were an unusual color of hazel, flecked with light and dark shades of amber, but the noteworthy thing about Avery's eyes was their forthright expression.

"You were in the séance room with Tilda, Myrna, and your daughter, not long before the fire."

"Yes. You and I talked about that yesterday morning." Faye had a thought so unexpected that it came out of her mouth before she'd fully examined it. "Did we talk about the fact that Myrna and Tilda communed with the dead in that very same room after dinner every single night?"

Avery couldn't hide her surprise. "No, we didn't, and Myrna hasn't told me."

"She probably didn't think to mention it. Nightly séances aren't abnormal in Rosebower."

Avery was making notes. "You're right. I need to remember that I'm working in the Downtown of the Departed."

She looked up again. Faye saw concern on her freckled face, but she couldn't read the woman well enough to suss out its source.

"I've been thinking through the sequence of events leading up to the fire." Avery paused, as if to give Faye a chance to do the same thing. "It seems obvious that someone barred the door to the séance room and set the house on fire."

"By throwing the burning lamps at the door?"

"Yes. You saw the evidence. And then the killer threw some more accelerant around, just to make sure the fire was big enough to do its job. I took samples to identify the accelerant and to confirm my suspicions, but the burn patterns are pretty clear."

"So the accelerant means that an arsonist intended to burn the house down. And the barred door says that the arsonist thought someone—presumably Tilda, since it was her house—was still in there. It also says that the arsonist thought she should stay there while the house burned. That's premeditated murder."

As Avery nodded, another thought struck Faye. "Anybody who lives in Rosebower would know that the Armistead sisters went in that room every night and closed the door behind them. Do you think the killer thought they were both in there? Myrna told me she went home early, because their time with us had been all the spiritual communion she needed for the day. She blames herself for Tilda's death, thinking that she could have helped her sister if she'd been there."

"Look at her. She can barely help herself."

"I know, but I'd feel the same way in her shoes. Do you think it's possible that someone wanted them *both* dead?"

Avery gestured at the folding camp chair beneath her. It looked insubstantial under her powerful legs and trunk. "I could type up my notes a lot easier if I went back to my office and worked on a computer with a real keyboard. But you see that I'm sitting here. Also, my house is a lot closer to Rosebower than that place where you and your daughter are staying, yet you're commuting in every day and I'm not. There's no logical reason I can't drive home when I finish working this afternoon. Why do you think I'm sleeping over there again tonight?" She pointed at Rosebower's overpriced inn.

"So you can keep an eye on Myrna?"

Avery nodded. "I've spent the last couple of days sitting here, watching who walks up and down these sidewalks. When I checked into the inn, I asked for a corner room that overlooks Walnut and Main. It gives me a view of everything that goes on late at night in metropolitan Rosebower."

"I'm guessing that nothing goes on here late at night. Look at the demographics. There's no work for young people, so they're all gone. This is, for all intents, a retirement community."

"That makes my job easy." Avery extended her hands slightly to the left and right, encompassing the length of the sleepy little street in front of her. "If I see any activity at all on this street late at night—in this neighborhood, actually—it's automatically suspect. I didn't sleep a lot last night. I saw exactly nothing."

"Thank you for looking out after Myrna. She's special."

Avery nodded again, but held her silence. She seemed to be waiting for Faye. Faye must have looked as clueless as she felt, because Avery prompted her. "There *was* one unusual thing happening in Rosebower this week, even before the fire."

It took a second for Faye's cluelessness to fall away. "*We're* unusual. Amande and me."

Avery still didn't speak, so Faye knew she needed to dig deeper. "In this town…on this street…everything we do is noticeable." *What was the link Avery wanted her to find?* "We stick out. People know who we are and they notice what we're doing. Someone almost certainly saw us go to dinner at Tilda's, and maybe they told somebody else. Maybe that somebody told somebody else."

Avery's meaning came clear, and it was so obvious that Faye knew she'd been hiding it from herself. "The arsonist thought Tilda was in the séance room. He or she had every reason to believe that Myrna was in there, too, because she's in there every night after dinner. And in a little town, gossip is a way of life. It's entirely possible that the arsonist thought Amande and I were still in that room, too."

The image of someone nailing Amande into a room and trying to burn her alive drove reason away. "Somebody may have been trying to kill my daughter and me. Or maybe the arsonist just didn't care what happened to us, not if the goal of killing Tilda or Myrna or both of them was important enough."

Finally, Avery's unveiled eyes said that Faye had reached the right conclusion. "How long have you two been in town? Hardly more than a week. That's not much time to make enemies, but I heard you got crosswise with Ennis yesterday. Do you make a habit of confronting strangers?"

"No! Well, sometimes…anyway, we've hardly spoken to anybody but Myrna and Tilda and Samuel. And that retired physics teacher, Toni, and the elder from the church and Dara and Willow. And yeah, Ennis and Sister Mama…which means that everybody who saw Amande stand up to Ennis knows who we are, but I think they're on our side. Everybody likes Sister Mama and nobody seems to like Ennis. So maybe we *have* met a lot of people, but it's not hard. These people are bored with each other, and there's no point in talking to a tourist who's going home tomorrow. Amande and I stand out."

"It's just such a coincidence…." Avery mused.

"You're not thinking *we* had anything to do with the fire?"

Avery shook her head. "Myrna told me the clock was striking eight as you left, and that's such a poetically old lady thing for her to remember that it's gotta be true. We have you on video getting gas at 8:07. Julie remembered serving you and your beautiful daughter ice cream just after that, so we know you're telling the truth about what you did between the gas station and the hotel."

Faye wasn't sure she remembered as much about her evening as Avery knew, even thought she had lived it. It was profoundly disconcerting to be interesting enough, in a law enforcement sense, for an investigator to compile a timeline of her activities. And knowing that video existed that showed her obliviously pumping gas creeped her out completely.

Avery continued cataloging Faye's activities. "So, let's figure fifteen minutes for ice cream and forty minutes for driving. Your 911 call came through at 8:59, so maybe you sped a little. There's no way you had enough time to burn down a house with somebody inside."

"But somebody did. Where was everybody else in Rosebower at eight o'clock?"

"There's no doubt about where the tourists were. Dara and Willow start their show at seven sharp, and they finish at nine sharp every night. I'm told you can set a clock by the traffic leaving their parking lot."

"That gives Dara and Willow an alibi."

"Yes, it does."

"I suppose I'm the alibi for the convenience store clerk. And for Julie. I don't remember whether we saw anybody else."

"The convenience store clerk doesn't need your help. We have him on video for the entire evening. Julie's alibi is decent. I don't think she would have had time to run over to Tilda's and set the fire after you left. Even if she had, her boss has vouched for her."

"And she's vouched for the boss?"

"Dwight? Yeah. Not airtight alibis for either of them but, like I said, decent."

"Samuel told me he was home alone, so no alibi for him. I don't think Myrna could hold a hammer, much less nail the door shut, and no one could make me believe she would do anything to harm Tilda. Sister Mama couldn't get her wheelchair up Tilda's porch stairs if she tried, so she hardly needs an alibi. Ennis, on the other hand…"

"Ennis has no alibi. None. His aunt was asleep. I do give him credit for not trying to get his aunt to alibi him, though God only knows whether she can still keep track of time well enough to be a credible witness. He can't even show that he was on the Internet or on the phone at any time that evening. He says he was watching TV, and maybe he was."

Faye started to speak, but Avery held up a hand to quiet her. "I'm going out on a limb to share these things with you, but you already knew everything you did that evening, and it's not hard to speculate about alibis in a town where most of the citizens were in bed when all hell broke loose. You're an important witness and you think like an investigator, so I may come back to you with questions, but I have to maintain the integrity of my investigation."

"I understand. If there's any way I can help, I will. Tilda was my friend. But this is your job."

"You seem to know your way around an arson investigation." Avery held up a hand to shield her face from the bright sunshine. She and Faye had been talking so long that the sun had begun its afternoon dip, clearing the canopy of their shade tree. "Do you want to tell me why?"

"I survived a house fire a few years back, and I helped out informally in the investigation. Archaeology is a lot like arson detection, in some ways. You find clues, you take samples, you send the samples to a lab and hope they tell you what you want to know. In the process, you destroy a little piece of the evidence and you can never get it back."

"I never thought about it that way. You're an investigator and, in my way, I'm an archaeologist. I dig through ashes, looking for the truth about the past."

"That's why your work interests me so much," Faye said. "Besides, the last time I watched an arson investigation, a friend of mine had died, so I was personally involved. That's true again this time. Helping with that other investigation helped me deal with my friend Carmen's death."

"And you're thinking it might work that way this time." Avery handed Faye her card. "Well, I can't promise to say much back, but I can listen." Her eyes followed Faye's hands as she tucked the card into her wallet. "I'm trying to watch over Myrna while I do my job, but I'm only one person. I can't follow you and your daughter everywhere you go. There are things going on here that I don't understand. Yet. Please be careful, Faye."

◇◇◇

Amande wondered if Ennis had ever in his life been alone with a woman. The man just would not stop talking, even though he was still standing half a room away from her. It was entirely possible that he was more scared of her than she was of him. This was saying something, since she was still clutching a weapon in her lap.

She now knew that after thirteen years of on-again-off-again parenting, his mother had chosen drugs over him and disappeared. Since her mother had only taken a year to make that decision, Amande thought she was the winner in the shitty-birth-mother contest. She wondered if he'd figured out yet that when shitty people leave a person's life, they make room for someone wonderful to come in. And this took her full-circle to the question of whether Ennis appreciated that Sister Mama was wonderful for stepping into his life when his shitty birth mother stepped out.

She'd also learned that the only thing Ennis had gleaned from his expensive private school education was that rich people could be as shitty as poor people. Since it took him a while to explain this, she'd had plenty of time to wonder whether she should alert the Nobel people so they could fly him to Oslo to accept his Peace Prize.

Ennis had made sure she knew how good he was at running his aunt's business. As best Amande could tell from his rambling monologue, his management skills were not nearly as fabulous as he thought they were. His understanding of the concepts of "accounts receivable" and "profit margin" seemed to be about as vague as her father's, which is why Faye had the final financial word on their family's business and its finances.

Amande did give Ennis credit for one important skill, maybe the most important one in his line of work. He could sell things. In person, his twitchy personality would scare the bejesus out of customers, but he must be doing something right online. Ennis had been quite believable as he described how quickly he was building his great-aunt's business.

Sister Mama's hoodoo products apparently brought in way more cash than Ennis spent making and shipping them. Thus, the amount of money retained in the company's bank account grew every month. This was all Ennis knew about their financial status, and it seemed to be all he wanted to know.

It occurred to Amande that a business could coast for a very long time on good sales, even if its manager was a total idiot. The day would come, though, when the sales dipped or an unexpected expense loomed. That was when a good manager would save the day. She hoped Sister Mama was still in good enough shape to deal with the next crisis when it came, because her heir apparent didn't seem up to it.

Ennis must have run out of things to say, so he took a step forward and said, "Hey," just as he'd done when he first arrived. Amande didn't know whether she wanted him to come closer or not. In a panic, she decided that she didn't. She reached for a pencil with her left hand, signaling that she needed to get back to work and that it was time for him to leave. In her lap, she shifted her grip on the weapon. Suddenly, his nervous head twitched in the direction of the window behind her, and his whole body was in motion.

This was the moment Amande had feared when she had palmed the spear-point, but something wasn't right. He was running faster than she'd have ever suspected such an awkward man could move—evidently his twitchiness also expressed itself in terms of quick reflexes—but he wasn't moving toward her.

He bypassed her desk and disappeared into the closet in under a second. She knew by the slamming sound of the service door that he was out of the building a heartbeat later. Two heartbeats after that, Amande was absolutely not surprised to see her mother enter through the usual door. If Ennis' courageous exit, triggered by the approach of a scrawny middle-aged woman, was intended to make her feel undying attraction, it wasn't working.

Ennis was sharp enough to know that the incident at the diner would not endear him to her mother. Rather than try to change Faye's mind about him, he hadn't stuck around long enough to do what a normal man would have done—shake her hand and charm her in preparation for the day when he might want to ask her daughter out. But why should she expect Ennis to do what a normal man would do? Any fool could see that he wasn't normal. And any fool could see that Amande would be an idiot to go out with him, although that's what he seemed to want.

Amande saw no need to worry her mother with this knowledge.

◇◇◇

Faye settled herself at her worktable, proud to see how focused Amande was on her work. She wanted badly to ask her how far she'd gotten with the transcription of the Armistead letter, but she held her tongue. Parenting a toddler was so vastly different from parenting a young adult that they might as well be two different activities. Two-year-olds were tiny people with a death wish. If parents didn't meddle with their every desire, they might not live to see three. Michael's recent encounter with a sharp stick was proof of that.

By contrast, meddling with an adolescent's every desire was a virtual guarantee that one's child would head for the hills at age eighteen, never to be seen again.

Nope. Faye wasn't going to fall into that trap. Amande was a responsible young woman. She'd have her job completed by the end of the day and Faye would hear about it then. Faye nodded in her general direction and set to work on her own tasks.

◇◇◇

Amande took a deep breath and blew it out slowly. If her mother had come snooping at her desk, she'd have realized that not a single word of the Armistead letter had been transcribed while she was gone. This would have triggered a barrage of questions about what she'd been doing or, worse, a long reproachful look. Amande hated Faye's reproachful looks.

Grateful to have dodged both those bullets, she squinted at her computer's clock and felt encouraged. She could absolutely finish this letter before the end of the workday. Thus, she could safely keep Ennis and his unsettling visit to herself.

This was good. If Faye were privy to any knowledge of this visit, the barrage of questions might last until her twenty-first birthday, unless Amande cracked and committed matricide. Since she loved her mother and wanted to keep her alive, Amande focused on transcribing the letter and on keeping her mouth shut until quitting time.

Chapter Twelve

Faye couldn't remember the last time she'd seen a white-haired lady, decked out in a polka-dotted dress and pearls, bawling out a middle-aged man who was taking his punishment with his head held high. Probably she'd seen her grandmother bless out a wayward plumber or two, but this man wasn't dressed like he was ready to unstop a drain. He was wearing a suit and tie, and neither was cheap.

"Miss Myrna…" he was saying, "Miss Myrna, you know I grew up in this town. I'd never do anything that wouldn't make you proud."

Faye couldn't say exactly what emotion she saw on Myrna's face, but she was pretty sure Myrna wasn't proud of this man and whatever it was he was planning to do. Amande stood speechless at Faye's left elbow.

At one point in her tirade, Myrna gathered herself well enough to leave aside Victorian ejaculations like "Well, I never…" and "You are no gentleman," and construct a sentence of her own. She did this with style. "Gilbert Marlowe, my ancestors are rolling over in their graves right this minute. If Tilda were here, she could tell you what they thought, but I can guess right well. I don't have her talents for talking to the departed, but I know what they'd tell me if I did. They'd say to tell you, 'No.'"

Marlowe seemed to be waiting until she finished venting. He didn't look like he made a habit of listening to opinions that differed from his own, but he stood his ground, silent. Eventually, he seemed to decide that he had listened to Myrna sputter things like, "The very idea!" and "How dare you suggest such a thing?" for a respectful amount of time. Saying simply, "I hope you know how sorry I am for your loss," he took his leave and returned to his waiting limousine. Limos did have a way of catching the eye, even for people like Faye who had no burning desire to ever ride in one.

Myrna fired her parting shot at both the fleeing man and his companion, unrecognizable through the darkened glass of the limousine's rear window.

"Tell your chauffeur to drive that fancy car back to Pittsburgh, and for the love of God, take this week's hussy with you. I have yet to meet one who was fit to cross my threshold."

As the limousine pulled away from the curb, Faye and Amande ushered Myrna across that threshold and waited for her to quit talking long enough to catch her breath. After the limo had receded into the distance, Myrna was still sputtering. "Can you imagine? It would be like…like Disneyland…with little mechanical things dressed up like our ancestors. And Tilda not cold in her grave."

It took two cups of tea, which Myrna insisted on brewing herself, to find out what the man had said that was so upsetting. Gilbert Marlowe had made a career in Pittsburgh as a developer, and a successful one, but he wanted to come home to build the development that would cap his career. Resort hotels, an Ayurvedic spa, a huge theater for Spiritualist meetings and speakers, a golf course, a children's museum complete with carnival rides…if there was a way to separate metaphysics-minded tourists from their money, this man was planning it for Rosebower. If he had come to Myrna hoping for the Armistead family's stamp of approval, he had undoubtedly left without it.

"Tilda was tougher than me. I don't know how many years she held that seat on the town council. I couldn't have done it, myself. I lack her moral fortitude and her ability to speak truth to fools, but I did pay attention when she talked politics."

Faye wasn't sure she agreed with Myrna's assessment of her own ability to deal with fools.

"My sister would never have voted in favor of Gilbert's tawdry scheme, and she kept the other councilors in line. If the wrong person takes her place on the council, Gilbert will be able to do as he pleases." Myrna set her teacup down because her hand was trembling too much to keep it aloft. The cup trembled and clattered on its saucer, making Myrna's frailty audible. "Oh, Faye. The truth is that there is no right person. With Tilda gone, there's no one with enough gumption to take her place. Gilbert has won. So why did he come here? To rub the whole thing in my face?"

Myrna's point was well-taken. Based on her description of local politics, Tilda's death had left a power vacuum in Rosebower, but Faye couldn't imagine that Myrna would be the one to fill it. If Tilda's replacement on the town council was to Gilbert Marlowe's liking, then there was nothing to stop him. Still, if he were really a power-mad scoundrel who destroyed small towns while tying defenseless women to railroad tracks, why had he just scuttled away from a sick lady who was past eighty? Something didn't add up.

Faye was, by nature, protective of elderly people. She didn't like to think of Myrna as a pawn.

Amande was tapping her on the arm, hard. "The letter. You told her about it this afternoon, right?"

The letter. It was the reason they had come to Myrna's house after quitting work for the day. A full hour had passed since Amande had finished transcribing it. If the girl didn't get a chance to read her transcription to Myrna soon, she was going to burst. And then she was going to have a nervous breakdown.

"Great-great-great-aunt Virginia Armistead's letter? You brought it?" Myrna's face shone in a way that her fellow Spiritualists might have called supernatural.

"No, I didn't bring the letter. It's too fragile to take out of the museum," Amande said. "But I copied it for you. Do you want to hear?"

"Indeed, I do. And I hope you two will join me for dinner afterwards. I threw a little something in the oven while the tea was steeping."

Faye had thought she'd felt something savory strike her nose. The plan had been to grab a bite at the diner, but this smelled way better. They'd have to eat and run, though, if they were to keep their appointment with Toni for an evening spent watching Dara and Willow strut their stuff. Amande had been cautioned not to mention this to Myrna. Faye didn't want to get into the middle of any family dynamics she didn't understand.

"We didn't come here just to get some of your cooking, but yes. Thank you. We'd love to stay." Faye nodded at Amande, saying, "Would you like to read?"

Amande was already pulling a neatly folded sheet of paper from her purse. She looked up to see if Myrna was ready for her to begin.

Myrna beamed, resting her arms on the table and letting them take the weight of her slumping torso.

"My dearest Hosea, I do so wish you were with me. When one is blessed with a partner in life, one does not wish to be without him on days of great import...."

Faye always loved the sweetness of Amande's voice, darker and deeper than most girls her age, but she was struck by the change in tone as she read Virginia Armistead's words. It was as if the formality of an overeducated Victorian woman had invaded the girl's speech. Her enunciation was clearer and her delivery was remarkably deliberate for a young person. Like Myrna, Faye rested her elbows on the table and enjoyed the words of a woman who had long ago disappeared into the afterlife in which Spiritualists believed so fervently.

"We women will soon raise our voices for the things that are our due—the right to own the things that are ours, the right to independent thought and action, and most of all, the right to speak our minds and be heard by our own government. These are not unreasonable requests. You have freely given me such independence as is yours to give, every day of our lives together, but you must understand that the word 'given' rankles. Am I entitled to none of the privileges that were yours by right at birth?" Amande's voice gained the urgency that Virginia Armistead had set to paper so many years before. "You do not treat me as a lesser being, but society does, and it is time for this to stop. It is time for us to be heard."

Myrna burst into spontaneous applause.

"Wait! There's more," Amande flapped the paper in the air.

"I know. But it just seemed like a good time to cheer for Great-great-great-aunt Virginia. Never mind me. Carry on."

The low, sweet voice resumed. "I haven't yet had the pleasure of seeing dear Mrs. Stanton. I am given to understand that she has been at work with her pen...."

As Amande read, Faye let herself relax into the sound of her daughter's voice and the feel of Myrna's warm home and the smell of the coming meatloaf. Some moments were so simple and perfect that Faye's nattering brain was able to be quiet and enjoy them. This was one of those moments.

◇◇◇

"Thank you for finding my great-great-great-aunt's letter. And thank you for coming to tell me about it."

Myrna patted Amande on the arm, and the pleasure on her face made Faye realize how rare the company of young people had been in the woman's life. "When Tilda was your age, she used to help Father in his work. People came—my, how they came—and Father would put them in touch with their loved ones. He and Tilda would take them in the séance room while I waited upstairs with Mother, out of the way. After their time with Father and with their ancestors, our guests simply beamed with happiness. Imagine! Communing with a loved one who had passed over, someone you missed very much." She put a hand to her own ample breast. "I miss Tilda so."

They paused in Myrna's front door. Faye knew they needed to go. Toni was waiting for them, but it felt wrong to walk away from Myrna's grief.

"Sometimes, when Father didn't need her, Tilda came over here and helped our uncle with his readings. I wanted to be part of helping those people; truly, I did, but Tilda was the one with the gift. She was only a year older, but even when we were little girls, I could see that she had something I didn't. But enough of that. I had Tilda, and she was a wonderful sister. And my parents and my dear niece Dara. And now, you! I have so many friends. Why else do we live, except to love other people? Love like that can't possibly be stopped by something as meaningless as death."

Amande hugged Myrna impulsively and thanked her for the fabulous meal, then Faye did the same. As they hurried, anxious to be on time for Dara's show, Faye was left to wonder how women of Myrna's generation had acquired the knack of plunking a fabulous meal on the table half an hour after extending an invitation to unexpected guests. Maybe Myrna's freezer was full of the homemade version of TV dinners, ready at a moment's notice.

Amande must have been thinking the same thing, "I thought she said Tilda was the good cook in their family. Did you notice a difference?"

Remembering the tomato sauce dripping over the sides of Myrna's meat loaf, Faye shook her head. "If Tilda's cooking was better, my taste buds aren't good enough to tell."

Toni was waiting for them outside the auditorium where tourists stood in line to see Dara and Willow do their thing. The moonlight sparkled on her steel-rimmed glasses and the scattering of silver strands in her black hair, and Faye was struck by the lack of wrinkles and age spots on her pale face.

It was not that the woman did not look her age. Rather, she seemed to be little damaged by it. Faye supposed that a lifetime in the classroom was the ultimate sunscreen. Toni had the complexion of a bookworm.

"Are you two ready for the psychic reading? Or maybe I should call it a show? Actually, I should probably call it what it is—the gullible public's daily fleecing." Toni spoke quietly, glancing around to make sure she wasn't heard.

"You really know how they do their tricks?"

Toni quieted Amande by putting a finger to her own lips. "Most of them. I keep going to their shows, trying to figure out the rest, but I have to space out my visits. I shouldn't be going again tonight, when I was just here on Monday, but I can't resist watching their shenanigans with you two. You're so…rational. In Rosebower, rational people are refreshing."

"Why do you have to space out your visits?" Amande asked. "You're paying good money for your tickets. What's the harm?"

"I don't want anybody to notice me. For professional reasons. But don't worry, I'll manage, eventually. Dara is no more supernaturally gifted than any of the rest of us. She's slick. That's all."

"What about Willow?" Amande asked.

"He's not even slick. He's just slimy."

Amande said nothing, but Faye could tell she didn't like Toni's criticism of her handsome new friend.

Leaning in even closer, Toni whispered, "I'm going to help you two look past their misdirection. I'll sit between you, so I can give you both an unobtrusive tap on the arm. When I tap once, I want you to look to the left of whatever it is Dara or Willow is doing, no matter what's happening on stage. I'm talking about your left. Don't try to remember which way is stage left. When I tap you twice, look right."

Faye supposed that figuring out magicians' tricks wasn't the weirdest hobby a physics teacher could have.

◇◇◇

Willow trained the hidden camera on the audience. There she was, just to the right of center and near the rear of the house. Toni the Astonisher. How anyone thought it was possible to hide from the Internet in this day and age was beyond him. And this was a person who had actively sought publicity for decades. He supposed that people of her generation had a blind spot when it came to privacy, or the lack thereof. He still had friends in the world of illusionists, and he'd been asking some questions. Toni the Astonisher could be trouble.

This was at least the sixth time she'd come to the show. He and Dara were good at what they did, but they weren't that good. There was a reason she kept coming back, and Willow couldn't think of a good reason. This camera fulfilled its function very well. It gave him a way to study the audience before a show, so that he could choose the most rewarding dupes. It was amazing what could be discerned by the body language of someone distressed enough to make life decisions based on the pictures on the faces of tarot cards.

Maybe everyone had a blind spot when it came to privacy, or the lack thereof, since every single human walked the Earth in a body that told watchers everything. A slump of the shoulders. A melancholy tilt of the head. A devil-may-care gleam in the eye. Willow knew how to work all these things to his advantage. He'd already chosen tonight's mark, so now he could train his camera on Toni the Astonisher and leave it there for the rest of the evening.

He'd already done this once, and an after-show viewing of the video had revealed much. She had stood out visually, among a crowd of other watchers, because she was never looking at the same thing they were. All the other eyes in the auditorium stayed focused on Willow and Dara, where they should be. Toni's eyes wandered up and down. They focused in directions Willow did not want them focusing. Toni could not be misdirected. This was dangerous.

Tonight, she sat with Dr. Faye Longchamp-Mantooth and her remarkable daughter. These, too, were not people who could be readily fooled. Willow wasn't sure what to do about these three women and their refusal to be distracted. He trained the camera on the rear of the auditorium, just right of center, and set it to record. Maybe after he'd watched them watch him he would know how to proceed.

Chapter Thirteen

Faye did not need a retired physics teacher to tell her that Dara and Willow employed a defined strategy. They liked to baffle their audience with bullshit. The auditorium was small, and the décor was inexpensive but flashy, with lots of glittery upholstery and wall hangings that distracted the eye from the serviceable industrial-grade carpeting. The stage was decorated with a dome-shaped brass-and-glass cage.

No, that wasn't right. The scientist in Faye couldn't honestly use the word "dome" to describe the structure. It was constructed of flat panes of glass, some of them mirrored, and it encompassed a volume that was actually more like half of a dodecahedron, with its faces made of glass and some of them left free of glass so that Dara could walk through them to enter the space.

A table and chair sat at its center, and the table was laid with ceremonial items. They were too small to make out from a distance, but a video screen overhead revealed them clearly. There was apparently a camera hidden somewhere, because Faye could see that Dara would be working with a deck of tarot cards and a large glass bowl full of something clear.

The stage set was the closest thing to a crystal ball that could be constructed of flat glass. *Half a crystal ball*, insisted Faye-the-geometry-freak. If it had been a full ball, there could have been no floor for Dara to walk on.

She couldn't deny that the effect was fairly spectacular for something that could be easily constructed by a building contractor with an on-staff window specialist and welder. Her admiration for the couple's ingenuity increased when the dome began to spin slowly on a large turntable. Again, the effect was exceedingly dramatic relative to the cost of a motor to run the turntable. The auditorium was equipped with standard overhead theatrical lights that glinted off the spinning frame's glass facets in several colors.

Faye had been prejudiced against Dara and Willow by Toni's insistence that they were frauds, but she was inherently fair. The couple's performance space gave every indication that they were excellent showpeople. This did not mean that they were dishonest.

The house lights dimmed, and the rotating glass cage sparkled yet more brightly in the beams of rising footlights. Willow stepped onstage and it slowed to a stop, as if waiting for the real star to take her place at its center. A spotlight picked Willow up as he moved down from the stage and out into the audience. He wore a wireless microphone attached to one ear, and his well-cut black suit contrasted crisply with his pale shoulder-length hair. Faye could hear Amande's little sigh from two seats away.

"Welcome, dear friends, to Rosebower, where the boundary between the living and the dead is tissue-thin." Willow spun to his left, eyes fixed on a fifty-ish woman wearing a flowered sundress. The hidden camera must have swung toward her, because her face suddenly filled the view screen. The damp traces on her cheeks shone in the reflected glow of the floodlights trained on Willow.

He grasped her hand warmly. "Whom do you seek? I feel that he is near."

More tears flowed down the wet tracks on her face. "My husband. Is Kevin here? Do you…feel…him?"

"Oh, Madame. Don't you? The aura of love around you is unmistakable. He misses you so."

Toni was doing no arm-tapping, so she must think that Faye could figure out this part of the show for herself. The woman was on the front row, so she would have been among the first to arrive. Willow would have had a chance to watch his target ever since the doors opened, maybe for as long as a quarter-hour. He would have had plenty of time to see the tears. Also, even Faye could tell that the woman had come in alone, just by the physical positioning of the people sitting on either side of her.

A weeping woman who has come alone to see psychics, especially psychics who claim to be able to put her in direct contact with the dead? There could be no easier mark.

Faye had felt the crowd warm to Willow when he guessed that the woman's loved one was male, but it was easy to see that the odds were in his favor. In any case, gender was a fifty-fifty shot. A woman well into middle age would likely have lost one or both parents, but men marry later than women and they die sooner. At age fifty, the odds that she had a dead father were greater than the odds that her mother was dead, and this would be true for a few more years yet. Fifty-year-olds have also entered the time of life when a dead spouse grows more likely, and heterosexual women far outnumber lesbians. These facts, too, pointed to the probability that this woman's tears were for a man. The possibility of her having lost a child was real, and the gender in that case would have been a coin-toss, but a dead husband or father was so much more likely.

Faye couldn't have calculated Willow's odds of guessing right when he used the word "he" for the sadly departed Kevin, but she thought they were way more than even. Maybe as much as seventy-five percent. Another sigh coming from the direction of Faye's own daughter said that the heterosexual women in the audience would have forgiven handsome Willow, even if he'd guessed wrong, and the audience was way more than half female. All of the demographics were in Willow's favor.

"It hasn't been long, has it? Since you lost Kevin? And your name is…"

"Debbie."

Faye wanted to stand up and ask him why he couldn't read Debbie's name, if he was such a damn fine psychic.

The woman's tears flowed again, and they made Faye angry. Of course it hadn't been long since Kevin died and left Debbie behind. Any fool could see that the woman was still traumatized. Debbie was not yet of an age when she could be expected to be a long-term widow. And Faye had watched Willow feel up Debbie's left hand, which still bore the rings that Kevin had put on her finger. Willow was shooting fish in a barrel, and the gullible crowd was letting him.

Faye cast an eye-rolling glance in Toni's direction, but Toni responded with only a slight shake of the head that seemed to say, "Just wait."

So Faye waited. Willow dried Debbie's tears by telling her that Kevin was watching over her, and that he was happy where he was. He said they'd be together again on the other side, which drove Debbie to tears of joy. Then he let her sit down as the crowd applauded...something. But what? Willow's talent? Kevin's steadfast love? Debbie's cooperativeness in providing entertainment for them all?

Faye couldn't say.

Willow moved on to a man who had come to Rosebower in hope of relief after years of pain. Willow correctly guessed that the man's pain was in his hip. Had he seen the man favor his hip as he rose? Who knew? But Willow got a big round of applause for putting his hand on the offending hip, while looking appropriately intense for a minute or two. Maybe the man's hip felt better when he sat down, but he didn't say so.

Then Willow told a teenaged girl that the boy she was dating was wrong for her. The right man would cross her path in five years, he would have red hair, and he would love books. By this time, Faye was getting bored.

As if sensing that he was losing his audience, Willow announced that he felt called to return to Debbie. As he returned to her front-row seat, he pulled a small box out of his breast pocket, ostentatiously breaking the seal close enough to his face that the microphone hanging from his ear picked up the sound of tearing paper. From the box, he produced a deck of tarot cards, apparently unused.

He shuffled them so expertly that his hands barely moved. Faye noticed Toni sit up straighter, craning to see his every motion.

"My wife has a gift for reading tarot. I want to know more about your future, Debbie, now that Kevin has passed over, and I think you do, too. We all do, don't we?"

The crowd applauded warmly and a few people expressed their empathy for Debbie vocally. "Yes! We do!"

Willow held up the newly opened tarot deck, and the rapt crowd settled. "Let us ask the cards for guidance. Dara will tell us what they say."

He fanned the cards open and urged Debbie to pick a card, then a second one, and then a third. Holding her three cards in one hand, he snapped the fanned cards shut with the other, before sliding the unused cards back in his pocket. Then he handed the three chosen cards back to her, one at a time, without looking at their faces.

"You drew them in this order. Don't show them to anyone. Hold them over your heart while my wife does her work." On cue, the spangled curtain at the rear of the stage parted.

Dara took the stage. In so doing, she woke up the room. If Willow's stage presence was a warm, steady glow, Dara's was like a laser beam. If pressed, Faye might have been willing to say that Dara's presence was like a thousand laser beams fanning out in all directions. She owned the stage.

Her brilliant red curls danced. The scarlet scarf tied around her full hips glittered. The jewel-toned panels of her long flared skirt swirled as if she were dancing, though she was doing nothing more than walk. She stepped through one of the huge glass dome's open panels and paused beside the table at its center. On cue, the globe began to spin slowly, and Dara went with it.

She let it make one full revolution before speaking or acting. Standing relaxed and confident, Dara looked less disoriented by the movement than Faye felt. It seemed unnatural to watch a performer onstage, turning her back to the crowd and then reappearing. This was an act that *wanted* its audience to feel unnatural, off-balance, disoriented.

Dara slid gracefully into the chair and laid her hands on the table where a tarot deck waited. She scattered them across the table, moving them randomly and occasionally sliding a card to the side. After laying her hand atop that chosen card for a moment, she would go back to sliding the other cards around in circles and spirals.

Once, she paused and stared deeply into the glass bowl centered on the table. Using a slender brass rod no longer than her thumb, she disturbed the surface of the water in the bowl and studied the ripples. Then she went back to sliding cards around, choosing one and sliding it aside, then changing her mind and sliding it back.

The room was dead silent. When Willow was performing, the audience had been attentive and interested. Maybe even fascinated. He was very good at what he did, no question about it. But Dara was better. There were no feet shuffling on the floor, no butts shifting in the seats. There was almost no motion at all. The crowd sat as if they'd been hypnotized.

Except for Faye. Maybe. She wasn't completely sure whether she'd been hypnotized or not. And except for the physics teacher at her side.

Faye felt Toni move slightly, placing one hand on her arm. Looking at Amande, she saw that Toni had a hand on the girl's arm, too.

One tap means "Look left."

She looked to her left and all she saw was Willow. Willow seemed to be doing nothing but working his suit. He spent a few long minutes with a hand on his right hip, which caused the beautifully made jacket to gather behind the hand and drape gracefully. Then he shifted his weight and put the other hand on his left hip. The changes in position came slowly, so he didn't look fidgety in the least. He looked like a male model doing a photo shoot.

Faye shot a look at Toni. The woman's eyes were fastened on Willow, and she seemed to be counting on her fingers.

Then Dara said in a deep voice completely unlike the one she used when gossiping with her sweet Aunt Myrna, "Now!"

She raked almost all the cards onto the floor, holding three flat on its surface with her right hand. One by one, she flipped the three remaining cards over.

Willow extended a hand and Debbie looked at it, as if awakening from a trance. She handed him the cards she'd been clutching to her bosom.

He showed them to her, one by one. "Death."

Debbie put her hand to her chest.

"The Ace of Swords."

Debbie was shaking now. Willow put a hand on her shoulder to calm her.

"The High Priestess."

Dara sat at her table, staring into space as if she hadn't heard. She disturbed the water in her glass bowl again, and studied the patterns on its surface. Then she flipped the three cards in front of her. She did this silently, because the camera focused on the cards did her talking for her.

There was no denying the cards on the table. Faye could see Death, a skeletal rider on a pale horse. The Ace of Swords was unmistakable, with its single blade reaching for the heavens. The High Priestess, shrouded in blue robes, stared implacably at the camera.

Faye glanced at Toni, whose face did not show the victory of a scientist who has discovered how something mysterious was done. Toni looked frustrated.

Dara stared at the cards in front of her without acknowledging the audience. She and the stage set continued to spin slowly, sometimes facing the audience and sometimes giving them her back. Still speaking in an odd, husky voice, Dara began to interpret the cards in front of her. "Death is not the cataclysmic card that it seems. It signifies change, rebirth, a total break from the past. For you," and now she finally looked at Debbie, "whether you like it or not, Death has brought a new beginning."

"The Ace of Swords is a card of hope, but it is a hard and sharp hope. It demands focus. It cuts to the heart of a problem. It points to the future, demanding that you rise to the occasion.

You have the strength of will to start again, now that the Ace of Swords has separated you from your past."

Faye could see Debbie's back shaking. The poor woman had progressed from simple tears rolling down her cheeks to full-out weeping.

"The High Priestess shows that you are your own haven. You need to retreat into yourself for a time of healing, but you need to listen for the voice that will tell you when the healing is done. When that day comes, wield the Ace of Swords. Do what you need to do to be happy again."

With this, the house lights went out and the dome stopped spinning with Dara facing front. Only the floodlights on Dara and the glassy dome remained…until something else appeared. The audience let out a collective gasp.

Transparent and dimly lit images flashed around Dara, so quickly that Faye couldn't distinguish them all. Sometimes she saw colorful orbs very like the ones that had visited her during her session with Tilda. Once or twice, she thought she saw human shapes, tiny but fully formed.

Then the floodlights came up again, drowning out the flickering images. Dara was speaking. "Is James here?"

A voice answered her from the back.

Dara faced the direction of his voice, saying, "Your grandmother…or perhaps it is your mother…is aware that you have broken the truth. Go and make amends."

Dara looked deep into the glass bowl, then she reached to the floor and picked up a discarded tarot card without looking at it.

"Someone here is seeking to repair a marriage." She looked straight back into the darkened room, and two people sprang to their feet as if they had no choice in the matter.

"Justice," she said, holding the card to the camera. "Can you both honorably say that you have shown the other justice? If not, then do so. If you have exhausted the limits of your own justice, then the court will wield it for you. Would you rather make your peace with each other and enter the future in justice and love? Or would you rather watch a judge divide your lives? Decide."

And on it went. Dara called out to audience members, sometimes by name and sometimes by situation, saying "Speak up, Jennifer, and tell me why you're here," or "Someone here is carrying a deep guilt." Somebody was always willing to stand up and take the medicine Dara dished out, and Dara always had a tarot card ready to sweeten that medicine.

The Four of Pentacles proved that Jennifer was clutching at the past because of her need for security. The Nine of Wands showed the guilty person that he had behaved badly because he felt threatened, and that he shouldn't run away from the results of his actions. Faye found herself wishing that Dara would call on her, but the flamboyant psychic never said, "Stand up, unbeliever, and let me solve all your problems for you." So Faye stayed in her seat.

On and on she went, and never once did Dara lose her theatrical presence. Just when Faye wondered how long the woman could do this, the floodlights dimmed again and she noticed something luminous swirling on the floor around Dara's feet. It was more than fog. Faye could see shapes coalesce in the light, then vanish. They were reflected in the lenses of the glasses perched on Dara's nose.

Dara picked up one more card from the floor and laid it on the table for the camera to see.

"This card is for us all—The Chariot. Events are rushing toward us, breaking over our heads like waves. If we are strong, we will take these things as they come. We will make each new difficulty our own and vanquish it. Only a fool lets life roll past, unheeded."

The stage went black, the house lights came up, and the people in the audience were left to find their own way out. Willow was gone.

Faye looked Toni in the face and said, "Tell me what I just saw."

"I will. Most of it. I haven't quite figured out the card trick yet. But we can't talk here. Look at all these people." She gestured at the dazed people walking slowly out of the building. "You know how much you paid to get in the door. Multiply that number by a full house attending nine shows a week. Dara and Willow are raking in some serious money. They do not want me to explain to you how they do it."

Chapter Fourteen

Toni's rental house was almost as old as the homes of the Armistead sisters, but it was smaller and less sumptuously furnished. Somehow, though, its old wood floors and white plaster walls managed to give the modest house a solid and prosperous feel. Its tiny kitchen proved perfectly adequate for brewing tea and opening a box of store-bought cookies. As Faye lifted her thousandth cup of tea of the week, she wondered whether the residents of Rosebower were trying to poison her with theophylline and tannins.

Amande could hardly wait for Toni to set down the teapot. As the retired schoolteacher leaned back comfortably in her chair, the girl demanded impatiently, "So how did they do it?"

"I presume that you use the word 'they' out of politeness. Willow didn't actually do anything."

Amande bristled.

"Yes, I know that he is a very pretty man. But did he tell poor Debbie anything that you couldn't have guessed?"

"Um…no."

"Are you psychic?"

The words flooded out. "I wish I was! Their show was just so mysterious. And exciting!"

"You mother paid thirty dollars for the two of you to watch Willow play his guessing games. Now, I'll grant that Dara's part of the show may be entertaining to the tune of thirty dollars, but how many hours would you have worked to earn your fifteen-dollar ticket if your mother hadn't been so generous? Do you get minimum wage?"

Amande nodded.

"Less payroll taxes?"

She nodded again.

"Did Willow really do anything that was worth more than two hours of your time?"

After a pained moment, Amande said, "No."

"You're a wise girl. So now let's look at Dara's performance."

This was what Faye had been waiting for. "The floating orbs and the tiny transparent people. How did she do that?"

"Have you ever been to Disney World? Specifically, have you ever been to the Haunted Mansion?"

Faye nodded yes and Amande shook her head, saying, "No, but I've seen pictures."

"Have you seen pictures of the dining room, where you can see through a bunch of waltzing green ghosts?"

"I always heard those were holograms," Faye said.

"Did they have holograms, way back in the sixties when Disney World was built?" Amande asked.

Toni-the-physics-teacher shook her head. "Not moving ones. And not at theme parks. The notion that the Haunted Mansion uses holograms isn't a new one—it's all over the Internet—but the geniuses who built the Haunted Mansion didn't need cutting-edge technology. They used a magician's technique that goes back to the 1600s. It's called the Pepper's Ghost illusion. All it takes is a pane of glass and a hidden room with control-lable lights."

Faye closed her eyes and pictured the auditorium. "Dara was surrounded by panes of glass. Where was the hidden room? Under our seats? Or was it above the ceiling, hidden from us but in full view of the stage?"

"Yes and yes. Very good. I'm sure that you both noticed that the mysterious images were very small. They flickered on and off, and they didn't last long."

Faye and Amande nodded.

"I think there are spaces below and above the stage. They're not tall enough to be called 'rooms,' but they serve the purpose for the Pepper's Ghost illusion, if you're willing to settle for tiny images. The items she wants us to see are in those spaces. She's got miniature human figures and 'floating' spheres, for sure. My guess is that the spheres are actually hanging from fine wires. A fog machine or two is probably enough to make those swirling colors at her feet. Those spaces above and below the audience must be fitted with lights that are set on timers synchronized with Dara's spinning cage. When she wants you to see a person or a sphere, the lights come up."

"When that happens, the hidden object is reflected in the glass?"

Toni smiled at Amande and said, "Precisely. Have you taken physics?"

"Last year, I took high school physics. I'm taking an advanced placement course this year."

Toni kept smiling. "Then you know more than enough optics to understand the Pepper's Ghost illusion. So tell me this: Why doesn't Dara use the technique throughout the show?"

Faye shrugged. "I have an answer, but it doesn't have anything to do with physics, just with common sense. If magicians have been doing this Pepper's Ghost thing for hundreds of years, then you're not the only person who knows about it. Given time, anybody with eyes will eventually notice that they're only seeing ghosts when they're looking through a glass pane. She doesn't want to give the audience a chance to figure it out."

"Bingo. You can only misdirect an observant person for so long. Dara is shrewd. She baffles the crowd, then skedaddles before they figure out her secrets."

"But the tarot cards." There was a furrow between Amande's eyebrows. "How could she have known which cards Debbie drew? Then how could she have drawn the same three cards herself? That was amazing."

"I'm still working on that trick, but I'm certain of one thing. Dara and Willow are not doing magic. Think about it. People do card tricks because they're easy to handle. They're flexible. You can palm them. You can stick them up your sleeve. But they only work for close-up magic. That's why Dara has a camera to show people her tricks. If she could do the same thing with... say...china teapots or books or flaming torches, then that's what she would do. Big, bulky objects would look way better onstage than a few cheap cards. Have you ever seen a book trick?"

Amande shook her head.

"Well, that's why. Books are too big to stick up your sleeve. Never believe a card trick. If the performer could really work magic, why waste it on something flimsy like cards?"

Faye had never questioned why magicians used cards. They just did. They also pulled rabbits out of hats. Why? Probably because a hat was an easy place to hide something the size of a rabbit. Accepting the status quo without question was generally the first step to being fooled.

"But you don't know how they're doing the card trick?" Faye asked, hoping she was wrong.

Toni shook her head. "No. But I can guess. First of all, Willow has to know which cards Debbie drew. Maybe he did something to force her to pick those three cards. Or they could be marked. More likely, he took a peek, maybe through sleight-of-hand or maybe with a mirror. Just because I didn't see him do it...again... doesn't mean it didn't happen. After that, all he has to do is let Dara know which cards his sucker drew."

Faye had been trying to figure out why Toni signaled them to look at Willow at this point in the show. Amande must have had the same question, because she asked it. "He's telling Dara which cards to pull by using body language, isn't he? That's why you wanted us to watch him work that suit like a runway model."

Toni laughed out loud. "The man does have style, I admit. Yes, I think he's using body signals, but I haven't cracked his code yet. There are four suits in a tarot deck, so he could easily signal one of those. For example, moving his right hand might be his way of saying, 'Wands.' His left hand might say, 'Cups,' his right foot could mean 'Swords,' and his left foot might be 'Pentacles." Each suit has fourteen cards. That's a lot, but I'm sure there are ways to position your body to communicate the numbers."

"All the numbers are two digits, and the first digit is going to be one or zero," Faye pointed out. "It wouldn't be that hard to come up with a digital system."

"No, it wouldn't, but I want *their* system, so I'm buying a lot of fifteen-dollar tickets trying to crack it. Remember, there are also twenty-two trump cards, and Willow would need an individual signal for each of them."

Toni reached in a drawer behind her and pulled out a tarot deck. She turned them face up and fanned them across the table. "In case you haven't done the math, Debbie—or Willow—pulled two trump cards and an ace. No boring little twos or fives for the Reigning Couple of Showmanship. The odds against that special combination are high. Not astronomical, but high. So how did he tell her what those unlikely cards were? I didn't see him slash his finger across his throat to signal the Death card, so their code is something more subtle."

Amande reached out and used her left hand to sweep half the cards into her right hand. "There. I just divided the number of signals by two. We don't know that he was holding a full Tarot deck. Maybe he was holding two identical half-decks. Two Death cards. Two Aces of Swords."

Toni considered the idea. "He'd have to be able to control his victim's draws. Otherwise, somebody would pull Death twice."

"And then they'd drop dead of fright." Faye looked at the other two women, both sitting silent. "That wasn't even funny, was it?"

Amande shook her head in her mother's direction and went back to studying the cards. "So maybe he's got a limited deck and maybe he doesn't. Unless he's forcing the person to draw three specific cards, he has to signal the actual cards to Dara, and then she's gotta pull them out of a face-down deck. Her cards *have* to be marked. His probably are, too."

Faye started to laugh. "Of course, they're marked, and I think we have proof. How old is Dara? Mid-forties?"

Toni joined her in laughing, while Amande looked blank. Faye reached in her purse for her brand-new reading glasses. "Was Dara wearing glasses when we met her?"

The girl shook her head.

"And she wasn't wearing glasses on any of the other times I've seen her perform," Toni said, triumph in her voice. "She has just now reached the age when she can't see the markings on the back of her cards. I remember when that happened to me."

"The camera…" Amande said.

Faye nodded. "If she makes the markings on the cards bigger, the camera will pick them up. Dara is too vain to wear those glasses unless she really needs them, and she probably doesn't need them yet at any other time—only when she's cheating at cards. Look at these." She waved a tarot card in the air that was bigger than her hand. "Even without my glasses, I can see that this is the Two of Cups. Dara doesn't need glasses if she's doing an honest trick."

Amande yanked the Two of Cups from her mother's hand and studied it, back and front. "You're right. Dara's cards have to be marked. The glasses prove it. Now you just need to decode Willow's part of the trick, Toni, and you've got the whole thing."

Toni said nothing, but she had a victorious air as she shuffled the oversized tarot cards. Deftly cutting the deck, she flipped a card in front of Faye.

"The Queen of Swords. She is independent, resilient, and calm in times of trouble. When a decision must be made, she makes it as surely and quickly as a falling sword." Toni cocked her head in Faye's direction and asked, "She is you. True?"

Faye couldn't argue.

"For you," she said, squinting through her bifocals at Amande as she flipped another card. Above a floating, unearthly being was a caption that read "The World." "Of course. There could be no other card for someone of your youth and abilities."

Then she handed the deck to Amande, who seemed far more interested in the filigreed designs on the backs of the cards than in the phantasmagoric art on their faces. Setting three of them side-by-side and studying the designs for differences, she said, "Those two cards were too perfect. They suit my mother and me too well. Are these marked?"

All Toni would say was, "I'm not talking," but she shoved her glasses absent-mindedly up her nose with her middle finger. Faye wondered if Toni's subconscious was saying, "I need these stupid things to read my marked cards." Maybe magicians weren't always able to squelch the unintended signals of a subconscious that knew all their secrets. Or maybe Toni touched her glasses on purpose, to help Amande figure out the cards' secrets all by herself.

Toni let Amande study the cards for a moment, reaching into the bag of cookies and handing Faye two more. Faye was glad to see that they were heavily studded with pecans and chocolate chips. Toni might not make her own cookies, but she bought the good stuff.

Leaving Amande with the cards, Toni came to sit beside Faye. "Is there any chance of talking my way back into that museum, or do I have to wait until you and Amande finish your work? I'm quiet, and I clean up after myself."

"I'm sure that's true, but..." Faye paused, hesitant to say no to someone who was in the act of showing her some gracious hospitality. "I just can't. I still haven't unpacked everything. I keep finding new stashes of old junk. It wouldn't be professional to let someone else come in and stir up the very artifacts and files I'm trying to organize. It just wouldn't work."

Faye could tell that Toni wasn't happy about this, but the woman had far more than minimal social skills. Her only gracious option was to say that she understood Faye's position, so that's what she did.

After disappointing Toni, Faye moved away from the dining table, sitting in a comfy armchair to watch Toni entertain Amande by teaching her to palm cards and do false shuffles. Her daughter was frighteningly adept at sleight-of-hand. While they shuffled and dealt and giggled, Faye amused herself by wondering why the former physics teacher cared about the history of this little town so much. She also wondered why the chicanery of Dara and her husband made Toni mad enough to buy a stack of fifteen-dollar tickets that was already tall and was still growing.

Chapter Fifteen

"Mom. *Mom.*"

Faye realized that her daughter was trying to get her attention, and that she'd been doing so for some time now. Amande couldn't be blamed for being bored by the current topic of conversation—health insurance options for retired and self-employed people. Neither could Faye and Toni be blamed for finding them fascinating.

"Mom. The diner's still open. I think I'll walk down there for a cappuccino." Anticipating Faye's response, she said, "It's only a block and there are lots of streetlights."

Toni, who had offered them a very hospitable variety of beverages, jumped up to make a pot of coffee, but Faye held out a hand to stop her. Amande didn't want coffee. She wanted to escape the tedious company of grown-ups.

"Go. Have a banana split. Text me when you get there."

"It's not even ten and I'm walking one block."

"A text is a small price for freedom. And a banana split. Go."

◇◇◇

As soon as Amande knew she could no longer be seen through the bay window of Toni's living room, she pulled her phone from her pocket. Its bright screen displayed the two-sentence text message that had arrived while her mother and Toni were deep in boring money talk.

Meet me in my aunt's garden. I have something to show you.

How did Ennis get her cell number? Maybe from Samuel but Amande would say Myrna if she had to guess. Myrna would probably adore the chance to be a matchmaker.

As Amande walked past the diner, she made good on her promise to text her mother when she got there. Then she kept walking.

◇◇◇

Amande lingered at the garden gate. It was covered with vining plants, and the thicket of leaves on the other side was so dense that she wasn't sure it would swing open when she pushed. The sense that these vines were reaching out for her kept her from taking the last step toward the gate.

Amande was not crazy about overgrown gardens and weedy lawns. She had the feeling that anything could be lurking in the unkempt greenery. This was stupid, because she had spent her childhood mucking about the swamps in Louisiana. These days, she could kill an entire Saturday afternoon with her dad in the pristine woodlands of Joyeuse Island, braving ticks and chiggers for the thrill of seeing the year's first blooming dogwood.

Nevertheless, she liked the area around a house to be tidy. Not necessarily manicured, but tidy. Perhaps this vulnerable feeling went back to the days when nomadic people needed to be able to see whether a predator was creeping up to their tents. And perhaps this meditation on nomadic people might only occur to the daughter of two anthropology-types.

The phone in her hand vibrated and its screen lit up.

Where are you? I'm in the middle greenhouse. Hurry!

She could have called out an answer to him, but she was still in a cautious mood, fit for lingering. Texting felt safer.

I'm almost there.

The vines resisted, but she forced the old gate open. Using her phone as a flashlight, she crept through the lush garden on the other side. A shadowy figure stood in the second of the three greenhouses on her right. That must be where Ennis was waiting. Led by the glow of his phone, she picked her way to where he stood. He waited in a narrow walkway between the shelves where Sister Mama grew medicinal herbs that weren't happy with New York's weather.

"Hurry!" She wondered why he was whispering. Maybe because it felt like there was nobody else awake in Rosebower. Except, of course, for her mother and Toni, who were a good bit more than one block away.

Then she saw it. In the phosphorescent glow of his phone's screen was a flower, large and white. It was opening before her eyes.

"I told you to hurry. You're just in time. It's a night-blooming cereus," he whispered.

It seemed unnatural to watch a plant move. Without the help of a breeze or a human or some other animal, a plant is supposed to sit still. Yet here this one was, stretching its luminous white petals into the air. Minute by minute, the flower formed itself, large and lovely. It loosed a penetrating perfume as it took shape.

"Beautiful, right?" he said.

Amande could hardly breathe, but she nodded.

"If you like that, you need to see the night garden."

Amande wondered why he thought she'd she want to leave the cereus before it finished opening, but she followed him outside into a dimly lit fairyland. The flowers in this corner of the garden, mostly white, had been chosen because they were beautiful in the dark. Ennis moved here and there, illuminating various blooms with his phone.

"Here are the moonflowers." He pointed to a vine loaded with luminous palm-sized blossoms. "They bloom when the sun goes down. You can see them open, just like the night-blooming cereus. You should come back tomorrow at sunset and watch."

His attention span for flowers was shorter than hers, because he quickly moved on to a bed of large-leaved plants topped with clusters of starry flowers. "See how white the nicotiana petals are? That's the scientific name for flowering tobacco. Sister Mama designed her night garden so all the flowers show up in starlight. And the leaves, too."

Surrounding the flowering plants were mounds of ornamental foliage, variegated in white and all shades of green. Their leaves glowed in the dark night, and they were as lovely as the flowers.

Ennis was still giving his flashlight tour. "And she picks the plants that smell the best, too, because it's important in the dark. A blind person could enjoy this spot."

This was true.

"Look. These four o'clocks glow like fire. Sister Mama says they got their name because they don't open till four o'clock in the afternoon."

The tiny trumpet-shaped flowers were magenta and yellow and white. Some of the flowers were splashed with all three colors. They looked like fireworks, and they did absolutely belong in a night garden. Bending down close, she could smell something sweet that was neither nicotiana nor cereus.

"Sister Mama loves the way her plants look and smell, but those things are just bonuses. She's not big on wasting garden space. The nicotiana is good in poultices and you can make bugkiller out of it."

"It kills bugs, but you'll put it on somebody's open wound?"

"It's all in the dose and in how you give it. That's true of store-bought medicine, too. Foxglove'll kill you. Digitalis will save your life."

"And the dose is different for different people. What would cure you, might kill me?"

"Exactly."

"What about these other things?"

"Leaves from four o'clocks help people who are holding water. Sister Mama might make a tea or give them a poultice. Either way, they take the swelling right down. The seeds are poison, though." He was still whispering, so Amande had to lean close to get her answer.

"The cereus? How does she use it?"

"It's not like she's taught me everything she knows. Not yet. But it may be that she grows the cereus just because it's too pretty to be called a waste of garden space. Sister Mama does what makes her happy. Want to go look at it again?"

Amande did want to see it again. Very much. As they turned to go, a muffled grunt startled her. It came from an open window on the back of the house.

"Was that your aunt? We should check on her."

"She talks in her sleep. A lot. We should stay out here and let her do that."

The sound came again, and Amande headed for the house's back door. Another noise came, and this one didn't sound like a human voice. It was more like one solid thing striking another solid thing. "Don't you hear that?"

"Hear what? No, Baby, I don't hear a thing."

The back door was unlocked and Amande was in the house before Ennis could take another shot at keeping her outside with him. It wasn't hard to figure out which room belonged to the open window. Once Ennis saw that she wasn't going to linger romantically in the greenhouse with him, he was right behind her.

Sister Mama's bedroom held little more than a bed and a chest-of-drawers. A handful of fragrant flowers sat on top of the chest, spilling gently over the edge of a wide-mouthed glass bottle. Her wheelchair sat in the corner and she herself lay under a worn patchwork quilt. One hand picked absently at loose threads hanging from the quilt. The other pawed at her face, as if someone were trying to suffocate her. Nobody was there.

Ennis hurried to her bedside. "Sister Mama. Sister Mama, are you okay?"

The woman didn't respond. Eyes closed, she continued plucking at her face and at the quilt. Amande tried to put a calming hand on her arm and she could feel the muscles spasming.

"Call 911," she said. "Hurry."

Sister Mama's breath caught in her throat and Amande wasn't sure she was getting any air. Maybe her throat muscles were spasming, too. She tried to lift the woman to a sitting position, thinking it would help her breathe. Sister Mama wouldn't bend.

All her muscles seemed locked up tight, except for the ceaseless motion of her hands and forearms.

Amande couldn't check Sister Mama's airway, because her mouth wouldn't come open. She noticed that Ennis had begun massaging his aunt's abdomen, maybe to help her breathe and maybe to loosen up the muscles so that she could sit.

"911?"

He pointed at the phone clutched to his ear. He had been massaging his aunt with one hand while he thumb-dialed. He was already talking to an emergency responder, but Amande was too frantic to listen to what he was saying. What was she going to do if she couldn't help Sister Mama breathe?

Since she couldn't get the suffering woman's mouth open, Amande went for her nose, trying to see whether air was coming in and going out. Something felt wrong.

One nostril was stiff and distended. The other, thankfully, seemed to be clear, but Sister Mama was still flapping her hand around her face. Amande eased her own hip onto the bed and forced the hand under it. If she needed to sit on it long enough to see what was happening to Sister Mama, then so be it.

"I think she's getting air," Ennis said. "Stand back and give her some room to breathe."

Amande stayed put, palpating both nostrils. "Turn on the lights." When he hesitated, she said, "Do it." He did.

There was something in Sister Mama's right nostril. Amande had heard of little children putting beans and rocks up their nose, but could a woman in Sister Mama's condition have done that? And had she regressed to toddlerhood? Amande had spent only a single lunch with her, but she didn't think so.

Now that the lights were on, she could see something barely protruding from the nostril. It was such an unnatural shade of orange that Amande knew it couldn't be part of Sister Mama. She grasped it between her finger and thumb and yanked hard.

As the squishy orange thing came out, every muscle in Sister Mama's body relaxed. Her eyes found Amande's and said thank you.

Amande looked at the thing in her hand. It was fairly large to have come out of a nostril, but sponges can be squeezed into remarkably small places. Why had Sister Mama had a chunk of kitchen sponge up her nose? And how long was it going to take the paramedics to show up?

She turned her head to look at Ennis. He gestured to the phone that was still stuck to his ear and said, "They're coming."

Amande took Sister Mama's hand in hers, hoping the gesture was comforting. Then she thumbed her own phone, one-handed, until the first person on her speed-dial list answered.

"Mom?"

◇◇◇

Faye didn't remember saying much more to Toni than, "Amande... Sister Mama," as she lunged out the door and ran for the car. Even in Rosebower, there were times when a car was the way to go. Driving five blocks was a lot quicker than walking five blocks. But why was her daughter four blocks further away than she was supposed to be? How did she find herself in the bedroom of a sick woman who was struggling for life?

◇◇◇

Faye rushed past Ennis to Amande. The girl stood silently, watching a paramedic examine Sister Mama.

"Mom. You wouldn't believe how much better she looks. She's pinking up by the second. She's breathing well. She's relaxed. She's sitting up. I don't even think they're going to take her to the hospital. Why do you think she shoved a sponge up her nose?"

Sister Mama couldn't talk to the paramedics, but Ennis assured them that this was normal for her. Other than being unable to answer their questions, she obediently responded to every instruction. She raised both hands, individually and together. She looked to her left, she looked to her right. She correctly answered questions intended to assess her mental function, by using gestures. Faye could see that the paramedics already had one foot out the door.

"Where's the sponge?"

"Right here on the floor."

Faye handed Amande a tissue. "Pick it up and bring it with you. I need you to step outside and explain some things to me."

Chapter Sixteen

Faye stood outside Sister Mama's front door, fiddling with her phone and delaying the moment when she'd have to ask Amande to explain herself. Amande opened the discussion herself.

"We were just looking at flowers."

"Then why did you lie?"

"Because you wouldn't have let me go."

"Not good enough."

Faye went back to fiddling with her phone. In a way, she was the one acting like a teenager. She was ignoring her daughter because she couldn't think of the right thing to say and because she was pretty sure there was something on the internet that she needed to find. Something about the sponge up Sister Mama's nose triggered Faye's memories of a favorite class in the history of science. The Romans had impressed her as ingenious people, particularly in their approach to the medical arts.

She asked the Internet to remind her of what she once knew about soporific sponges.

◇◇◇

Amande expected her mother to keep talking about the fact that she'd lied. She wasn't sure whether she wanted to acknowledge the lie or do an end run around it, by railing about the silliness of tracking her whereabouts by text. She was seventeen years old, and she'd been wandering around Barataria Bay alone in a boat when she was twelve.

But hey. She'd lied. There was no denying it.

Since she was inarguably guilty, why hadn't her mother gone in for the kill? Why was she standing there studying her phone like its screen displayed the answer to all life's questions?

"A soporific sponge. Just what I thought."

Amande was accustomed to weird polysyllabic utterances from her mother, but "soporific sponge" might be the weirdest of all.

Faye handed her phone to Amande for perusal. "I took two semesters of 'History of Science' in grad school. The second one focused on medicine. In the old days, people spent a lot of time worrying about pain relief. It's not like you could run to the drugstore for an aspirin in the Middle Ages. And surgery… the ancient Romans knew a lot about the human body, and they knew how to fix some parts of the body when they broke, but can you imagine having a tumor removed while you were awake?"

Amande shook her head.

Faye brandished the phone. "Look at this web page. It says that medieval writers described something that sounds almost like a magic potion—poppies, mandrake, henbane, hemlock, and probably a lot of other stuff. The potion was brewed, then left in the sun to evaporate off most of the water. When someone needed to be unconscious, a sponge soaked full of that stuff was stuck up their nose. The Romans are thought to have used something similar."

"Did it work?"

"Supposedly. Maybe not as well as modern anesthetics, but that is a list of some very powerful natural sedatives and painkillers. A sponge up the nose would administer them as inhalants, just like our modern general anesthetics, but they could also be absorbed through the mucous membrane. If I knew somebody was planning to cut me open, I'd figure it was worth a try. Let's go talk to the paramedics about this. And no. We're not finished talking about the honesty issue. It can wait, because this is more urgent. Slightly."

◇◇◇

The paramedic looked tired. He was probably coming up on the end of a very long shift. "I hear what you're saying, but I don't think you understand how many weird things I've seen in people's noses. And other parts. Usually, it's kids that do this kind of thing, but you'd be surprised."

"So you're not going to take her to the hospital?" Faye asked.

"For what? Look at her. Does she look worse than she usually does?"

Faye had to say no.

"I don't know what to say about the sponge. You lost me when you started talking about 'herbal alkaloids.' I'm here to treat the patient. I did that. There is no longer an emergency. If you weren't here, I'd have already gone. Since I've got another call, I'm going to do that now."

Faye didn't want to discuss this issue, or anything else, in front of Ennis, so she followed the paramedic out of the house and she kept walking.

"Where are we going?" Amande asked.

"To the inn down the street. I want to talk to Avery. Someone has already killed a woman in this town, using a bizarre method. People don't get locked up and set on fire by antique kerosene lamps every day of the week. In that paramedic's world, people may get kitchen sponges stuck up their nose all the time, but not in mine. I'm not comfortable with bizarre events, not when it comes to a person's safety. Avery needs to know about this."

"What are you going to do? Get her to run a tox scan on a snot-covered sponge?"

"Maybe. If it was soaked in an opium derivative, a toxicology lab analysis aimed at heroin or codeine would probably pick it up. Hensbane, mandrake, and hemlock? I'm not so sure about that. But even a screening test could probably tell us whether there are unexpected chemicals soaked into that sponge, even if it can't identify them." She picked up her pace, as if all the mysteries of the week would be solved if she could just get an orange chunk of sponge to Avery. "I'm betting they do find something. Why else would she have started getting better as soon as you took it out? My guess is that it hadn't been in there

long, or she would have been unconscious when you found her.
And, no, I don't think she stuck it up her own nose."

"Who'd want to drug Sister Mama?"

At last, Faye made eye contact with her daughter. "Maybe the
man who gets fed up with taking care of her? She's less trouble
to him when she's asleep."

"Mom. That's just…awful. Ennis wouldn't do that."

"And you know this how?"

"You weren't there. He was so upset to see her that way."

"Then let's get back to your question. Who else would want
Sister Mama drugged? Or dead."

"Dead? Why do you say that? Dead?"

"Sister Mama is very frail. A real doctor probably wouldn't
consider putting her under modern anesthesia in her condition.
You don't think exposing her to a random mix of primitive
anesthetics—any one of which could kill her with a big enough
dose—might be a murder attempt? Haven't you ever heard of
Socrates being poisoned with hemlock?"

Amande started to say, "Where would anybody get—" then
she gave up. They both knew that any plant-based pharmaceuti-
cal in the world had at least some possibility of being in Sister
Mama's garden and greenhouses.

"Why would Ennis invite me over while he was in the process
of killing his great-aunt?"

This was a point that Faye would have to concede, though
with a caveat. "He probably wouldn't, but murderers are crazy.
Maybe he wanted some company while the poisons did his dirty
work for him. Maybe he wanted an alibi. Or maybe he wasn't
trying to kill her. Maybe he just wanted her to be quiet while
he tried to romance you. If you think somebody else did it, you
need to tell me how they got past you and Ennis."

"The windows were open. One of them was on the side of
the house that we couldn't see. Somebody could have gone in
and out of there before we got there, and Ennis might have been
watching TV. He'd have never heard. Or…Mom! I heard a noise

right before we went in the house. It was like a thump. I bet it was somebody going out that window."

"You say *you* heard the noise. Where was Ennis?"

"He was right there. It was after I heard Sister Mama groan the first time."

"He didn't hear either noise?"

"No."

"Maybe he didn't want to hear. Maybe he knew his great-aunt was in there dying."

Amande gave a frustrated teenager screech. "You just want him to be guilty. You're trying too hard to make him be a killer. I think he's not."

"Who found the sponge?"

"I did, but it was easy for him to miss. Only a little bit of it hung out where I could see it."

"Maybe he was hoping you wouldn't notice it."

Amande's glare spoke for her. They had reached the front door of the inn. Faye said, "I guess we should call Avery and let her know we're coming. And we're bringing a snotty sponge with us."

◇◇◇

Ennis sat at his sleeping aunt's bedside. She looked better and her breathing was regular. She was as healthy as she'd been the day before, but that wasn't saying much. She still couldn't walk and talk. She couldn't tend her garden and mix her potions. He couldn't tell when she was happy or sad. He didn't know if she was ever happy these days.

This might have been the evening that Sister Mama took her leave of this earth. Maybe it would have been better that way.

◇◇◇

Faye's daughter looked at her and said, "Avery said she'd get some labs run on the sponge. Are you happy now?"

Not particularly, no. Faye wasn't happy at all. Avery had listened to her, which was more than she could say for the paramedic. She hadn't called Faye's soporific sponge idea stupid, so Faye had to give her credit for being open-minded. She'd just said, "I'd have done the same thing in the paramedic's shoes, but he hasn't spent most of the past week in Weirdbower, New York. Neither has the sheriff. He lives on the other side of the county, which might as well be another continent. If I call him, he's going to want to know whether I think he should investigate every time somebody has a fainting spell. However."

Faye had liked the sound of that "however."

"The forensics lab manager owes me a favor. I actually don't know whether he's got a handy-dandy test for hensbane, but you said 'opium.' If there's opium on this sponge, I'm sure there's a tox screen that will find it. Let me see what he's willing to do for me."

So now Faye and Amande were in the car, making yet another drive back to the bed-and-breakfast. Returning to Amande's "Are you happy now?" question, she said, "Of course I'm not happy. I'm worried about Sister Mama and I'm worried about you. We are only here for a few weeks and there's no need for you to start something up with a questionable man like Ennis LeBecque. You are not to see him again."

Great. Now she'd wandered into the most treacherous part of parenting a teenager. She'd issued a dictum that she might not be able to enforce.

Working notes for Pulling the Wool Over Our Eyes:
An Unauthorized History of Spiritualism
in Rosebower, New York

by Antonia Caruso

*Dara Armistead has done it again. She is enjoying my
fifteen dollars and I still don't know how she does her
stupid card tricks. Willow is such a good cheater that,
once again, I couldn't catch him peeking at the cards
he used to fleece that defenseless widow. Still, I do
think that's how he does it, and I do think he used body
language to tell Dara which cards the widow held. Or
maybe their sound system is set up so that Dara could
hear when he tapped on his earpiece.*

*Was she wearing an earpiece, too? I must remember
to check next time.*

*Morse code would be too obvious, but a combination
of taps and body signals would do the trick. (Ha. I'm a
magician and I just said "trick.")*

*Whatever code they're using, it's not overly sophisti-
cated. It wouldn't have to be. It's entirely possible that
they did nothing more than memorize a different signal
for every card in the deck, because they were afraid that
a suspicious retired schoolteacher would one day be
sitting in the audience and they wanted to make her life*

as hard as possible. Even better, they wanted her to buy as many fifteen-dollar tickets as she could afford. They wanted her money.

Money.

I've heard the word all my life. I've earned money all my adult life. I've spent it. I've saved it. I've never been scared of it before.

I have seen people prostitute themselves for money before. This may not be the first time I have seen some-one do it mere days after a parent's violent death, but I'll have to say that watching Dara perform as if nothing had happened was a sight that raised the hair on the back of my neck. What would it have cost her to take a week to grieve? Nothing but money.

How much money do Willow and Dara need? Unless I miss my guess, Tilda possessed an inherited fortune, and now it is Dara's. If she is sufficiently in love with money to choose raking it in over grief for her mother, then maybe she was sufficiently in love with money to kill her mother for her fortune.

Do I have evidence for this? Do I even have evidence that Tilda Armistead's death was no accident? No.

All I have is the sick feeling in my stomach that comes from watching two people cheat an audience when those two people should be grieving.

Chapter Seventeen

Faye was still unsettled by Sister Mama's mysterious illness, but she couldn't deny that the discovery of Virginia Armistead's letter had brought a spark to her work life. She could see that Amande felt it, too. At any moment, one of them could find something else equally awesome. This possibility was more stimulating than the caffeine in the double-shot of espresso that had washed down her breakfast.

When Samuel showed up at the museum, mid-morning, she realized that she was a full twenty-four hours late in telling him that they'd found something significant. It wasn't that he expected a minute-by-minute report of their work, but he *was* paying the bills and he *was* passionate about history. He deserved to know about the old letter while it was still news.

To find her in the workroom, he had passed through the museum's displays, still cluttered by the same chaotic mess they had held when Faye arrived. The work room was in the process of getting worse before it could get better. This disarray made Faye feel a little sheepish when he asked, "Can we take a walk and talk about your progress?" She was glad she'd saved yesterday's good news to distract him from the pile of work left to do.

As Faye followed Samuel outside, she pointed Amande in the direction of some documents to be filed. Amande really didn't need the instruction, but showing the client that she was responsible with her employee's time was good business.

Nervous, she led from weakness, making excuses for her cluttered workspace. Samuel brushed her concern aside, saying, "It's been a strange week, Faye. We lost Tilda on Monday. Last night, there was an ambulance on my own street, coming to help Sister Mama. If those things put your project off-pace, I can't blame you. I've seen how you both throw yourselves into your work. You'll get it done."

Reassured, Faye jumped directly to the good news—fabulous news, actually—about the Armistead letter. "We found something significant yesterday, Samuel. Really significant. It's a letter written from the Seneca Falls convention, and it gives intimate, personal details about the women who attended. I can get a publishable article out of it that will get the attention of every women's studies scholar in the country. More than that, I think it's something that will have widespread appeal. This letter will get you coverage in the popular press. Schools will want to bring their kids to see it. It could put your museum on the map."

"It should already *be* on the map. We have some amazing things here. What have you found out about the Runestone? And the Rosebower spear? The Langley Object?"

Faye groped for something diplomatic to say that she hadn't already said. Samuel was one of those history buffs who couldn't be satisfied with plain old everyday history. He was convinced that the academic establishment was hiding the truth about medieval Europeans in North America and about Sasquatch and about prehistoric alien landings because…well, because they just were.

Samuel had never met a conspiracy theory that he did not love. History was not history unless it enflamed his imagination, and a simple letter from a woman who knew Elizabeth Cady Stanton wasn't going to do that. A scale from the hump of the Loch Ness Monster would be more to Samuel's liking.

Looking at his normally taciturn face, now bright with anticipation, she finally admitted to herself why none of her colleagues had outbid her for this job. She'd thought it was because they could find better paying work elsewhere. Now, she knew deep-down that the real reason she'd won this bid was because nobody else wanted to work for Samuel.

He was still talking, and he still wasn't making sense. "And the Langley Object? It's a bas-relief carving of an actual *flying saucer*. Please tell me you're getting it documented. *That* is the article you should be publishing."

Faye opted to backpedal and tell the truth at the same time. "I've looked at all the items you mentioned under magnification and I'm still working on a literature review. I also sent photos of the Rosebower spear to an expert on ancient American weapons."

She neglected to mention that this expert was her husband and that his opinion had been the same as Faye's. The spear point didn't deserve to be a focal point of this museum.

It wasn't junk, no. It was an utterly beautiful work of art. But it was not rare and it was not nearly as old as Samuel wished it to be. In Faye's professional opinion, it was a not particularly uncommon example of work done by Native Americans in the middle of the first millennium of the Common Era in the place that would be known as New York. Unfortunately, the huckster who sold it to Samuel told him that it was far older and that it was carved from stone only found in Europe, thus "proving" contact between the Old and New Worlds a thousand years before Columbus.

If Faye couldn't get Samuel to listen to reason, she would have to waste his money on laboratory results that said what she already knew to be true. Faye hated to waste money, even if it wasn't hers. Also, Samuel was not going to believe lab results he didn't like, so why pay for testing?

As for Samuel's fabulous "runestone," Faye didn't need Joe or a lab to tell her that it was a palm-sized sherd incised with decorations common to Iroquois pottery. It wasn't rare, and it was exactly what she would have expected to find in the countryside surrounding Rosebower. Samuel, however, believed with all his heart that it was something more. To him, those incised figures were Nordic runes proving that northern Europeans were living in America long before Columbus got lost on his way to the Spice Islands.

Most ridiculous of all was the "spaceship" carving on the "Langley Object." In this case, Samuel had been right to believe that he owned something that she wouldn't have expected to find in western New York. It was a piece of stone about half the size of a sheet of notebook paper, but only an imagination the size of Samuel's could see a spaceship in its stylized carving. It looked Mesoamerican to Faye, and she couldn't argue that it had traveled a long way to New York from the Yucatan Peninsula, but she didn't think it came to Rosebower by way of a flying saucer.

If she had to guess, she'd say one of Samuel's nineteenth-century ancestors had bought it while traveling in Central America, brought it north, and stashed it in the museum. Whatever its origin, Faye was really skeptical that the round thing on the central figure's head was anything more than a ceremonial headdress, but her client wanted it to be a spaceman's helmet. He wanted it bad.

Samuel wanted Faye to drape the credibility of her Ph.D. over work that would be called pseudoarchaeology in polite circles. In impolite circles, it was known as "bullshit archaeology."

Still dumping on the Armistead letter, one of the most significant finds of her career, Samuel asked, "Why are you wasting time on letters that passed between housewives? The Rosebower spear, the runestone, the Langley Object—these things could change the way we understand the world. And ourselves!"

Until this instant, when she finally understood the intensity of his misbegotten passions, Faye had not realized that she could give this client good service, yet still lose the job.

If she told Samuel what she thought about his "Runestone" now, she would soon be scurrying to read the fine print on her contract, because if it left Samuel the wiggle room to fire her, then he most certainly would. Since contracts generally favor the person who has the money, Faye was pretty sure that Samuel had retained some wiggle room.

Faye tried to examine her quandary dispassionately. She'd known Samuel had odd notions, but she hadn't expected the situation to spiral so far out of control. It wouldn't wreck her career if he forced her to leave this tiny, unimportant museum in a shambles. It would, however, hurt her professional pride.

Besides, the Virginia Armistead letter proved she could be walking away from truly significant things that ought to be preserved. American culture hadn't always done a good job of recognizing women's contributions. Here was her chance to help right that imbalance. Faye really wanted to salvage this situation.

Then Samuel put a toe over a line in the sand that Faye didn't even know she'd drawn.

He said, "Don't you see? My artifacts explain everything! There's no way that the Indians were advanced enough to build huge mound complexes like Cahokia in Illinois, much less the pyramids in the Yucatan. First the aliens came. Then the Europeans came years earlier than we thought. They built the cultures that Columbus and the explorers after him discovered. It's the only reasonable explanation."

Faye felt herself grow unexpectedly calm. She'd been willing to make allowances for Samuel's unorthodox ideas. She didn't share them, but everybody was entitled to an opinion. This last pronouncement, though, had a distinctly racist tone.

So the indigenous Americans, the ancestors of her husband and son and, in small part, herself, were incapable of building complex civilizations? Only aliens from outer space and Europeans were capable of such a thing?

She noticed that he didn't suggest American contact with ancient Egypt, so he probably figured that their civilization was built by aliens, too. Otherwise, he would have been forced to believe that the massive pyramids at Giza were built by Africans— Faye's ancestors, and her son's, and her daughter's. More than likely, Samuel wouldn't have credited Asians with any part in the globe-spanning cultural interchange of the deep dark past, either.

If, in her client's mind, otherworldly aliens and Europeans were the only beings capable of building a civilization, why was he willing to work with not-very-European Faye?

"You understand, don't you? When you find evidence of an advanced civilization, you have to look for early European contact. For so many years, we carried the rest of the world."

We. He had said "we." Samuel was standing right in front of Faye, yet he had no idea who she was.

Faye took a glance at the back of her hand. It was a distinctive pale brown. She was proud of her multiracial heritage. People who knew her were aware that her great-great-grandmother was a slave.

This man, who didn't know her at all, was color-blind in a backward kind of way. He had hired a woman, sight unseen, whose résumé had signaled him to expect a contractor who was smart and competent. Based on his world view, the only option when he met dark-beige Faye was to presume that she was a white woman with a really good tan.

Faye was poised to quit the job and walk away...until she saw the glimmer of a possibility that Samuel might be taught a lesson.

Improvising as she spoke, she said, "My expertise is really in historic archaeology. I can hold my own with lithics and ceramics, but I think artifacts as...notable...as yours should be handled by an expert. Fortunately, I know just the person. It'll cost you a plane ticket and a few days of this man's time, but he's really the best there is. I'm lucky that he's willing to consult for me."

They shook on it, leaving Faye eager to go wash her right hand. Then she returned to her computer to draw up a contract that Samuel would happily sign, because it would promise him a credentialed expert to look at his so-called "runestone."

She still did not intend to do any bullshit archaeology, so he would not be happy with her final report, but it would be prepared ethically and according to sound scientific principles. More importantly, every word of it would adhere to every last clause in the contract. She still might not get paid, but it would be entertaining to watch him try to wriggle out of her bill for writing it. If she decided to take him to court for breach-of-contract, she would have the pleasure of watching him try to convince a judge that Rosebower's original settlers were intergalactic alien space invaders. And Europeans.

At this point, she no longer cared whether she got paid, anyway. She just wanted to see what would happen if Samuel continued to spout racist crap in the presence of the credentialed expert he was flying to New York—her intimidatingly large Creek husband.

◇◇◇

Amande noticed that her mother had nothing to say when she returned from her talk with Samuel. Oh, she'd said hello and given Amande's upper arm a playful squeeze. She had peered over her shoulder and pretended to inspect her work, but Faye knew Amande had done nothing all day but sort through old letters. Unlike yesterday's find, today's batch of letters had *not* been written by someone watching history be made.

Most of today's letters had come from spoiled young people writing home to the late-Victorian parents who were paying for their grand tours of Europe. They were invariably some variant on this theme:

> *Dearest Mother and Father,*
>
> *Our tour down the Rhine was most inspiring. The castles on the hilltops above us had their romantic aspects, but I am told that even those still inhabited are no longer kept in the grand style, due to the difficulty of finding menials who are willing to do the work needed to maintain such establishments. I also find German wines much inferior to those of France.*

Amande always lost attention immediately after each insufferable letter-writer complained about non-French wine. She had tried to joke about these wine whines, but her mother had nodded and said, "Hmmm," so Amande had gone back to sifting through the stacks of boring papers.

What could Samuel have said to upset Faye so?

After an hour of listening to her mother fidget, Amande wasn't surprised to hear her say, "Time for a coffee break, but I'm not thirsty. Why don't you go to the diner and get yourself some of that cappuccino you like? I'm going to make a phone call."

Amande didn't get the sense that this was going to be a business call. This was a call prompted by the worries that were making Faye squirm so much that she'd probably worn the varnish off her desk chair. Amande figured that it was a coin-flip as to whom her mother would call to hash out her problems. Either it would be her dad, or it would be Magda.

Amande wished she had a best friend like Faye's. The one thing that Amande's new life with Faye and Joe hadn't given her was friends. She'd never had real friends while growing up. It hadn't been her poverty that had set her apart, because there had been plenty of poverty to go around in south Louisiana.

Part of her isolation had been her doing, because she'd never known what to say to the other kids. They'd wasted their time on playground bickering, as if they didn't know what real trouble was like. And they'd kept their distance from Amande, because they knew that she did.

She'd imagined that they were afraid to talk to her, for fear her bad luck would rub off. The combination of a runaway mother, deadbeat father, and weirdo grandmother was enough to render her socially untouchable. Worse, the almost-homeless existence of living on a houseboat was deeply scary to children who knew, at some level, that their own families might be one assistance check from an existence that was as tenuous.

Being adopted by Faye and Joe had been like having a fairy godmother drop down out of the sky with a pumpkin full of all Amande's dreams. She was a little lonely. This was true. So what? She'd be going away to college in a year, and that would be way different from living on an island with a couple of adults and a toddler.

She looked out the window. Faye had her phone to her ear and she was hunched over with laughter, so Amande knew exactly who was on the other end of the call. That was a best-friend kind of laugh, so her mother had called Magda.

Distracted by Magda's jokes, there was no way that Faye would have noticed the foot traffic on the sidewalk across the street behind her. If Amande hadn't been watching, no one would have seen Ennis walk by and then, five minutes later, walk past again. Amande guessed that he was hoping her mother would leave so he could come inside and pay Amande another visit.

If she took her mother's suggestion and walked to the diner for a cappuccino, she had no doubt that he'd follow her there. She thought maybe she'd skip the coffee. Or maybe she'd go for a walk and let him chase her.

Sometimes Ennis weirded her out. But sometimes…Well, sometimes, she thought he might be nothing worse than lonely and bored. Just like her.

Faye was still talking ninety-miles-a-minute to her cell phone, gesturing with her free hand as if Magda could see her. Amande wondered how long they'd been friends. She should ask Faye.

Her mother knew she was lonely. She kept talking about getting Amande a job in Sopchoppy or Panacea when they got home, so that she could spend time with people her age. Amande was very good at real-world math, and she knew that the fuel costs to get her ashore to that job would eat up every last dime of a minimum wage paycheck. Faye seemed to think she should do it anyway.

Amande knew she could have friendships like the one Faye shared with Magda, once she ventured off the island and put some effort into meeting people. Right now, however, she was a little scared of the big bad world. She thought she might hide out on Joyeuse Island for an extra year or so.

Chapter Eighteen

Faye could laugh and joke all she liked. Even on the other end of a cell phone connection, Magda Stockard-McKenzie could tell when her friend was stressed past her limits. The laughs came a little too quick, and the jokes fell a little too flat. Faye had not placed this call just to hear Magda's harsh and crow-like voice, but that was okay. Best friends didn't have to say what they were thinking, not until they were ready to say it.

The best friend code required Magda to pretend that Faye had really called to talk about work. No-nonsense Magda could play make-believe, when necessary, so she asked a work-related question. "So your client believes he's got a picture of an alien *and* he believes he's got a medieval Scandinavian shopping list proving that Columbus wasn't here first?"

"Yes, he does believe those things. I've held that stupid 'Runestone' in my own two hands. Oh, and by the way, Columbus *wasn't* here first. Keep talking like that, Madame Archaeologist, and I'm going to see about getting your Ph.D. revoked."

Magda liked to hear that familiar cocky attitude. If Faye could still make her laugh by insulting her, then things couldn't be all that bad. "I know Columbus wasn't first. Not two hours ago, I got an eye full of your gorgeous husband, and I am completely aware that his ancestors were waiting on the beach to tell the Europeans hello. Just think. If Columbus hadn't come over here and messed things up, this country would still be full of men who look like Joe."

"Yeah, but then your people would've stayed in England, so you wouldn't be here to goggle at Joe's."

"I'm sure we would have had an embassy with the Creeks. I could've gotten a job there, where I'd be surrounded by Joe clones. Trust me. I'd have found a way to get to this side of the Atlantic."

"I'm going to tell your husband."

"Mike knows that I love every hair on his…arms. Despite the fact that there aren't many left on his head and they're all gray."

These things were true, but the retired sheriff still walked and talked like the forty-year-old man he had been when he took responsibility for the safety of the citizens of Micco County, Florida. If the words "peace officer" had ever been true of anyone, they were true of Sheriff Mike. Magda loved the old coot for just those things.

She listened to Faye mentally backpedal through the conversation. "Wait. You said you'd just seen my husband. Did he come ashore for no reason other than to visit? Don't tell me he got lonely enough to admit it."

It had taken Faye long enough to ask that question. Magda decided that she really *must* be stressed. Everyone in Joe's world knew that he generally only left Joyeuse Island for work and for unavoidable errands, like grocery shopping. His hunting, fishing, and gardening kept their grocery bill to a minimum, but the Longchamp-Mantooth family liked milk. And ice cream. They were all big on ice cream. Short of learning to milk a deer, the island-dwellers' only choice was to come ashore from time to time.

"I happen to know that my husband bought groceries not two days ago. What was he doing in town today?"

"He got lonely," she said. "Imagine being alone on an island with a two-year-old for days and days."

The phone was silent while Faye took a moment to do that. Finally, she said, "Poor Joe."

"Yes. And he's never going to get over that emergency room trip with Michael."

"Did you get a look at his stitches? Do you think he's in pain? Does he even still have stitches?"

Magda interrupted Faye before she could embarrass herself with another question. "Hush. The child is fine. The stitches are still in. The cut looks good. Joe is a meticulous man, you know that. He cleans the wound and uses antibiotic ointment three times a day, like clockwork, just like the doctor told him. I watched him do it yesterday, after school."

"School? Yesterday? Joe was in town three days in a row?"

"When I saw him at the grocery store on Tuesday, I could see that the man was at the end of his rope. He was the sweet, calm, loving, and perfect dad that he always is, but he was at the end of his rope, nevertheless. Two-year-olds are…"

"Two."

"Yes, they are. I told him to come in early yesterday morning and I'd talk to the people at Rachel's preschool about letting Michael visit a few days a week. Just for the summer."

"So Michael started school and Joe was going to tell me this…never?"

"Settle down. Michael didn't start school without you. He just got some glorified babysitting and he had a good time on the playground. Mostly."

Magda mentally kicked her honest self. She should probably have kept Michael's playground adventures to herself.

"Mostly?"

"Um…Michael's homework is to remember that it's not okay to throw rocks."

As a mother of a five-year-old, Magda knew that it was possible to be absolutely humiliated by something she herself did not do. That sick feeling was in Faye's voice as she said "Rocks? He went to school with a bunch of little kids and threw rocks on the first day? Did he hurt anybody?"

"Nobody's hurt. He wasn't aiming at the kids, or somebody might've been. The teacher said he damn near took a squirrel off a tree branch. The rock whiffled right through the fur on its fluffy little tail."

It could have been worse. One inch in the right direction, and the playground could have been full of traumatized children watching a squirrel expire.

"I can't believe my child was throwing rocks at school."

"Faye. What does your husband do with rocks? There is a reason Michael likes to throw rocks, and the reason is not that his mother is a failure."

Her phone emitted the sound of Faye saying, "Ohhhh." Understanding had dawned.

"Joe spends days chipping rocks till they're razor sharp. Then he makes arrows, kills something tasty, and we have a great meal. Sometimes he skips the chipping and the bow, and he just uses his sling to throw any old random rock."

"Exactly. If Michael's rock had been an inch to the left, there would have been a squirrel waiting in your freezer when you got home. Faye. He'll figure out when it's okay to throw things and when it's not. Baseball players' children figure it out. A hunter's son can, too."

Faye was silent for a moment, but Magda waited for her.

"None of this makes it any easier to say what I called to say."

"I was wondering when you'd get around to that. Does it have something to do with your crackpot client?"

"It does. I need Joe to come up here and explain to my client that the Iroquois were perfectly capable of making his idiotic 'Runestone' and that the Mayans did not need prehistoric astronauts to help them build their pyramids. I'm on the brink of quitting this job, but it's just possible that Joe can help me save it. I need him. I was going to see if you and Mike could watch Michael, just for a week, but now I don't know. He's such a handful lately. I think it's too much to ask."

"Don't act stupid, Faye. Of course, we'll take our godson for a week. We were a little insulted you didn't ask in the first place. Mike needs an excuse to drag his model trains out of the attic, and I need an excuse to play games that Rachel thinks she's outgrown. And I solemnly swear not to let Mike teach him to shoot his service revolver. The child doesn't need access to any more deadly weapons."

Faye said what best friends say when they see that it's pointless to continue arguing. She said, "Thank you."

"Don't thank me until you see whether I give him back."

Chapter Nineteen

Why hadn't she thought to lock the door?

Amande did a mental face-palm. She had denied herself cappuccino so she could sit here and worry over whether Ennis was going to walk past her window again, but she'd left the service entrance unlocked. Stupid.

There he stood in the closet door, with his hands jammed in his pockets like he didn't know what else to do with them. Well, she couldn't exactly make fun of him for that. She was sitting at her desk, fumbling with a pen, because she didn't know what to do with *her* hands. Worse than that, she'd just smeared ink on her wrist. She dropped that hand to her lap.

Ennis looked scared. That made two of them. She'd be scared of making a fool of herself, even if Ennis were nothing more than a decent-looking twenty-year-old who had told her she was pretty. Since he might also be a man who couldn't be trusted with an old lady's safety, she was also scared that she was being a fool. She should open the window and call for her mother.

But maybe he wasn't so bad. Maybe she'd met him on the worst day of his life and maybe he was as torn-up about his aunt's near-death experience as she was. Maybe he was a nice-enough guy who loved his aunt, and he just wanted to talk to somebody his own age as badly as she did. Maybe.

If she was going to let him stay, she needed to say something, because he seemed to have run out of ideas. Since she didn't even know whether she liked him, she decided to treat these encounters as practice sessions for the time when she'd need to think of something to say to a man she *did* like.

"Did you always live in Rosebower? Before boarding school, I mean."

"No. *No.* Small towns aren't for me. I'm meant for the city. I come from Atlanta and I'm aiming to get back there when… when I can."

Amande gave him the tiniest bit of credit for realizing how poorly she would respond to something like, "I'm heading back to Atlanta as soon as my great-aunt kicks the bucket."

She said, "I'm not sure if I'd be happy in a city. I want to go to a good college next year, but I hope it's not too far away from my family."

"I don't want to waste my time in school, not when I've got a business to run. Sister Mama, she counts on me."

This did not make Amande feel good about Sister Mama's situation, but Ennis kept talking. He had perked up, like a young man who thought he was impressing a pretty girl. He had also walked across the room as he spoke, stopping just on the far side of her desk.

"She taught me how to run the greenhouse and take care of the garden before she got so sick. Now I'm taking care of all that and her website, too. And her patients, mostly. They come to me for their herbs."

"You're prescribing their herbs? Their medicine? I bet Sister Mama spent a lot of time learning to do root medicine. My grandmother knew all about it. She gave people weird stuff all the time, but I wouldn't. You can hurt somebody with that stuff."

"Relax, Baby." He reached a hand toward her hair, and she drew back. The hand hung in mid-air, still reaching. "I told you Sister Mama taught me a lot, back when she was able, and she's still pretty good at bossing me around. I only understand about half of what she says, but it's enough. I'm not hurting anybody."

His hand moved forward. Her head moved back some more. Then she saw his eyes flick toward the window.

"I've got some orders to deliver. I'll talk to you later, Baby." Ennis slipped out the delivery door about forty-five seconds before Faye walked in the front.

Amande could see that her mother's conversation with Magda had gone well, and she expected to hear about it, eventually. She wasn't sure whether Faye needed to know that Ennis had started calling her "Baby," or even whether she needed to know that Amande had been in the same room with him.

Probably not.

◇◇◇

Toni headed for her usual seat at the diner for a late breakfast, as she had done every day since arriving in Rosebower. Toni had the habits of a scientist, so she'd done the math on breakfast economy. She knew there was no way to justify the cost of a restaurant breakfast.

Eggs were running under two dollars a dozen, making them less than twenty cents apiece. Bacon was less than five bucks a pound these days, and there were twenty-ish slices in that pound, so maybe they cost a quarter apiece. The materials in a cup of bad coffee might as well be free, even if she added her customary spoonful of sugar. Any time she paid more than a dollar for bacon, eggs, and coffee instead of cooking them at home, she was hemorrhaging money. Even if the diner threw in a piece of toast and a pat of butter, she was getting no bargain.

Even worse, her favorite breakfast, French toast, contained a fraction of an egg, a splash of milk, a couple of slices of bread, and a dusting of sugar. Paying somebody to make it for her was sheer stupidity. Besides, her own French toast tasted better, because she was prodigal with the vanilla extract. Nevertheless, here she sat, throwing money around, because people are social beings and they don't like to eat alone. She never would have expected to feel nostalgic in retirement about all the meals she ate in the school cafeteria.

As she passed the cluster of retired dudes who always homesteaded the corner of the diner nearest the restrooms, she nodded and said, "Good morning, gentlemen." For the first time on record, she received utter silence in response.

This was new. These men were twenty years her senior, which meant two things: she looked like a young chick to them, and they were old enough to have lived in an era when sexual come-ons from strangers were considered goodhearted compliments. Sitting down to breakfast without being greeted by "Hey there, Sweet Lips," was unsettling.

Julie, the ponytailed waitress whom Toni had always envied for her ability to be happy working double-shifts at her dead-end job, left a napkin-wrapped knife and fork on the table with neither a comment nor a smile. This was hard to believe, considering that Toni overtipped her on a daily basis. Dwight, the owner, violated his policy of greeting every customer with a handshake, staying in the kitchen.

Toni sat in silence, wondering when Julie was going to take her order. She might as well have been at home, enjoying a fifty-cent breakfast of homemade French toast.

Time passed, and Toni wasn't even offered a cup of coffee. She found it difficult to face inexplicable social ostracism without the aid of caffeine. When Julie returned, arms loaded with breakfast for the old dudes, Toni tried to flag her down, but the woman disappeared quickly.

An instant later, Dwight appeared, smartphone in hand. "Is this you?"

Nothing in cyberspace ever really goes away. The phone's screen displayed the website Toni had decommissioned when she retired her magic act a year before. It featured a five-year-old publicity photo in which Toni looked far more glamorous than a fifty-ish woman has a right to look, but glamour is good business for a magician.

"Yes," she said. "That's me. Or it was me. I'm retired."

"Are you also retired from this?"

He hit a couple of links on the phone's screen, pulling up a series of articles she'd written for a high-profile journal for science educators. Publishing those articles had earned her quite a bit of praise from her graduate advisor, late in the twentieth century and long before the emergence of the Internet. She'd had no idea that they were available online. This was not good.

In those articles, she had spelled out exactly how fake psychics did their tricks, then she had developed in-class activities that let kids see the physics behind mysterious phenomena like floating séance tables. She'd even explained the Pepper's Ghost illusion. And, since she'd been younger and more fiery in those days, she had spared no scorn for the fakers she was exposing.

Worse, she had specifically targeted Spiritualism as a form of organized religion. Having spent face-time with Spiritualists since arriving in Rosebower, she wished she hadn't been quite so snide in debunking the faith of real people with real feelings, but the laws of physics couldn't be bent to spare people's feelings. Toni still stood behind the things she'd written in those articles.

Julie stood beside Dwight. Her order-taking tablet remained in her apron pocket and her hands hung by her sides. She said, "My father is an elder at the church down the street. He's never lied to anybody in his life." She turned on her heel and walked into the kitchen.

One of the old dudes said, "My wife still gives readings. I guess she'll keep on giving 'em till she passes to the other side herself. She can't retire, because people depend on her, and you know what? Her work put our children through college. Working for the county, it was all I could do to keep us fed. You're an insult to everything my wife stands for."

The man sitting next to him only looked up from his breakfast long enough to say, "What he said. If you was a man, I'd punch you in the mouth."

Dwight leaned down close and said, "You listen to me. Both my parents, God rest their souls, spent their lives serving people on both sides of death. They weren't fakers. They didn't cheat nobody. They used the talents God gave 'em, and I don't see anything wrong with earning a living by using your talents. It's what you did when you was a schoolteacher and it's what you did when you was 'Toni the Astonisher.'" His tone grew nasal and mocking as he pronounced her stage name. "How much good were you doing for the world when you charged people to watch you pull rabbits from hats? How much?"

A magician never really lets go of her preference for misdirection, even when she would be better served by going straight to the truth. Toni instinctively answered his question with a non-answer. "I never pulled a rabbit from a hat. Using animals as entertainment is abusive."

Dwight's voice grew quieter and he leaned even closer to Toni's face, as if he were afraid his restraint would make it harder for her to hear him. "And it's not abusive to insult people's beliefs? It's not abusive to attack the way they make a living? I bet Tilda Armistead is spinning in her grave to know that a person like you is here in the town her family built. You need to go home now."

He left her alone at a table made of chrome, sitting on a vinyl-upholstered seat. The linoleum floor was sticky under her feet. The diner, which had always seemed so inviting, suddenly went sterile. There was nothing in the room with Toni but hard, reflective surfaces and people who didn't like her.

She picked up her purse and, disoriented by the act of walking out of a restaurant without paying, reached into it for her wallet. Feeling stupid, she slipped her money back into her purse, but reached for the napkin-wrapped cutlery, because her brain had absorbed a certain restaurant routine: Sit down, eat, then deal with the bill left on her table. But there was no bill on the table, only silverware. Having never been kicked out of a restaurant—or a bar or a store or a school or anything else—Toni felt a confusion that made her sympathetic to aging people who behaved strangely because they lived in a world that had changed.

She left the silverware where it was and left with nothing but her purse. When she got home, she found a shattered bay window and a rock in her living room.

Who would do this? Ennis? He was her first thought because his actions merited suspicion, but also because of his youth. Rosebower showed an elderly face to the world for good reason.

The town was graying, mostly because there weren't many jobs there, but also because its social structure favored age.

A psychic could practice until late old age and, unlike most jobs, wrinkles and cataracts were an asset. Age signified wisdom and long experience in esoteric matters like contacting the dead. To a person looking for a guide through one of life's tough spots, Sister Mama's frailty made her look like a woman who'd already been around the same block. In Rosebower, age brought political power with it, too, resulting in a town council full of people who would be long-retired anywhere else.

Dara and Willow were by far the youngest successful practitioners around, even though Rosebower itself had denied them the right to practice inside the city limits. Ennis, Dara, and Willow were the most visible members of the younger generations in town, but they weren't alone. Younger people were outshone by the elderly Spiritualists who still ran the place, but they were there, if you knew where to look.

In any tourist town, there are service employees. In this town, they served an unusually old ruling class. These service employees, people like Julie and Dwight, were plenty young enough to hurl a rock through her window or to set Tilda's house afire. Toni was not fooled by Avery's silence on the matter of Tilda Armistead. Something about the woman's death made all Toni's logic circuits misfire. She could think of no rationale that would prompt someone to both kill Tilda and try to intimidate a meddling, nonbelieving physics teacher, but maybe she needed to think harder.

She wondered whether it was wise to stay in Rosebower, now that her secret was out. Maybe it wasn't just unwise to stay. Maybe it wasn't even safe. That rock could have cracked her skull open, if she'd been at home and sitting in the right place.

But could she write the book she wanted to write if she left? She had told Faye the truth when she said she wanted to write about the foibles of a little town whose residents believed they could talk to the dead, but she hadn't told her the whole truth.

Her intent was to expose hucksterism in all its forms, using Rosebower as a weird little case study. If she was able to parlay her (admittedly minor) show-biz connections into a contract with the right agent, this book could be big. And if she failed to grab the interest of a traditional publisher, no worries. She was pretty sure she would be just as good at building an Internet empire as Ennis LeBecque. She had an interesting hook—fake psychics—and her expertise as a magician gave her a very sturdy platform on which to build an online reputation.

Oh, yes, she could sell this book. But did she really need to spend a year as Rosebower's pariah to do it?

Working notes for Pulling the Wool Over Our Eyes: An Unauthorized History of Spiritualism in Rosebower, New York

by Antonia Caruso

*I don't know why they called this place "Rosebower."
I think they should have named it "Hornets' Nest." It
would have been more honest.*

*Think about it. Main Street is lined with cute little
Victorian houses and almost every one of them was
originally built with a private entrance to a "reading
room." Next to the door of the reading room is a tasteful sign announcing the name of the psychic who works
inside. The sign usually also gives some notion of the
proprietor's specialty. Tarot. Palmistry. Aura reading. Tea
leaf discernment.*

*Hell. For all I know, somebody in town is advertising
a preternatural ability to read chicken guts.*

*How can these people's gullible devotees fail to see
the obvious? Why would a person with true supernatural
powers need props? Wouldn't a real psychic be able to
look a person in the face and just know?*

*From Faye's description of the séance she attended, I
know that Tilda Armistead used props, but simple ones,
just a crystal ball and some incense. Then she closed*

her eyes and didn't even look at the crystal ball. I see a lot more honor in her style than I do in the antics of someone sloshing wet tea leaves around in a cup. Right or wrong, Tilda's readings came from inside her, not from a randomly flipped assortment of cards. Or from a steaming pile of chicken entrails.

Rosebower is going to miss Tilda and her unshakeable good sense. Specifically, she's going to be missed in her lifelong role as a local politician. The town council has ruled this place with an iron fist since God was a girl, and Tilda's death will not diminish its political power. Her loss will, however, obliterate its ability to govern credibly.

Imagine, if you will, the most head-in-the-clouds and daydream-believin' hippie you've ever met. Feel free to imagine three of the original hippies, grayed and wrinkled but still waving a fist at the establishment that provides their Medicare. Or perhaps you'd rather imagine a thirty-something neo-hippie who has never worked for anyone but his father. Or maybe you're pondering the image of a middle-aged woman who embraced the New Age and its mystic crystals instead of dealing with the emotional fallout of her empty nest. Even better, imagine all these people and two more like them, then try to imagine that they are able to run a small town.

You can't do it, can you? Well, neither can I. Without Tilda Armistead on its council, I think the town of Rosebower is in deep, deep trouble.

I have no idea who will be elected to Tilda's seat, but I do know what the first order of business will be for the new town council. They will begin to bicker over licensure requirements. If they make it more difficult to become a Rosebower-licensed spiritual practitioner, then people with established practices win, because they won't have to deal with new competition. If they relax the town's standards, new residents hoping to start a practice will be happy. And so will the wannabes who would move here tomorrow, if they thought they could get a business permit. The wannabes don't vote here, not yet, but the owners of the inn and the diner and the grocery store and those new teahouses do.

Any council without Tilda will eat itself alive from the inside, arguing over licensure and creating enmities that will last a lifetime. Tilda won't be there to make them do boring things like negotiate a contract for garbage disposal. She won't be able to make sure that there's enough money in the budget to keep up the parks. Institutional gangrene will set in, and there will be no one to stop the decay of a place that is unique, if a little loopy.

Bystanders like me will be treated to the spectacle of Spiritualists at war. The newcomers will press for their right to do business, and the old guard will entrench itself further, horrified that anyone would equate the practice of their religion with "doing business"...despite the fact that they all charge a hefty hourly rate for that practice. And the schism can only continue to grow wider.

This is when Gilbert Marlowe will stop looking like Rosebower's money-loving destroyer. Tilda Armistead was the only human alive who was capable of standing between Marlowe and a dollar. Give him a chance to clean up the parks and re-institute garbage pickup, and he will start looking like a savior. When that happens, the council will gratefully approve the plans for his tawdry resort and the fascinating history of this weirdo little town will come to an end.

His plans for developing a New Age Disneyland in Rosebower have brought the old guard to the edge of apoplexy. And he may be able to push them over that edge, because the staunchest upholders of Rosebower's storied past are uniformly elderly. It may be that he needs to do nothing more than wait for a few more funerals. If he stirs the hornets' nest a little more, his opponents may start dropping dead on their own. Only I don't think Gilbert Marlowe has any patience whatsoever.

I may think these people are wacky, but I do like the place. I will be sad when Marlowe destroys it.

Chapter Twenty

Faye was a finder by nature. She could hardly count the times in her childhood when she'd stumbled onto money someone had dropped on a department store floor. Her mother had always marched her straight to the service desk to turn it in. Her grandmother had been less consistent in her approach to good citizenship. If Faye found big money then, yes. Her grandmother had made her do the right thing. When it was pocket change—a quarter, or maybe even a dollar—her grandmother was capable of looking the other way.

This, Faye had decided, was the advantage of being a grandmother. Grandmothers could totally shuck moral responsibility on occasion, but mothers were saddled with it forever.

Faye's status as a finder held true outside the retail world, as well. She was not the best housekeeper in the world, but she never lost a critical piece of paper. If a bureaucrat asked her to produce one of her children's birth certificates, she could reach right into the heap of paperwork on her desk and pull out the folder labeled "Important Documents," while Joe and Amande watched in neatnik horror. And when they lost their keys or their phones in their own pristine private spaces, Faye could find those for them, too.

When tropical storms blew down trees on Joyeuse Island, Faye was the one who found arrowheads snared in their root-balls. She was the child who had explored the island's woods while her grandmother fished, and found the foundations of a slave cabin, obscured by weeds. What is an archaeologist but a finder? She'd been born with a talent for her profession, and her grandmother's windswept island had been the perfect place to develop it.

Faye knew the things that finders know. She knew that the eye rarely focused directly on the object being sought. Treasures lurked in the peripheral vision. She knew that trying too hard rarely yielded results, although workaholic Faye had passed forty without fully accepting that success didn't always rest on trying real hard. Most of all, she knew that major finds rarely came alone.

Within a week of finding that windfall arrowhead, little-girl Faye had stumbled onto a fifty dollar bill on the grocery store floor. (Her grandmother had absolutely made her give that one up to the lost-and-found.) The slave cabin's foundation had appeared beneath her feet within a month.

In Faye's life, big discoveries came in clumps. For this reason, she was not surprised when Amande opened a sagging cardboard box and erupted in a full-on war whoop. "Mom! I think I've got years of Virginia Armistead's private correspondence here! Not letters written by her, obviously. They would have gone out to the people she was writing. But look at all these letters written *to* her. And we found them! How lucky is that?"

So her daughter was a finder, too. Maybe some talents aren't passed along genetically. Maybe two people can be so well-attuned that their traits just rub off on each other. Faye hoped she was soaking in some of her daughter's natural capacity for joy.

Right now, Amande was doing some kind of hip-hop-inspired victory dance that involved a deep squat, followed by hunched shoulders and strange hand gestures, culminating in eight twitches of her left shoulder as she rose to standing. Rinse and repeat.

Faye was tempted to join her, but opted for a hand jive she remembered from her teens, done to the beat of Amande's chant.

"We found 'em! We found 'em! We found 'em, found 'em, found 'em!"

Shortly before Faye used up all the dance moves she remembered, Amande quit her shoulder twitches and snatched up the box. "Look, Mom! There's so many of them. We'll need to split the work between us."

Faye held up her hands, sheathed in white cotton, palm out and fingers wiggling. "Bring 'em on. We're going to get a major conference presentation out of these, and you're coming with me to help deliver it."

There was more than one way to get her daughter off their island and out into the wide world.

◇◇◇

Gilbert Marlowe was impatient. He was always impatient but, at this moment, he was irrationally impatient. He was impatient with the Rosebower elite who refused to succumb to old age and get out of his way, and he was humiliated that he had let Myrna Armistead push the emotional buttons that had made him revert temporarily to childhood.

Like any entrepreneur, Marlowe dreamed big dreams, and then he chased them like butterflies. Like any successful entrepreneur, he knew that he would catch some of the butterflies, but some of them would get away. Rosebower was an important butterfly and he didn't like it dangling just out of reach.

His limousine was large enough to hold a small business meeting. Two men sat on the bench seat facing his. They were not large men, and they looked nervous.

Marlowe himself was not a large man, but he made it his business never to act small. He pumped iron to accentuate his naturally broad shoulders. He stood straight. He spoke in a deep, firm voice. If he had intended to continue doing business with these men, he would have paid an image consultant to give them some gravitas, but he had no such intention.

The first thing he'd do would be to change the blond's name. Willow was no name for a man who hoped to be taken seriously. Then he'd send the image consultant to buy him a new wardrobe. Not that Willow's current wardrobe was cheap or ill-fitting. This was a man who liked to look at himself in the mirror. No,

Willow's problem was that he looked stealthy and insubstantial, despite the fact that he had the muscles of a man who went to the gym daily because he liked to look at himself in the mirror.

Ennis, too, was better-built than his thin frame suggested. Maybe his muscles came from lifting his aunt in and out of her wheelchair and pushing it around. The right haircut could do quite a lot with his face, which was pleasantly symmetrical but a little too intense. He was very young, but Marlowe sensed an inherent instability that age wouldn't fix.

The bottom line was that Marlowe enjoyed looking at these men and their soft-edged handsome faces more than he wanted to admit, but he would not want to be doing business with them very much longer. Hence his impatience.

"When can we break ground on the project?"

Willow and Ennis explained about the town council and they explained about the transfer of titles and they explained about the land permitting and they explained that they needed more time. That's another thing Marlowe could have taught them, if he'd had plans to keep them around: Never explain.

"Gentlemen," he said, interrupting them abruptly, "I am nearly out of patience, but I have plenty of projects I'd like to do. If the Rosebower deal isn't going to be profitable, and soon, I can take my business elsewhere. I'll still be making money, but you two will be out in the cold. I can take care of the land permitting, because the county government is much more easily bought than Rosebower's town council. There are more pressing legal issues that you two need to address. Willow, how long is it going to take to settle your mother-in-law's estate?"

"It should be a formality. My wife is an only child."

"I have no use for the word 'should.'"

Willow pursed his lips but was wise enough not to answer.

"Your great-aunt, Ennis. Has she given you power of attorney?"

Into the vacuum of Ennis' silence, Marlowe inserted a single short sentence. "I've asked very little of you two geniuses, relative to the payoff you'll be getting. So why are you sitting in my car wasting space? I want to hear a detailed plan for how we are going to get from here to a finished project. I want it before the end of the week. By Sunday, the two of you are going to guarantee that there will be no legal impediments or I will walk. Do you understand? Tie up the loose ends or I'm finished with this deal."

◇◇◇

It was coincidence that Faye raised her head at just the right time. It was coincidence again that Amande had chosen the desk that sat catty-corner to the window, putting Faye in the desk that had an unobstructed view of the street. In a way, it was coincidence that Gilbert Marlowe's limousine was passing at the time she lifted her eyes.

Or maybe it wasn't. A vehicle that size, dark and sleek, carried its own gravitational pull. It commanded attention. It drew the eye. Perhaps the limousine itself attracted Faye, tugging on her with enough force to make her look.

It was glossy, like a dark mirror, and its very blackness gave off an aura of stealth. The window tint was so intense that Faye wondered if its transparent darkness was legal or even safe. Glass couldn't be both opaque and functional. She got a blurred glimpse of people in the back seat, then she caught sight of something white that swung like a pendulum. It was something she recognized.

Willow's hair. The person nearest the rear window on Faye's side of the car was Willow. Why was Willow talking to Gilbert Marlowe?

◇◇◇

The limousine had disappeared behind Ennis before he finished opening the garden gate, and he hadn't even seen it go. Marlowe didn't seem anxious to be seen with him, nor with Willow. They picked their way through Sister Mama's garden, unable to avoid treading on the plants that were stretching themselves over the packed-dirt path. If a plant wasn't packed with healing essences, Sister Mama didn't grow it, so every step they took released fragrant essential oils from the leaves crushed underfoot.

Some of the plant smells were minty, some were flowery, and Ennis thought that some of them frankly stank, but Sister Mama still remembered what they all did to the human body. When a favorite client asked, she would even prescribe their oils for an ailing pet, though her imperfect knowledge of non-human reactions to root medicine worried her. On days when she was feeling good, Ennis rolled her chair into the garden and she practiced medicine by pointing to a plant, then pointing to a name on her client list. This method seemed to be working. They hadn't killed anybody yet, but there was always next week.

Ennis was thinking of taking Dara and Willow into the business. When Dara was a teenager, she'd worked for Sister Mama after school. She remembered a lot of the herbal lore she'd learned as a kid, and she had his great-aunt's way with plants. He could almost see them sending out green shoots and leaves as she tended them.

Willow, too, was taking an active interest in root medicine, and he had more of a head for the accounting side of business than Ennis. If the three of them teamed up—with Willow watching the dollars-and-cents and Ennis handling the web sales and Dara making the products—they would be unstoppable. He thought maybe handling plants might make Dara happier than handling audiences did. He wasn't sure about Willow. He fed on the love of an audience, but he liked money an awful lot, too.

Sister Mama might not be crazy about this possible business arrangement, so he hadn't mentioned it to her. He also hadn't worked up the nerve to ask Gilbert Marlowe for financial backing. Once the resort project was underway, Marlowe would be a lot more reasonable. In the meantime, Ennis thought maybe Willow would help him put together a business plan. Men like Marlowe liked business plans.

It was time for Sister Mama's morning dose of magical good stuff. Ennis pulled a large stoppered bottle off a shelf filled with bottles made of glass in all shades of brown and blue. When her speech had started to fail, he'd gone to Dara, asking if she'd help him tinker with the formula. Dara had twiddled with the recipe until she came up with something that Sister Mama didn't spit out as soon as it hit her tongue. Now Willow came over regularly to help with the weeding and bring some new recipe his wife had concocted.

Willow was twice Ennis' age, but he was the closest thing to a friend he had in this godforsaken little town. Ennis looked forward to his visits, and he did think that Dara's tinctures were helping Sister Mama. If nothing else, she'd been a lot quieter lately.

Chapter Twenty-one

Amande looked up for the first time since she started work on the transcription of Virginia Armistead's correspondence. "Mom. There's something a little weird about these letters."

"I saw it, too."

They both hesitated. The truth was uncomfortable, but somebody had to say it.

"Are the letters in your box dated from the 1880s?" Faye asked.

Amande nodded.

"By that time, Spiritualism was well-established and Virginia Armistead was a *grande dame* of the movement, if only because of her illustrious last name. Her husband and children were active practitioners. And she was decades into her marriage."

Amande nodded again.

"Then why is she carrying on an extended correspondence with Piruz Takhat? The man was a notorious fraud and a womanizer."

"I'd never heard of him, so I looked him up. Whoever wrote the Wikipedia article makes a big deal about proving that Takhat's names don't even match."

"Yeah, I think Takhat is Farsi and Piruz is used by Sikhs. Or maybe it's the other way around." Faye's knowledge of non-American cultures was embarrassingly spotty. "Even worse, his stage name was 'Sultan Piruz Takhat,' but he is known to have been born in Detroit to American citizens named Sullivan. The odds against his being a legitimate sultan are pretty steep."

Amande rolled her eyes. "'Sullivan' *sounds* a little like 'Sultan.'"

Worse than his phony claim to sultanhood, however, was his habit of misusing his very real talents of hypnotism and masculine charm to seduce a legion of women. His supposed psychic abilities had been thoroughly debunked by Harry Houdini. Even Sir Arthur Conan Doyle couldn't be convinced to believe in him.

Faye tried to picture an upper-class lady who was an adult in 1848 indulging in a long correspondence with such a shady man in the 1880s. Mrs. Armistead must have been in her sixties by that time. "What have you learned?" she asked Amande.

"I've read three of his letters. If he calls her 'my lady' or talks about her 'chaste beauty' one more time, I'm going to barf."

Faye had been treated to a sentence that included the phrase, "the luminosity of your Grecian brow and flawless bosom." She had almost barfed herself.

"Do you think they were sleeping together?" Amande asked.

The phrase "sleeping together" sounded so crass after spending an hour reading Victorian love letters. *Affaire de coeur* or *liaison dangereuse* seemed more period-appropriate. Nothing sounded tawdry when pronounced in French.

Faye was unaccountably relieved to be able to say, "I see no evidence of it." Why was she relieved? The woman had been dead for more than a century. Maybe because she wouldn't want Myrna to know that one of her ancestors had misbehaved before she passed to the other side.

Though she saw no evidence of a physical affair, she saw plenty of evidence of a one-sided emotional affair. The "sultan" spared no compliment, and he missed no opportunity to ask Mrs. Armistead for money. Faye knew she had sent him money, probably many times over, because all three of the letters she'd read so far expressed his gratitude for her recent "donation to the cause of furthering my work."

Faye was particularly unsettled by the ways he had used her gifts. Takhat made no effort to hide the fact that he was using it to scam his audiences. He'd bought materials for elaborate boxes with places where assistants could hide when they "disappeared." He'd used Mrs. Armistead's money to hire contortionists who could slither into any hiding place and wriggle out of any restraints. He'd even used it to construct a Pepper's Ghost setup, sending Mrs. Armistead an itemized receipt for large panes of glass.

Most damning of all were the diagrams. Takhat had repeatedly sent Virginia detailed plans of how to construct these trick boxes and "escape-proof" restraints. Worse, he'd repeatedly explained how her family members could use them to fool their gullible clients.

Faye knew that Takhat had promoted himself as the real thing. He didn't earn his money in public magic shows. He earned it by scamming grieving parents into thinking they had seen their dead children, when they were really only looking at Pepper's Ghost. Reading Takhat's letters made Faye want to wash the lies out of her brain, yet he didn't even try to hide his tricks from Virginia Armistead.

Takhat's letters were evidence that all the Armisteads hadn't been as honorable as their heiress, Tilda. If this knowledge made Faye feel sad and disillusioned, how would Tilda have felt if she'd known about it? How would it make Myrna feel now?

◇◇◇

Faye asked for the waitress to pack their lunches to go. It was far too gorgeous a day to eat in the diner. Also, Ennis was seated in the exact middle of the dining room, feeding his great-aunt with unctuous patience, and Faye wasn't in the mood to watch his floorshow.

"There you go, Sister Mama. Do you want some squash? Let me mash it up for you."

He nodded in Faye's direction, then flashed a big smile at Amande. The girl got so flustered that she dropped the napkins and straws she'd been gathering for their picnic. What was wrong with her? Until last night, Faye would have said that her daughter didn't even like this man.

While waiting for their food, Faye scanned the bulletin board by the door. Most of the postings were business cards and brochures, but she couldn't miss the big orange flyer urging residents to attend that evening's town council meeting.

"You should go to that, Mom. They're going to elect Tilda's replacement."

Faye wanted to go, but she couldn't think of an excuse that would justify sending Amande to the airport to pick up Joe, so she asked, "Why?"

"Because you're not going to be happy until you know what happened to Tilda, and that meeting will be full of suspects. I'll pick up Dad."

There were extra copies of the flyer on a table by the door, so Faye grabbed one. If she was going to snoop on an entire town, she might as well learn as much about them as possible.

The waitress presented them with two white paper bags. One of them already showed a transparent greasy glow, evidence that Faye's Reuben was in there. Amande's turkey sandwich was keeping its scanty fat to itself.

"Hang on a minute, Sister Mama. You got to give me time to cut this roast beef up for you, and I need to pour gravy on it. Since I know that's how you like it."

Faye could not fail to see how Ennis' eyes followed them out the door. She was glad to leave him behind.

The trees in the park looked manicured to Faye, who was accustomed to live oaks shawled in Spanish moss. She thought the northern landscape looked unnaturally neat, as if harsh winters killed off everything messy and weedy. Stone picnic tables and benches were scattered along the lakeshore. Here and there, a moss-covered piece of statuary punctuated the grassy lawn. Rosebower's park looked like an inviting and useful cemetery.

One of the tables was occupied. Toni sat alone, eating a sandwich brought from home and wrapped in waxed paper. A bag of green grapes sat at her elbow. She looked glad to see them.

Scooting over on the bench to make room for Amande, Toni said, "How's the museum biz, ladies?"

"*Awesome.*" Amande pulled her sandwich out of the bag. "We found a stash of letters that you are not going to believe. One of the Armistead ancestors was carrying on a long-distance love affair with a fake sultan. The only way this could be better is if there were pictures."

"Amande…" Faye said. She hoped the girl realized this was code for, "It's not real ethical to blurt out sensitive information until you've figured out whether your client really owns it and you've shared it with the donor's heir." Which, in this case, was probably Myrna. Faye could just imagine how an elderly spinster would feel about such family laundry being aired. A married Armistead woman corresponding with a philandering charlatan? Myrna would be apoplectic.

Amande didn't pick up on her mother's coded message of "Please be quiet now." She kept talking. "And he wasn't just a fake sultan. He was a fake psychic working under a fake name. I love it!"

Faye put a hand on Amande's arm. This time the girl understood. Toni was holding a grape up, studying the sunlight glowing through its translucent green body as if that particular grape were the most interesting thing around. "So," she said. Her tone was so casual that she had to be faking it. "Those sultan letters sound…um…mildly interesting. May I…?"

Faye shook her head.

"Maybe they'll go on display in the museum. Maybe they'll be in an open collection where you can come read them. But maybe Myrna will ask for them back, so she can keep them private. The museum's records are such a mess that I can't begin to decide ownership issues."

Toni finally ate the grape. She said nothing.

Wondering if the woman was going to study every last everloving grape instead of making eye contact, Faye decided to push her a little. "Doesn't it bother you, living here among these people but knowing that they're going to hate your book when it comes out? Not just the book—they're going to hate *you*. I remember you said you were planning to sell your book in local gift shops.

That's ridiculous on the face of it. The residents of Rosebower are going to pretend that you and your book don't exist."

Finally, the magician gave Faye her attention. She also gave her a glimpse of the force-of-nature personality that might be expected from a schoolteacher who had once made a splash in low-rent show biz.

"Do you think I don't know how Rosebower is going to feel about my book? Maybe they feel that way already. Did you know somebody busted out my window this morning? That rock could have killed me. I'm thinking about leaving town. Maybe you should do the same."

"Maybe I will. But first, I'm going to find out all I can." Faye waved the flyer for the town council meeting in Toni's face. "Want to come?"

◇◇◇

Avery had asked Faye to sign some paperwork, in preparation for photographing the demolition of Tilda's house. The pile of forms indemnifying Myrna, Avery's employer, Myrna's insurance company, and the rest of the western world was truly monumental. If Tilda's house should accidentally collapse on Faye's head, she had no one to blame but herself.

As Faye plowed through the pile of paper, she said, "Do you know any reason for Willow to be spending time with Gilbert Marlowe?"

"The developer?"

"Yeah. I saw Willow in the back of Marlowe's limo this morning. Yesterday, I watched Myrna rip the man a new one over his development plans for Rosebower. I don't know whether Dara hates him as much as Myrna does, but Willow apparently likes him. Or, at least, he's willing to enjoy his cushy ride."

"Why doesn't Myrna like Marlowe?"

"She seems to have known him since he was a boy. Right now she's angry because he wants to build a resort that she thinks will ruin Rosebower. Tilda was against it, too, but she had some power to stop him. Myrna's just an old lady shaking a fist. I'm sure he'd like her to give his project the Armistead stamp of approval, but she can't keep him from doing anything."

"And Tilda could?"

"She was on the town council. With Tilda dead, Marlowe may soon get his way. Would you consider a business deal like this resort—golf course, hotel, spa, exhibition halls—a motive for murder?"

"A project that size? Hell, yeah. It's the only reasonable motive I've heard yet."

Faye reached in her purse and pulled out the town council flyer. "I'm going to this meeting tonight. You know Gilbert Marlowe will be there, along with most anybody else who might have killed Tilda. Wanna come?"

"You know I do."

Faye said, "I'll save you a seat," and went back to her stack of paperwork.

After she'd signed about eighty-five pieces of paper, Avery had led her over to a big pile of junk in the house's side yard.

"These are the things I had to pull out of the house to complete my investigation. I gave Miss Myrna a few trinkets I found upstairs that I thought she might want, but most things that didn't burn were ruined by smoke or water. What you see in this pile is… stuff. Bricks. Here," Avery said. "Have a brick for the museum."

Faye took it, knowing that even this bit of trash was going to need cataloging. And she'd need to get Myrna to sign paperwork deeding any donations over to the historical society. These archival requirements were the reason Samuel needed to stop taking everything that was handed to him.

Avery had picked up a stick and was using it to uncover new layers of debris. "Scorched wallboard, with the paper still glued to it. Nails left behind when a board burned. Is there any reason you archaeologists might want to look at this junk before I have it hauled away?"

Amande didn't even wait for Faye to answer. "Oh, yeah."

The three women, deeply immersed in discussing how to deal with the trash pile, didn't hear Dara as she approached.

"Willow and I were checking on Auntie. We've decided to take turns sleeping at her house, because she's not doing so well. I don't think she needs to be alone any more. Anyway, he's there to watch her and I saw you and I thought…well…I wondered what had happened to my mother's crystal ball. Please? If I could have only one thing to remember her by, that ball would be it."

"I haven't seen it," Avery said. "Or rather, I haven't seen what's left of it. The fire was centered around the room where your mother used the ball, so I'm assuming it was there. Glass doesn't do well in high heat."

A breeze ruffled Dara's curls and played with her full skirt. The midday sun revealed some lines around her mouth that Dara would probably wish away if she could, but Faye thought they made her seem more human. So did her need to recover a little piece of her mother.

"It wouldn't have been harmed by the fire. It wasn't glass. It was rock crystal, what scientists call quartz. You should have found it in the ashes. It was flawless, without a single internal fracture. You can't imagine its power. It's impossible to buy one like it these days. Our family has had it for generations. My ancestors' very souls are imprinted on its crystalline structure. I have to have it."

Okay, so maybe Dara sounded a little flaky, what with ancestors' souls and crystals and such, but still. She sounded like someone who believed in those things, not like the unrepentant faker that Toni saw when she looked at this woman, the last of the Armisteads. Faye wished Avery had found Tilda's crystal ball, so that Dara could have it.

Avery listened intently to Dara, without rolling her eyes at her airy-fairy talk of crystalline power. All she said was, "I can't explain why I would have missed something of that size in the debris, even if it had been broken. I found hundreds of tiny shards of glass. Even if your mother was using a fake—"

Dara bristled.

"—I still should have found pieces of glass or a recognizable puddle of plastic." Avery took a stick and poked the pile of junk she'd pulled out of the house. "There's nothing in this pile or in that house that could be your mother's crystal ball. If I'm wrong about that—and I'm not—I'll certainly let you know, but I can't tell you where it might have gone."

"Thank you." Dara twisted her hands in the gauzy skirt of her sundress. "I heard you talking about looking through the junk in this pile. I'll come back and see what you've found. Auntie will want to hear."

Still wadding fabric in her clenched fists, she said, "Speaking of Auntie, I have to go. She wants me nearby all the time, these days. It scares her when she has trouble breathing. It scares me, too. I don't like it that Willow and I both have to leave her when we do our shows. I want more time with her. I lost so much time with my mother. I—" She turned her head to look back at Myrna's house. "I have to go."

Dara walked away, her hennaed curls swinging far down her proud, straight back.

Faye waited until Dara was out of earshot before asking Avery, "You said last night that you'd been a paramedic?"

"I did."

"When did you last talk to Myrna Armistead?"

"This morning. I've seen her every day this week, some days more than once."

"What's your opinion of her condition?"

Avery touched her own jaw, as if to wipe off a drop of sweat, and her eyes focused on a spot somewhere behind Faye's left shoulder. Her body language said that she didn't want to tell Faye what she thought. Reading such gestures was the tool that Willow used to make people believe he could read minds and talk to spirits. Faye wasn't as good as Willow, because she was usually focused on the next thing on her to-do list, but she could read people when she tried.

Avery's hand still lingered on her jaw. "I haven't done an examination on Myrna, so I can only offer personal observations. That's no more than you could do."

"But you have medical training and I don't."

Avery inclined her head to acknowledge the truth of Faye's statement. She met Faye's eyes. Scholars of body language would say this signaled that she was preparing to tell the truth.

"As Miss Myrna's friend who just happens to have medical training, I can say that I don't like what I see. Her breathing is labored. She can hardly get up out of a chair. Her color's not good." She stopped talking, as if to see whether she'd satisfied Faye's nosiness.

Faye kept the persistent gaze of the person who hasn't heard all she wants to hear, and she said nothing. After a couple of seconds, Avery took a breath and spoke again. Damn. Faye was impressing herself by how good she was at this body language stuff.

"Ms. Armistead looks like a cardiac patient to me. Fairly well advanced."

"Can you make her family take her to a doctor? Can anybody?"

"There's no emergency, Faye, and she is an adult capable of making her own decisions. I can't chop her door down with an ax and haul her someplace she doesn't want to go. Nobody can. She has a right to decide about her treatment, and she has a right to put trust in her family."

Yes, she did. Faye hated being wrong, so she flung one last provocative question. "Even when that family includes a slimy creature like Willow?"

"I've seen Willow with Myrna. He's gentle. Affectionate. He gives her candy and tells her silly jokes. You don't like him, but that doesn't mean he's not good to Myrna."

"You don't like him, either."

"I never said that."

Faye saw that Avery was waiting for her to say, "But you don't!" So she didn't.

After a moment, Avery laughed and admitted the truth. "No, I don't like him, either. But Faye, people get old and, eventually, they die. If Myrna wants to do it at home, in the presence of her family, I'm not going to argue with her decision."

One more provocative question came to Faye. "If I wanted to kill somebody old, I'd do it here, wouldn't you? Nobody pays much attention when an old person's body gives up and dies. I think that's why there's so little talk around town about Tilda's death. Nobody but you, me, Amande, and the killer knows that it wasn't an accident. Everybody else is secretly wondering if her death was for the best. They're probably thinking they'd rather go out quickly, like Tilda, than spend miserable years slowly fading away."

"What are you saying? Do you think someone is trying to kill Myrna? Do you have some evidence for that?"

"Not a scrap. It was just an idle observation. But if somebody wanted to get rid of an old lady, this would be an easy place to go about it, because the people in charge of their elders' care don't seem to be paying much attention."

◇◇◇

Shortly—too shortly—after Faye and Amande walked away, a young man appeared and introduced himself to Avery as Ennis, Sister Mama's great-nephew. Avery had heard about Ennis. After the scene in the diner between him and Amande and Faye, everybody within ten miles of Rosebower had heard of Ennis. She judged that he had been waiting for the archaeologist and her daughter to leave before he approached her. Perhaps he'd been exercising good manners and restraint in doing so, but something about Ennis put Avery on her guard. The notion of him watching her and waiting felt icky. She was no happier about the notion of him watching Faye and Amande.

He'd hardly said hello before he launched into a complaint that made no sense. She heard him saying that somebody had been stealing things from his garden. Then he backpedaled. It wasn't his garden. It was Sister Mama's.

"They're digging stuff up. They're going in the greenhouses. They're—"

"Are the greenhouses locked? Is there a gate on the garden?"

"We never needed one before, but—"

"Have you talked to the sheriff?"

Ennis looked confused. "He doesn't listen. But you're here… investigating things. Checking out Miss Tilda's fire. You're not who I should talk to?"

"I'm a fire inspector."

"Aw, shit. I mean, excuse me."

"All I can tell you to do is to lock up your valuables. If somebody might want to steal your great-aunt's herbs, you need to make it hard for them. Criminals are lazy. If you make their life hard, they'll go find somebody who doesn't. Whether your valuables are diamonds or plants, it's all the same. Lock 'em up."

He nodded and walked away without saying goodbye.

Maybe Ennis was being straight with her. Maybe somebody had been digging roots out of Sister Mama's garden and he was worried about it. It was also possible, however, that he was trying to cover his tracks. If the tox screen said that opium, or something equally deadly, was on that scrap of orange kitchen sponge, then Ennis could be in a lot of trouble. It would be shrewd of him to spread the word beforehand that anybody in Rosebower might have been stealing from Sister Mama's garden.

Avery wished she knew what opium poppies looked like when they weren't blooming. She'd downloaded a book on the botany of medicinal plants and it would be her bedtime reading for the foreseeable future. It looked to be about as soporific as the poppies themselves.

Ennis was still in sight. He moved like a nervous man, and he also moved like a twenty-year-old who was not yet in total control of his body. As he cut a shaky path across a neighbor's grassy lawn, Avery wondered if he'd been sampling his great-aunt's wares.

Chapter Twenty-two

Five minutes before the council meeting, Faye settled herself into a seat that Toni had saved for her. She was glad Toni had gotten there early, because the council room was packed. Avery had wanted to stand in the back, maybe so she could keep an eye on various suspects.

The six surviving councilors sat at a table in the front of a room that had a church-like feel. Attendees were seated in long benches, much like pews, and the councilors' heavy wooden table reminded her of an altar. Three of the councilors were of Tilda's generation, one woman and two men. They spent most of the pre-meeting time with their heads together, muttering. The other three, a man and a woman in their fifties and a younger woman, were examining a stack of papers together, one page at a time. The room was full, and the town's cultural divide was as visible and obvious as the male and female seating areas at a Shaker meeting.

Instead of being segregated by sex, however, this room was segregated by age and, to an extent, by social class. Faye and Toni sat on the left. Faye had no idea whether or not Toni had intentionally chosen a seat that allied her with the defenders of traditional Rosebower. Myrna sat in the center of the left side of the room, flanked by ladies of her generation. There were a few younger people in the vicinity, but they were all wearing the conservative clothes of a flock of faithful churchgoers.

Across the aisle sat everybody else. The age range skewed much younger, and even those of retirement age were dressed casually. This group had embraced t-shirts and flip-flops and the soft filmy dresses Faye associated with New Age enthusiasts. Scattered among the more ethereal-looking attendees were the people who held down jobs in the service industry—Julie, Dwight, the owner of the inn where Avery was staying, the owner of one of the teahouses and his staff, the grocery-store owner and the man who sacked food for her. Faye was startled to see how many people in run-of-the-mill jobs were required to support the psychics and seers who were the stars of the Rosebower show.

The agenda said that the town would address its regular business, then nominate candidates for Tilda's empty seat and hold the election immediately. Faye could guess the number of nominees—two, one for the people on the right and one for the people on the left. She could almost count the votes by looking at the voters themselves. Women wearing pantyhose and men wearing ties would vote with Tilda's camp. Men wearing hiking boots and women wearing crystals around their necks would vote with the new guard. By Faye's count, the vote would be close.

A very slick brochure touting Gilbert Marlowe's development was being handed out. At first, Faye thought it was interesting that the resort would be contiguous to the auditorium where Dara and Willow worked, northeast of town. They would profit handsomely by the traffic. Was this good fortune due to Dara's family connections? Faye remembered seeing Willow in Marlowe's limousine, so maybe Willow was the one with connections.

After studying the map, she wasn't so sure that either of them had exercised any clout in the proposed location of Marlowe's development. There just wasn't any other place to put it. The lake would cut off access between the town and anything built to the east of it. A wide swath of land to the south and west was consumed by undeveloped woodlands designated as a national forest. The only piece of suitable property big enough for Marlowe's development lay on either side of the main road into town from Buffalo. Dara and Willow had gotten lucky.

After the meeting was called to order, the floor was opened for public input on issues to be decided by the council. The moderator seemed to be following an unstated rule: A comment stated by a citizen sitting on the left side of the room was followed by a comment coming from the right. Faye had spent most of her time in Rosebower with Myrna and the traditionalists who surrounded her, never hearing the complaints of their opponents. She had to admit that they weren't unjustified.

Dwight went first. He stepped up to a microphone near the councilor's table and said, "My son moved two hundred miles away, because there's no jobs here. What's wrong with progress? And let me tell you something else. My wife is as gifted a psychic as anyone in town, but the visitor's center hasn't ever referred a client to her. Not once. This council's in charge of referral policies. My Selma built a successful practice because she's talented and honest, but would it hurt you people so much to help somebody out, instead of sending tourists to the same people every day that rolls? Who's going to get all the new clients, now that you don't have Tilda Armistead to send 'em to? God rest her soul." His time was up, so he stepped down.

The moderator called on a woman anxious to speak, because she worked at the visitor's center and she wanted to respond to Dwight. "We always recommend three licensed practitioners for new clients to choose from, and Selma's on the list. We can't control which practitioners they choose."

Dwight got three words out before being shushed by the moderator. "There are ways…"

Faye agreed with Dwight. There were ways to sway customers toward one psychic or another. Put Selma's name last on a list of three, then gush about the talents of the first person on the list—Tilda Armistead, for instance—and people would take the hint.

The speaker continued to recite the visitors' center policy until her time was up. "We keep a list. When you get a recommendation, your name goes to the bottom of the list. The process is fair."

If Dwight's wife had truly worked her entire career in this town without a single referral from the visitor's center, Faye sincerely doubted that the process was fair.

Next, the moderator called on a man seated on the right. He was in his late sixties, vigorous and with a body like a bear.

"We need to revisit licensure requirements." He said it like an announcement, a fact, not merely a suggestion to be considered. Everyone on the right side of the room nodded vehemently. "You people," he gestured at the councilors, "hold all the cards. Rosebower was my dream. I've come here every year since I was a kid. I attended services every time I came. I've paid for readings with you…and you… and you…and both of you, and you all predicted great things." He pointed at several people on the left side of the room. One of them sat at the councilors' table. "You all said you 'sensed great power in me,' and I paid you a lot of money to train me to use that power. Just like you do. I'm starting to think you tell that to everybody…well, everybody with deep enough pockets to pay for training."

Mumbling rose from both sides of the room. People on the right mumbled about how they'd been cheated. People on the left mumbled that the people on the right were wrong.

The bear-like man still held the floor. "I trained for years so that I could come here and open a practice when I retired. I thought, 'There aren't many places where it's okay to be old, but Rosebower's one of them.' Then I got here and you wouldn't give me a license. That's when I learned that being old isn't what counts. Wisdom isn't what counts. It's who you know that counts, and how long you've known them. I'm in favor of Marlowe's development. He'll need people like me to do readings for his hotel guests. If he doesn't, I'll rent some space nearby and hang up a shingle. I don't give up easy. You people control what happens in Rosebower, but you've got zero clout as soon as I cross those city limits."

As the discussion dragged on, Faye saw that people like this man accounted for a surprising proportion of Rosebower's age-skewed demographics. There were many other retirees who had come first as tourists, and then been drawn back in retirement for the same reasons they'd vacationed here. The place was beautiful and they were fascinated by Spiritualism itself. Among them were people like the bear-ish speaker, who had retired here hoping for licensure, only to be denied just in time to see their 401(k)s evaporate when the housing bubble burst.

These people were hurting, financially and emotionally. They blamed Rosebower's council, and they blamed the long-term residents who ran the town as if the world hadn't changed and never would. No wonder they appeared to be ready to vote some new blood onto the council.

The moderator rang a little brass bell and declared the public comment period to be over. She called Gilbert Marlowe to the podium.

A hum arose as people on both sides of the room resumed their muttering. This was the first big event of the evening. The election of Tilda's replacement would be the next.

Marlowe's presentation was slick, and his video fly-through of the proposed buildings was way more entertaining than the usual seven-screens-and-done PowerPoint presentation. He emphasized that Rosebower itself would be unchanged by his development.

Faye disagreed. She shared Myrna's feeling that the project would change Rosebower forever. She realized that, even if she accomplished nothing else with her work at the museum, she would be preserving the memory of an evocative place that was slipping away. Whether it succumbed to Gilbert Marlowe or to the demands of new residents or to time, Rosebower could not remain as it was for much longer.

To distract herself from Marlowe's seductive promises, she studied the brochure in her hands. It bothered her, and not just because she wished Gilbert Marlowe would go away and leave Rosebower alone. Something about the lovely diagram, with its blue sweep of lake and its green computer-generated trees cradling the town and resort, didn't work. The area to be developed, crammed tight with the hotel and its associated buildings, looked small compared to all that nature. Faye couldn't decide what was wrong with it, but it bothered her. Folding the brochure into a small square, she slid it into the pocket of her jeans to examine later.

"This lovely town, a lasting symbol of simpler times, will remain as a time capsule from the earliest days of Spiritualism. The town council will retain control of everything within the city limits, especially the licensure of practitioners. I have no influence on the government of this town. I own no property within the city limits. Therefore, I can't vote."

Faye hoped everyone here saw this empty promise for what it was. Power and money could do more to influence the people on the council than one measly vote. And surely they all realized that Marlowe's project would neutralize the competitive power of any license issued to practice as a psychic within Rosebower's boundaries. Anyone could throw up a shack outside the city limits and start charging money for reading tea leaves. Essentially, that's what Dara and Willow had done. Increased tourist traffic to the resort would make it possible for others to join them.

Suddenly, Faye did a mental backpedal. Marlowe had said, "I own no property within the city limits," and this was true. The brochure in her hands told her that the entire project would be outside Rosebower proper. So why was Marlowe here?

Why was he riding around in a limousine with Willow? And why had he been bothering Myrna? What, really, did Marlowe need from these people? He could use their goodwill, but he could do without it.

Was this what had bothered her about the brochure map? Maybe. But something was still not right. Marlowe's behavior told Faye that she was missing something.

He was saying, "The most conservative projections say that my development will quadruple tourist traffic."

If this was true, Marlowe's resort would soon be surrounded by businesses set up by the people who had been rejected for licensure by the town. There would be no governing body to ensure that they conducted their business with respect for the religion underlying it. Faye had a vision of a tiny Las Vegas Strip leading into Rosebower, with flashing lights and tacky billboards touting bargain-basement spiritual readings. Myrna's horror at the tawdriness of Marlowe's plans may have been dead-on.

Marlowe's voice gained strength and presence as he built to a concluding pitch that would close this sale.

"This development will be built outside the town, so I am not here to ask permission. I am here to propose partnership. I am willing to establish a position on my management team in Pittsburgh to be held by one of Rosebower's own. This job will be compensated at standard industry rates for such a responsible position. In return, I'd like the town to consider electing me for the open seat on this council. I want us—all of us—to embrace the twenty-first century together."

After a second of silence, the room erupted as people reacted to this proposal. After a moment of people-watching, Faye reassessed her judgment. All of Rosebower didn't react. Only Myrna's half of the room did. Now she saw what Marlowe was planning. He didn't need Rosebower's voters to make his project a success, but the combined drawing power of the museum-like town and his cushy resort was far more than either could generate on its own. Marlowe aimed to be in charge of both tourist draws. She finally understood what he'd been doing in town the past few days. He'd been building a power base with Rosebower's progressives. Counting heads, Faye wasn't sure whether his base was big enough to carry the election.

And now the lifelong businessman drove his pitch home.

"My proposal makes economic good sense, but it promises more than money. Rosebower has a gift for the world. Think of the spiritual power you could wield by showing so many people how to live in peace with themselves, with those around them, and with those who have crossed to the other side. Your principles are based on wisdom and kindness. Is it kind to leave so much of the world in the dark?"

Myrna's friends were plucking at her sleeve, trying to keep her in her seat, but she was an Armistead. It was impossible to tell her what to do. She was wheezing when she reached the front of the room, but she got there under her own power.

"You will *not* sit in my sister's seat, Gilbert. Maybe we can't stop you from destroying our way of life, but that doesn't mean we have to help you."

Myrna stood with her legs slightly apart, which was not the way that ladies of her day were taught to stand. She had no other option. Without a wide base of support, she was too weak to stand without toppling over. Her head sagged and her jaw gaped open as she gasped for air, but she held herself upright.

"If nobody else will run for that seat, I will."

No one in the room thought that Myrna Armistead would still be standing when the next meeting rolled around, but no one in the room was willing to say so. Faye was glad to see someone else on Myrna's side of the room rise. Somebody…anybody… needed to get her to see reason and sit down.

Faye's heart sank when she saw that the person striding toward the microphone was no savior. It was Ennis.

He didn't shove Myrna aside. In fact, he stood politely until she stepped away from the podium. He even cupped her elbow in support when she staggered a little. It was the gesture of a man who was well-versed in caring for the elderly. If she hadn't seen Ennis with his own great-aunt, Faye would have been fooled by this instinctive act of kindness.

Ennis raised the microphone, so that he could speak into it without stooping. "Sister Mama and I will vote for you, Mr. Marlowe. And I'd like to put my name in the hat for that job on your management team. Rosebower has been pretending like the future isn't coming, and where has it got us? No jobs for young people. No money for anybody. A few tourists stop by every now and then, and every cent they bring gets snapped up by the few that've got licenses. I think we should all work together. It's time."

No argument on Earth would be sufficient to convince Faye that this "surprise" announcement had not been planned.

Tumult ensued, despite repeated bangs of the gavel. Faye could see all six sitting council members scanning the crowd. The reason was obvious. They were recounting votes, trying to decipher whether or not the election would go their way, now that Ennis had shifted his family's allegiance and upset the natural order of things. Ennis himself was being besieged by right-sitting citizens, anxious to welcome him into the fold. Those on the left were more reserved. Some sat in silence, while others huddled in small groups to talk political strategy.

In an action that surely violated Robert's Rules of Order, the councilor holding the gavel banged it three times and declared that the meeting would be adjourned with no further discussion.

Myrna was alone, sidling slowly away from the crowd around Ennis. Somebody needed to go get her before she fell.

Faye looked around for Dara, wondering why she hadn't already rescued her aunt, until she realized that Dara and Willow were doing their performance. They had a lot riding on the results of this meeting, but the show must go on.

Myrna's peers didn't look capable of whisking her out of harm's way, so Faye took action. Slithering through gaps in the crowd, Faye reached the front of the room swiftly and took her friend by the arm. It was one of those situations where being small and determined paid off.

Avery was right behind her. They ushered Myrna out, then Faye sat with her on a streetside bench while Avery went to get her truck. As far as Myrna was concerned, the two-block walk home might as well have been twenty miles.

Chapter Twenty-three

Toni walked alone on the sidewalk of Main Street. Rosebower was in the process of eating itself alive, and she had left early because she couldn't bear to watch. She didn't know whether the evening's events saddened her or sickened her. These were people who claimed to be in contact with spirits on a higher plane, yet they tore at each other like jackals.

Toni was pretty sure that if she were able to speak to her dead parents, they would say, "Love one another while you're all still alive." They wouldn't say, "Go after every cent you can grab while you can. We wish we had."

It was almost time to leave Rosebower, but she had one or two things to do before she went.

◇◇◇

Faye and Avery had positioned themselves on either side of Myrna. They each had a shoulder in one of her armpits, giving her enough support to walk up her own porch steps. The three women were having a repetitive conversation. Faye and Avery had both spoken several sentences that included the word "doctor." Myrna had displayed an astonishing ability to find different ways to say, "No."

As they made their way across the broad porch, a light flicked on inside and Dara opened the door. Her face was oily slick, because only a heavy, greasy cleanser will remove stage makeup. The wet washcloth in her hand was already beige, black, and red, but Faye could see that she still had more cleansing to do.

"Auntie, what's wrong?"

"I'm just tired. I'll feel better with a cup of tea, and please dear, would you put a generous splash of Sister Mama's home brew in it? I keep a bottle in the back of the pantry to serve to guests. You'll know it when you see it. Her handwriting is on the label."

"You want a drink? With *alcohol* in it?"

Myrna shook off her protectors, making her own way into the parlor so steadily that Faye knew Dara would never believe that her aunt was sick enough to be hauled to the doctor against her will.

Lowering herself into a chair embroidered heavily with crewel work, Myrna slipped off her shoes and rested her swollen feet on a matching footstool. "Yes, alcohol. You can check my ID if you like, but I assure you that I'm of age." Her breathing sounded much better, as if being at home calmed all her body's systems.

Dara knelt by Myrna's chair and rubbed her aunt's hands. Faye could see that they were swollen, too.

"I'll get you some tea and some home brew. How about some of your special candy?"

Myrna gave a firm nod. "And don't forget my bedtime dose of whatever it is that Sister Mama prescribed. Her herbs and roots help me. I can tell."

"Would you like some spiritual time with me afterward? I can move this comfy chair into the séance room for you."

"No." Faye had never heard Myrna snap at Dara, but there was a distinct snappish tone to her "no."

"Whatever you say, Auntie."

"If Tilda has a message for me, she'll come out and say it. There's no need for the two of us to sit in an airless little room and wait for her to come. She's here." The swollen hands gestured to include the entire room, all of Rosebower, maybe all the world. "Those of you with spiritual gifts set too much store in the trappings of it all. Crystal balls are silly. They're just lumps of rock."

Myrna closed her eyes as if to end the conversation, but she let a few more words escape. "Faye and Avery, I'm grateful for your help. Dara, I'll be grateful for the tea and candy, but I'll be way more grateful for Sister Mama's handiwork. It's hard, preparing for a career in politics. I may need to take up cigar smoking." With a sigh, she settled into her rest.

On her way to the kitchen, Dara beckoned for Avery and Faye to join her. "Politics?"

Faye knew no other way to say it. "Rosebower imploded at the council meeting tonight. Myrna has decided that running for Tilda's seat is the only way to save the town."

"I wish I'd been there to stop her. Working every night gets old sometimes." She remembered the condition of her face and grabbed a paper towel. A few swipes across her face did a decent job of taking off another layer of greasepaint. "Oh, who am I kidding? Nobody can stop Auntie when she's on a mission. She looks pretty good tonight, doesn't she?" She directed the question at Avery. "Better than yesterday?"

"Better than an hour ago. Lots better. You do realize that she's sicker than she thinks she is," Avery said.

"I'm sleeping here tonight. Willow will be here tomorrow night. One of us needs to stay at our house to walk the dogs and do all the chores that old houses need you to do, but we can swap off. Auntie will only be alone for a couple of hours a day, while we're performing. As for a career in politics…let's see how she feels between now and the next council meeting. In the meantime, I'm glad you're both here. I was planning to ask for a favor."

Faye couldn't imagine what kind of favor would involve both her and Avery, but she said only, "What kind of favor are you talking about?"

"I'd like to talk to my mother."

So would I, Faye thought, *but she's just as dead as yours.* All she said out loud was, "I'm sure that would be a comfort to you."

"I'd hoped that she would come to me on her own, but it's been days. I want to hold a séance and ask her to come."

Of course she wanted to hold a séance. Now that Faye thought about it, she was surprised that Dara hadn't already done it. She was born to the Spiritualist faith. Talking to dead people would be a natural way for her to deal with grief.

"I can hardly sleep. I should have made peace with her years ago. I should have held my tongue. I should never have said anything to her, except, 'I love you, Mother.' I should—" she swallowed. "I want to tell her I'm sorry. I want to establish the kind of communion that we should have had in life. I never thought she'd be gone."

Surely Dara wasn't serious. Her mother had been over eighty. Believing that she'd never be gone had been the very definition of denial.

"I will attempt to contact my mother tomorrow morning. I'd like you and your daughter to attend."

Faye hadn't seen that one coming. Instead of blurting out "Why?" she asked, "Morning? Don't you have to do séances in the dark?"

"That's why Auntie's séance room has no windows. It's always dark in there."

Dara's brittle and off-kilter tone and her loopy smile reminded Faye of Billie Burke's rendition of Glinda the Good in *The Wizard of Oz*. As Faye grappled for a response, Dara kept talking in that strange, dissociated voice.

"You have to come. You were the last to see her alive. Your daughter and Auntie are just as important, as they shared spiritual time with her so close to her passing."

"So it would be just the three of us?"

"No, we need someone else to reach my mother, someone with rare power. She was so independent and autonomous. She will not necessarily come readily."

"Willow?"

"He will be there to assist. I'll need him to interpret and take notes, but he won't sit among us. We need someone else, someone strong. Sister Mama, I think. She has a powerful spiritual connection and she was close to Mother. We still need one more."

"Won't that little room be crowded?"

"It will hold six at the table, plus an assistant. I've seen it many times. And we obviously can't have five at the table."

Her reasoning wasn't clear to Faye. "Obviously?"

"Jesus had five wounds. This is why the pentagram is such a powerful symbol. There can be any number of participants at a séance, except five."

Faye choked on the words, "If you say so," because she could already hear the sarcastic dismissal of Dara's religion that would be in the tone of her voice. Instead, she said, "My husband will be here. He could come."

Dara wasn't listening. "You, Avery. You will come," she declared in a voice that didn't invite discussion. Her persona had morphed from ditzy Glinda the Good to the commanding presence that dominated a stage every single night. "There's a reason you're still in Rosebower, though you never say what it is. If this fire had been routine, you'd be gone. You're still here because you have questions. Whatever they are, I want to see them answered as much as you do. My mother knows the answers. You'll be the sixth person at the table."

When the decision was reached, Dara's mood shifted again. The stage persona dropped away. She reverted to a middle-aged woman wiping cleanser off her face while she worried about a loved one. "I'm very grateful to you both for bringing Auntie home."

A moment later, Faye found herself standing with Avery on the front porch, having been hustled out the front door almost by magic.

Faye pulled her phone out of the pocket and checked the time. "It's nine-thirty. Let's say we got here at nine-fifteen. Dara looked like she'd just gotten home from work, didn't she?"

"Yep. And she couldn't have staged that face-washing routine for our benefit, because she didn't know we were coming. Unless they ended the show early on the night of the fire—and wouldn't it be stupid to create a whole room full of witnesses who knew she and her husband left work early enough to kill her mother?—I'd say that Dara and Willow are in the clear."

"Maybe."

"Are you just saying 'Maybe,' because you don't like them?"

"Maybe."

Avery pulled her keys out of her purse. "Where are you planning to wait for Amande to pick you up? The diner? Would you like a ride?"

"It's only a few blocks. I can be there before you get your truck out of that tight parallel parking spot."

Avery jingled the keys in her hand. "Let me ask you something. How well do you know Toni Caruso?"

"As well as I know anybody in Rosebower, including you. I met her less than a week ago. I like her. She's one of the most interesting people I've ever met, but it's not like we've had a bunch of heart-to-heart talks. Why?"

"I noticed you sitting with her tonight. I was a little surprised to see her show her face, when you consider the rumors flying around town about her."

"Rumors?"

"You haven't heard about her getting kicked out of the diner yesterday?"

"Kicked out? For what? Did somebody find out about her book?" They had reached Avery's truck. Rather than unlock it, Avery leaned against the driver's door and considered her answer to Faye's questions.

"I don't know about any book, but the whole town knows she's a magician who is on record as saying that Spiritualism is a pile of horse crap." At Faye's raised eyebrow, she said, "Well, she probably didn't use quite those words, but she has been informed that she is not welcome at the diner, and she's probably not welcome in any business owned by a true believer in life on the other side. I'm guessing that this is why she disappeared after the meeting, rather than coming with you to help Myrna. Nevertheless, people who disappear at strange times make me suspicious."

Faye had been too caught up in helping Myrna to wonder where Toni went. "So the old geezers hate her, and the New Age upstarts hate her, too?"

"Pretty much."

"Is that why you were asking me about her?"

"I asked because I'm very curious about what she was doing on the night that Tilda Armistead died. She's like you, in some ways. She doesn't fit into the usual Rosebower patterns. She's a wild card."

Faye remembered Toni's hands, making cards appear and vanish for Amande's amusement. Toni's profession made her naturally secretive. This didn't make a killer. "I can't imagine Toni hurting Tilda, but that's no help to you, because I can't imagine anybody wanting to hurt someone so gentle. Yet somebody did. I do know where Toni was on Monday night, though."

"She wasn't with you, because I know where you were."

"No, she wasn't with me. She told me she watched Willow and Dara perform that night."

"It's better than nothing, but I'm not sure I can get any witnesses, since the audience is generally full of tourists who would be long gone by now. If she paid for her ticket with a credit card, there would be a paper trail."

"Even if you prove she bought a ticket, that's no guarantee she actually went to the show."

"No," Avery said, "but it's a start." She gave Faye a short good-bye wave. "Go. I know your daughter drove to the airport to pick up your husband, just so you could stay here and watch Rosebower be dysfunctional. You want to be at the diner when they get there. Go tell him hello, and leave the investigating to professionals... um...to one professional. Me. I can handle it, Faye."

◇◇◇

Joe and Amande arrived at the diner before Faye had finished her apple pie. Dwight was a man of his word. The pie had been free, and so had the cup of decaf that came with it. This was good because when she saw Amande pull into a parking slot, she was out the door without a thought for paying the bill.

It had been hard, being without Joe. Faye could take care of herself and she could take care of her kids. What she needed in a partner was a man who shared the load. She buried her face in Joe's thick coarse hair.

He said, "I planned this trip right. Here I am on Friday night, with a weekend to play before we have to work."

She went on sniffing his hair while she said, "Sorry, dear. We're working tomorrow. You need to talk some sense into our client. Amande and I have letters to transcribe. Oh, and Amande and I need to be here early, because our assistance is needed at a séance."

His big hands gripped her shoulders as he placed a kiss on the top of her head. "I knew you were going to say something like that."

Working notes for Pulling the Wool Over Our Eyes:
An Unauthorized History of Spiritualism
in Rosebower, New York

by Antonia Caruso

*I need to rethink this book. Maybe I've gathered enough
data to write a credible narrative. Maybe I haven't. Maybe
it's not safe for me to be here any longer.*

*Even if this is true, I'm not willing to give up my book,
but it may need restructuring. Maybe I only have enough
background on Rosebower to fill a single chapter, but
I could find other longstanding deceptions to debunk.
There is no shortage of them. I can still write a book that
will show the world's fakers to be the cheats that they
are. It might not be the book I came here to write, but
it will do its job.*

*If I leave, and I suppose I shall, I have a few things
to do before I go. I want badly to get my hands on the
letters that passed between Virginia Armistead and her
sultan friend. Faye Longchamp-Mantooth is not going
to give me access to them until they're accessible to the
public and other scholars. I will need to file an advance
request with Samuel so I can have access when that
time comes. Because I think he is no more capable of
running a research facility than a toy poodle, I will also*

ask Faye to let me know when the museum is open for business. I think she'll do that, as a matter of professional courtesy. If not, I shall badger Samuel until he gives me the right answer.

The other two things I need to do while I'm in Rosebower can be accomplished at the same time. The first one is simple. They're both simple, actually.

First, I want video of Dara and Willow as they perform. I will never crack their code without watching the tricks over and over again, back to back. Hidden cameras are awkward and they carry a risk of discovery. Until now, I haven't wanted to take that risk, but I've already been exposed as a magician and I'm leaving town. What do I have to lose? The only risk I will incur by taping tomorrow night's performance is being publicly embarrassed. I'm fifty-six years old. I will survive a little embarrassment.

I own a concealed camera that looks like a wristwatch. (You may be asking why I own such a thing. Well, a magician wants to keep up with her competition, and if an illusion is good, even the best practitioner may have trouble figuring it out on the first viewing. I only steal from the best.)

If I am not welcome at the diner, then I assuredly will not be welcomed by Dara and Willow at their show. Fortunately, I am a very fair disguise artist. Early in my career, I was often hired to be the assistant planted in the audience, waiting for the magician to "randomly" pick me. My disguises were always more elaborate than the situation required, because I love my work too much. Tomorrow night, a "man" whom Dara and Willow could not possibly recognize will be sitting in an aisle seat, recording the proceedings with "his" wristwatch—that is to say, with my wristwatch.

My second goal tonight is even simpler. I want to see how long Willow actually participates in the nightly shows. Unless I miss my guess, his part of the act is over *in under an hour. Dara carries the rest of the show on her back, alone. I find it interesting that Willow has an hour every night to move around Rosebower, unsuspected. Once I know exactly what time he leaves the show, I will tell Avery. She can compare this information with the timing of Tilda's housefire and draw her own conclusions.*

I'm looking forward to tomorrow night's masquerade. A girl never gets too old to enjoy a good game of dress-up.

Chapter Twenty-four

Skipping the breakfast at a bed-and-breakfast is not the best way to get the most for one's money, but Faye, Joe, and Amande had no other choice. They needed to get to Rosebower for a day that included an early-morning séance, a stint of photo-taking at a burned-out house, and probably an uncomfortable meeting with their client. The B&B's proprietor, grateful to save the money and effort involved in cooking their breakfast, gifted them with granola bars and travel mugs of coffee as they hurried out the door.

The reason for their murderously early departure? Dara had declared that the spirit world was most accessible when the day dawns and when the sun sets. Every sunset of the week was consumed by her stage show, so dawn was the best time for her to make contact with her mother. Faye yawned as she drove, wishing that Dara had been so willing to inconvenience herself for her mother when Tilda was alive.

Amande was asleep in the backseat, sagging against her shoulder restraint. Joe sat beside Faye, studying the agenda for the previous night's council meeting and the brochure for Gilbert Marlowe's proposed resort. Faye had been telling him about the goings-on in Rosebower since her first day on the job, but she knew he understood things better when he could see and feel them. The two documents spread across Joe's lap gave a succinct summary of Rosebower's issues and, even better, the brochure included a map. If Joe could picture the town in his head, he could function there. That was the way his mind worked.

As they neared the town, Joe looked at the map, then looked out the window, time and again. Was this one of the ways he gave his learning disabilities the runaround? If so, it was one that Faye had never noticed.

Finally, she said, "Are you ground-truthing that map? It's based on the tourist map they gave me at the visitor's center, which has been working pretty well for me. I haven't gotten lost once."

"The streets look fine. It's the trees that bother me."

"I can't tell you anything about the trees. The map shows me which streets will get me from Point A to Point B, and that's all I use a map to do."

"I'm just wondering why Marlowe's map shows trees where there's not any. This stretch is open country, mostly pastures and row crops. It wouldn't have been hard to get his map right. A few seconds with Google Earth and boom. You know where the trees are and you know where the farms are. It ain't rocket science."

"He probably just hired a lazy mapmaker. Why would Marlowe fake something like that?"

"For starters, this map is drawn to make it seem like there's no other place in the whole world to put that development. Nobody likes to cut trees, so maybe Marlowe put trees on all the other land to take our mind off it."

"Maybe."

"Except I think he needs that land, trees or not. Didn't you say he was planning a golf course? Where's he going to put it?"

Faye risked a car crash by yanking the map out of Joe's hands. Now she knew why this map had bothered her so, when she first saw it at the council meeting.

Joe was right. She'd heard talk of a golf course from more than one mouth, but Marlowe had failed to mention it during his presentation and he'd left it off this map. If he planned to build one, he needed the land that he was hiding under all those fake trees.

Faye had just two questions. Did he own it? And why was he trying to distract people from it? If she had learned anything from Toni the Astonisher, it was the importance of misdirection.

◇◇◇

When they arrived at Myrna's house, the séance room was already set up for a crowd. Myrna and Sister Mama were seated at the table holding a pretty decent conversation, considering that Sister Mama couldn't actually talk. Myrna's skill at interpreting her meaning probably came from fifty years of friendship and the power of love. Or maybe she was more psychic than everyone believed. Sister Mama looked the same as she had all week. It was as if the encounter with an opium-soaked sponge hadn't happened.

Avery beckoned for Faye to join her on the back doorstep. "Do you understand what's going on here? We're recreating the circumstances of Tilda's death. What's to stop someone from nailing *us* in *this* room and setting *this* house on fire?"

Faye felt very stupid for failing to consider this.

"Umm...the killer would have to want at least one of us dead. We have no reason to think that this is true. But we have no reason to think that it's not. Also, there are no convenient oil lamps sitting around, but a killer who means business will bring whatever it takes."

Avery nodded impatiently. "It's broad daylight, so that's another point in our favor, but still. Faye, this is not worth the risk."

"What reason will you give for calling this thing off? These people don't know that Tilda was murdered. They think she was killed by a random house fire."

"Unless one of them is the killer. But you're right. Calling off the séance would tip my hand."

Joe was standing in the back door, beckoning. "They're waiting for you."

"Here's our answer," Faye said. "We've got Joe. He's got nothing to do until his meeting with Samuel. I've told him everything I know about Tilda's murder. He can stand guard."

Avery considered it. "Okay. Joe, if you see anything…any-thing…unusual, your first priority isn't to chase the bad guy or take him down. If you see anything strange, your Priority One is to open the door to the séance room and let us out. If Tilda had been in hers like the arsonist thought she was, she wouldn't have even had the slender chance she did have. She wouldn't have been able to get in her car and drive to you for help. She'd have burned alive."

◇◇◇

Joe sat in the doorway to Myrna's broad porch. Her front door was open behind him, giving him a good view of the door to the séance room. He could see every corner of the parlor and the dining room, he could see out all the windows of both rooms, and he could see the hallway to the kitchen. Anyone coming in the back door and planning to nail seven people into a tiny room would have to navigate that hallway first.

From this vantage point, he could see a goodly stretch of Walnut Street in front of the house, as well as two blocks of Main Street. The hulk of Tilda's dead house dominated one corner of the intersection of Rosebower's two busiest streets. The house, the street, the town were all as quiet as death.

Few people were out of their houses so early on a Saturday morning. Silence enveloped Rosebower. There was nothing to keep Joe and his hunter's ears from picking up on unusual noises. The thin leather of his moccasins left him open to the house's vibrations beneath his feet. If he'd been standing on the ground, the whole world would have vibrated against his soles. Joe felt good about his ability to keep those people safe.

At such times, when the world was quiet and he needed his senses sharp, Joe liked to tap into his own spiritual practices. There were talismans in the leather bag hanging from his belt that he couldn't have explained to anybody else, but they helped him commune with things that cannot be seen. Turning those talismans over in his relaxed hand helped him modulate his breathing and seek focus. All these things sharpened his senses, and seven people were depending on those senses right now.

He was also making use of the spiritual tool Faye hated most. Tobacco. Was it his fault that white men had turned tobacco into a deadly indulgence?

Joe smoked on rare occasions, but this was not one of them. People were in pain because fire had claimed Tilda Armistead. This was no time to use fire to gain clarity. Instead, he had tucked finely ground tobacco into his lip, and he held a favorite spit cup in his hand. If he was lucky, Faye would limit his punishment for this transgression to an hour of the silent treatment. He knew she'd missed him, and also she liked to talk, so his sentence would probably be light.

He spat in the cup and thought of Tilda Armistead. He invited her to come, if she was lonely. He invited her to fly away, if that would bring her peace. Then he did nothing but sit and spit and watch and breathe.

◇◇◇

Willow closed the door to the séance room. The tiny candle in front of Dara was the only relief from utter darkness. It occurred to no one—not Willow or Dara or Myrna or Avery or Sister Mama or Amande or even Faye—that, by leaving Joe on the front porch, they might be shutting out the only person among them who truly had the ability to commune with the spirit world.

◇◇◇

"Cramped" was not the right word for the overcrowded séance room. Faye thought that "claustrophobic" might not have been going too far. Any of the six people sitting at the table could have leaned her head back and felt it hit a wooden wall.

A small candle in the center of the table cast a feeble light on their faces. Near it, directly in front of Dara, sat a large crystal bowl. It was not the fine, hand-blown type of crystal that Faye's grandmother had loved, wafer-thin. It was heavy and thick and its surface was ornate with deeply cut patterns. Willow stepped forward and poured two decanters of clear fluid into the bowl. Based on the way they separated into two phases that each glowed differently in the lamplight, Faye guessed that the decanters held oil and water.

He opened a small jar and scattered green leaves over the liquid. Sister Mama leaned forward and breathed deeply, as if she knew them by their smell. Probably she did.

And then Willow drew a knife.

Faye, Amande, and Avery all jerked backward. Faye could hear the other two scrabbling with their feet as they tried to push back from the table, away from the knife. Their struggles were stilled by the sight of Willow dragging the blade across his own palm. He let several drops of blood drip into the crystal bowl, then he wrapped his hand in a handkerchief and withdrew to his spot under the staircase.

Dara looked eerily like her mother, gazing into the bowl the way Tilda had searched her crystal ball. Faye almost thought Dara hadn't noticed her husband and his knife until she said, "Blood draws spirits." Her tone was abstracted, distracted. Absent.

Faye supposed they left the bloody part of the ritual out of their public act because it was too intense for the masses. Then Willow cut the lights and they were left in a darkness too black for the public. Any reasonable fire code would have denied them the right to put an audience into darkness so deep. It wasn't safe to hide an emergency exit so well.

Faye turned her head back and forth, looking for a single sparkle of light. There was none. She was sitting in a room built for this very purpose. Solid construction and copious caulk were capable of blocking all light. She sat with six invisible people in utter blackness.

Dara instructed them to join hands. Even in this small space, it took a few moments for them to find each other.

"Place your hands flat on the table, touching only at the pinky and thumb."

Again, there was awkwardness and confusion, but they managed it. She could hear Avery and Amande helping Sister Mama and Myrna get their hands where they needed to be.

There was nothing in Faye's sensory world but the chair beneath her, the table where she rested her hands, the tips of Amande's and Dara's pinky fingers, and Dara's voice saying, "Let us begin."

This time, Faye saw no glowing orbs. She heard no warm and loving words. Thumps and raps sounded in all directions. People were moaning, but she was almost certain that Amande wasn't one of them.

Dara's voice repeated the word "Mother," time and again. The word came at irregular intervals and it was different every time. A whisper, a groan, a hiss, a shout, and then another whisper. If Tilda was answering, Faye couldn't hear her.

A cool breeze kissed Faye's face. A moment passed, punctuated by a wordless hum from Dara, and then a distinct odor of roses wafted through the room. Faye wasn't exactly afraid, but she wanted very much to be somewhere else.

After an unknowable period of time, the table rocked and jumped beneath her flattened hands. It felt alive. Faye almost wished they could all raise their hands and let it fly, if that's what it wanted to do. Then a huge crash sounded behind her. It was so loud that Faye thought maybe the table had escaped and flown into the wall, but no. She could still feel its oak surface beneath her palms.

A tinkling bell sounded once, twice, and again, then the overhead light came on. It was bright, blinding, almost painful, but she could see Willow. He stood with his hand on the light switch. There were thick, sharp fragments of glass littering the floor around him. A few were caught in his flaxen hair.

"What did you do?" Dara was on her feet, shrieking. "She was here. My mother was here."

Willow pointed to the thick chunks of glass at his feet. "If that had hit six inches lower, it would have cracked my skull. She tried to kill me."

Dara wouldn't look at the broken glass. She would only look at her husband. She crowded Avery aside so that she could get in his face.

"But why did you ring the bell? It drove her away. The bell shouldn't ring till morning. You *know* that. A lingering spirit can come to the dreams of those who sleep in the house. I might have…would have…dreamed about her tonight."

Faye was thinking, "And this is more important than your husband's safety?" Nobody had asked her opinion, or anybody else's, but her sympathies were with Willow.

Willow said, "It would be madness to have her spirit walk this house for another second. Look at this." He gestured at the sharp bits of glass, then he was willing to say no more.

The door burst open and Joe's big frame filled it. "What's happening in here?"

His eyes flicked around the room. When they lighted on Faye and Amande, both safe, his body relaxed slightly. He grabbed them each by a wrist and tugged them toward the door, but there were too many people in the way, so he changed his strategy.

Avery, sitting nearest the door, helped him get Myrna out and into her easy chair. Joe brought Sister Mama's wheelchair as far into the room as it would fit, helped her into it, then parked her next to Myrna. Only then could he reach his wife, who had been penned into the far side of the room too efficiently to allow her to help with the people standing between her and the way out.

Dara and Willow remained where they had been, standing beside the light switch and glaring at one another.

◇◇◇

It had seemed prudent to give Dara and Willow some time alone, so Joe, Faye, Amande, and Avery had retreated to the front porch.

"What just happened?" Joe asked as he emptied his mouth into his spit cup. He looked at Faye as if to say, "You want me to protect you from a murdering arsonist, but I can't have a little tobacco now and then?"

Faye gave him a look that would curl every last one of his yard-long hairs.

"Either we were visited by an angry ghost or somebody wants us to think so." Avery's voice was even but strained. "It was like something out of a movie. Flying tables. Ghostly knocks on the wall. Weird sounds and smells. Those things are hokey, if you ask me. If a spirit can do all those things, why can't it just say, 'Hey. How ya doing?'"

"Because it's easier to make a table fly," Joe said. "Did you notice whether the woman was wearing sandals?"

Faye remembered a conversation about sandals and tables, held with Amande and Toni just before Amande wandered off to an assignation with a scary young man. She pictured the table in the séance room and imagined herself in sturdy sandals. By lifting her toes and sliding the sandal's soles under the two nearest table legs, it wouldn't have been hard to lift those two legs off the floor. By pressing down with her own hands, she would have had some ability to leverage the other two legs into the air. She might have had trouble holding it steady, but a wildly rocking table that occasionally makes noise by striking a leg on the floor is quite dramatic. Maybe even more dramatic than one that simply levitates.

Another point in Dara's table-tipping favor was the fact that five other people were pressing down on the table top, giving her a steady resistance to manipulate. It was all simple physics. No wonder Toni loved this stuff. "Yep. She always wears sandals."

Amande grinned at Faye, while Avery just looked blank.

Faye walked over to a white wicker end table sitting next to Myrna's porch swing. She wasn't wearing sandals, but her boots had a thick heavy sole that protruded slightly past the toe, making a small ledge. It would do.

She placed her hand flat on the table top and jammed that ledge beneath a table leg, then lifted her foot. The table wobbled, but it rose.

"That's not much of a trick," Avery said, "but it fooled me."

"It's been fooling people for a century or two," Faye said, "but I can't believe anybody would ever have been fooled by the rapping and cool breezes and smells floating around that little room. Willow was there to knock on the walls and open a bottle of perfume. He probably has a little paper fan he uses to move the air around that room. He could do anything he liked. It's pitch-dark in there."

"But the bowl…." Amande's voice drifted away as softly as Willow's rosewater perfume.

"I bet you didn't notice the wet spot beside Dara's chair, did you? It was hard to see from where you all were sitting." Joe's smile was sly. Faye hadn't seen it often enough lately. She reminded herself that she was angry with him. "What was in that bowl when the lights went out?" he asked.

"Water. Oil. A few drops of Willow's blood." Avery was trying to deliver that last phrase with the professional tone of someone whose work had shown her a lot of death, but Faye heard a faint note of discomfort escape her. Seeing the body of someone who died in a fire was truly horrible. Watching a small cut bleed slightly was not, but watching a man purposely harm himself was discomfiting in a different way. Faye understood how Avery felt.

"I bet they dumped in a whole bunch of herbs, too."

Faye wondered if maybe Joe was the real psychic, until he said, "The herbs are still in there, if you want to check. There was a lot of wet, slimy, green stuff stuck to that wet spot on the floor. She must have dumped the bowl after the lights went out, but before she made you hold hands. She did make you hold hands?"

They all nodded, but Amande asked the big question. "Who threw the bowl? Dara couldn't have done it. Mom had Dara by one hand and Avery had her by the other. She couldn't have let go of your hands long enough to throw the bowl. Neither of you would have let her."

"I sure didn't," Avery said. "Did Willow throw it at himself? Or did he maybe stand up next to the wall, holding the bowl in both hands, then bang it on the wall over his head? It was a thick bowl. I think it would be hard to break it that way. And it would be dangerous. He could cut his hands *or* his head, and the cuts might be a lot worse than the one he made on his palm."

Joe contradicted her. "Dara threw the bowl."

All three women asked, "How?"

"After the lights went out, and before she took your hands, she dumped it on the floor behind her. Then she put it on her head upside down. Like a hat. If you went in there and looked at her, I bet you'd see that her hair was a little wet."

Amande looked doubtful. "She's still gotta throw it."

"Sure she does. But she don't need her hands."

Joe held out his empty hands and mimed putting an invisible bowl on his head. Then, his upper body made a quick forward-and-back motion from the hips. Simultaneously, he flipped his head forward like a whip. "You wouldn't believe the power you can get this way, when you put your whole upper body behind it. It's like using a slingshot the size of yourself. You bet she could throw that bowl hard enough to break it against the wall."

"That explains Willow's reaction," Faye said. "He looked really surprised and really angry. He's a good actor, but he didn't look like a man who felt safe. He looked like a man who didn't know what had just happened. He also looked like a man who was pissed off at his wife. If he thought Tilda's ghost threw the bowl, why would he be angry at Dara?"

Faye remembered the shock in his voice when he said, "She tried to kill me." In the context of a séance, Faye had assumed he meant Tilda, the spirit being called. She peeked through a window and could see that Dara and Willow were still standing in the same spot, shouting at each other. In the context of a troubled marriage, maybe the "she" who had tried to kill Willow was his wife.

Chapter Twenty-five

Faye had been keeping an eye on the window, so she saw Willow turn his back on his wife and leave. He headed toward the kitchen and, presumably, out the kitchen door. Dara crossed the room and put a hand on Myrna's shoulder. A word passed between them and Dara lifted her eyes toward a window that looked out onto the porch. Faye took a step back, but she knew Myrna had told them they were there.

She was not surprised when Dara opened the door, with Myrna right behind her, so she was ready with innocuous questions. "How are you, Myrna? Should we call Ennis to come get Sister Mama?"

As she asked the innocuous questions, she noticed a few glittering drops of oil clinging to Dara's hair. Joe was a genius.

"What happened in there?" Amande looked hardly able to contain her curiosity, despite the fact that her father had just explained precisely what had happened. The deceitful child was playing Dara for information. "How did that bowl fly into the wall? It looked like it was worth a lot of money."

Amande was right about that. Everything in Myrna's house looked like somebody had spent a lot of money on it, way back when Queen Victoria was on the throne. Breaking a bowl in this house was a bigger deal than it was in Faye's.

"It was just a bowl. I've used it in my work for a long time, but it can be replaced." Dara smoothed her hair back from her face and, in the process, smeared away most of the oil droplets.

"I've heard of using a bowl instead of a crystal ball," Joe said. "But why? Is the ball too obvious? Too hokey?"

"Hokey? *No.* A practitioner must use the right tool. When the right tool is in the right hands, magic is not too strong a word. For me, a bowl of water, oil, and my husband's blood carries more resonance than a simple piece of quartz. There is only one crystal ball that would enhance my abilities, and it belonged to my mother and years of Armisteads before her. There is no other like it. I would trade all my mother's legacy—the money, the land, and every last jewel in her safety deposit box—for that ball. And, if by some miracle, I did have that ball, I would trade it for a single moment with my mother."

Money, land, and jewels. These sounded to Faye like classic motives for murder. Now that Tilda was dead, these things were Dara's. Willow's, too, presuming he stayed married to her. And, in Rosebower, maybe a singularly powerful crystal ball belonged on that list of motives for murder.

Joe directed his next question to Avery. "I just spent most of an hour sitting on the porch, looking at the wreck of poor Miss Tilda's house, and I've got something to ask you. Have you looked under the doorsteps?"

Avery looked confused by the question. "No, I can't say that I've done much more than shine a flashlight into the crawlspace and under the porches. People were smaller when these houses were built, and maybe the house has settled. I don't think an adult could get into those crawlspaces now, if anybody ever could."

"I'm not talking about the house or the porches. I'm talking about the doorsteps that take you up to the porches. Or any doors, really. I only know what little I've read about Spiritualism, but I know a lot about hoodoo. I grew up with people that set a lot of store in it. My wife tells me that you've got a root doctor right in there." He glanced through the open door at the silent Sister Mama. "Seems like the whole town's serious about hoodoo and root magic."

Dara said simply, "Sister Mama is a gifted woman."

"Here's what I know about hoodoo. One way to work on another man's future with hoodoo is to work your magic on his path. Maybe you sprinkle graveyard dirt someplace where he'll have to walk. Maybe you don't do anything but draw a big X in his path when he's not looking. Lots of hoodoo hexes bury things under doorsteps. In the rest of the world, this would be weird for me to say but, in this town, I think we should look under those doorsteps."

Avery shrugged as if to say, "I've heard odder suggestions this week," and they all followed her across the street. She was a tall woman, broad-shouldered, and the only way she could see under Tilda's doorstep was to lie on the ground, cheek to the grass.

When she said, "Somebody hand me my camera. It's in my purse. And somebody go get Sister Mama," Faye knew that she'd done a good thing when she sent for Joe.

◇◇◇

A dried-up lemon. A few nails. Several pennies.

Avery had photographed them in place. Now she had spread them on the grass and was squatting beside them, taking up-close photos. She squinted up at Sister Mama.

"Did you do this?"

Sister Mama shook her head firmly.

"Do you know who did?"

She shook her head again.

"Do you know what it means?"

She gave a vigorous nod, as if she were glad to know something useful. She held up one palsied hand, thumb down. Her meaning seemed clear. A person who buried a lemon under another person's doorstep was not casting a good-luck charm.

Sister Mama wasn't finished. She wanted to speak very much. She began with "Ehhhh...," then frowned. Trying again, she exhaled hard enough to form an "h" sound.

"Hehhhh..."

Her arms moved in agitated jerks. She wanted to say more, but couldn't. Finally, she managed another "Hehhhh..." and ended the sound with a broad gesture of her right hand. It made a swoop downward to the left, then rose high again to make another swoop crossing the first one.

"X?" Amande asked.

The old woman nodded and repeated the sequence. "Hehhh..." and following it with an "X" in the air.

"Hex?" Faye asked. "You're saying someone tried to hex Tilda?"

Sister Mama swayed and laughed. "Yeh."

Faye let her eyes travel over Tilda's ruined house, thinking that perhaps the person who hexed Tilda Armistead wielded the most potent magic in Rosebower. Then she let her eyes rest on Myrna. The morning sun cast every last crease on her face into sharp relief. Each breath seemed to come harder.

Without speaking or even thinking, Faye ran back across the street. Being smaller than Avery, she could squeeze most of her torso beneath Myrna's doorstep. This effort brought her face to face with another desiccated lemon, more rusty nails, and more pennies. Faye would never have thought that a little garbage could make her so blindingly angry.

She heaved herself back into the sunlight, calling out, "Get that camera over here." Then she ran for Myrna's kitchen door, the entrance she used every day. As she expected, she found another lemon, more nails, more pennies. But she didn't expect to see something else resting just past the lemon, glinting at arm's-length in the darkness.

She felt more like an archaeologist under this house than she'd felt since she arrived in Rosebower. There was a story here, and she couldn't afford to mess it up. Carefully, so carefully, she backed out from under the steps. If there were clues in this dust, she wanted them to stay.

"Avery. The camera."

"Another lemon?"

"Yes. And a crystal ball."

◇◇◇

Faye and Avery worked together to document the site of Tilda's crystal ball. Technically, Faye supposed, it could have been somebody else's crystal ball, but Dara and Myrna swore that it was the same size and of the same rare clarity. Maybe some of the fingerprints on it would prove to be Tilda's.

Close observation had gleaned some clues to support their opinion. An easily visible trail led through the dry dust under Myrna's steps. It led from the grass to the ball's resting spot, as if someone had rolled the crystal like a bowling ball. The stair treads weren't water-tight. With the next rain, that trail would be gone. This meant that the ball had been placed in this spot since rain fell. A quick check of a weather website said that it had been less than two weeks since Rosebower saw rain. The ball itself had gathered very little dust, which also supported the theory that it hadn't been outdoors for long.

Joe had brought a chair outside for Myrna, so that she could watch Faye and Avery work. Sister Mama couldn't be convinced to go home and rest, and Dara was still hovering over them both. Faye wasn't sure she'd ever had such an attentive audience while she was trying to work, and she knew she'd never worked in front of someone like Myrna. Every five minutes, she asked, "Faye? Avery? Would you like a cup of tea?"

At last, she and Avery agreed that they'd collected all the evidence they were going to get. Avery stooped to pick up the ball, but Dara got there first. She cradled it in her arms like a baby and cried.

"That's evidence—" Avery began.

Myrna didn't let her finish. "And it's mine." She took the ball from her niece and clutched it to her own chest.

Myrna spoke in the sing-song voice of a woman half-tanked. She must still be taking Sister Mama's alcohol-laced tinctures. Willow's 150-proof estimate seemed low. "I've got more stuff than anybody needs, but the fact remains. Now I've got even more. Tilda made me her only heir years ago. You're *my* only heir, but this ball and everything else your mother owned is mine for as much time as I have left."

Dara looked as if she'd been slapped, but she was born for the stage. She revealed nothing.

Myrna reached her hand out to pat Dara's and almost missed. "I'm sorry, dear. So sorry. Why couldn't the two of you kiss and make up? She was my sister and I know she was…prickly…but she wasn't that bad. Not that bad. Really."

Dara took a few slow steps backward and then ran away, her sandals slapping on the sidewalk's pavement.

"I love that child, but sometimes she wears on my nerves." Myrna handed the ball to Avery. "If you need it for evidence, keep it. My sister left all she had to me, including this useless lump of rock. She must have had her reasons."

Chapter Twenty-six

The building housing Rosebower's museum was utterly unpretentious. So why did it scare Faye?

It was a single-story wood frame building dating to the 1940s, originally built as a house. Samuel's father had established it as a museum in the 1960s. The bathroom looked exactly as one would expect it to look, tiny and utilitarian. Its vintage sink and tub contrasted with a replacement toilet in a groovy shade of avocado green. The rest of the building showed the same historical mishmash. There were gorgeous heart pine floors in the display rooms, but the vinyl flooring in the work room was ugly enough to keep a weary archaeologist awake on the job.

It was not a beautiful building, but it wasn't a frightening one. Nevertheless, Faye lingered on the sidewalk outside, her heart fluttering in her chest. It was time for Samuel to meet his new consultant, the one who was going to tell him that the centerpiece artifacts of his museum were worthless.

Okay, maybe they weren't worthless, but they weren't what he thought they were and they weren't anything special. Faye had set Joe up for a difficult meeting. It didn't help matters that she and Amande would be working in the next room while it happened.

Joe put a hand on her waist and started walking, herding her along with him. Amande followed behind, as if she knew Faye was thinking of retreat.

◇◇◇

Faye sat at her desk, wondering whether Samuel would throw a tantrum and whether she'd be able to hear it through the wall. Maybe her company was destined to lose its only current contract within the next twenty minutes. Even so, she wasn't the type to go down without a fight. She might as well make those twenty minutes billable.

She picked up a box filled with carefully packed china, enough to serve a party of twenty. There was no denying that the plates and cups were pretty, festooned with pink roses and blue scrolls, but they were probably mass-produced. Or they could also be as rare and valuable as Myrna's irreplaceable antiques. Faye bet herself that she and the Internet could ferret out the truth before Joe and Samuel finished talking.

◇◇◇

As Faye had expected, American antique stores were crammed full of rose-trimmed china plates just like the one in her hand. Twenty minutes of her billable time had been spent proving that Samuel didn't need to waste shelf space on it. She supposed this was valuable information.

"Amande, can you catalog these pieces and pack them properly for storage?"

"Sure. I'm ready to go on the clock now."

Her expression said, "You're supposed to ask me what I've been doing and why I wasn't on the clock," so Faye obliged her.

"I wasn't asleep when you and Dad were talking in the car. How'd you like to know who owns the property surrounding Mr. Marlowe's development? You know…the land he needs if he's going to build that golf course he wants? Well, it just so happens that there is one name on the deeds of all the tracts that touch the property he owns now."

She was still wearing her "Ask me!" face.

Faye was interested, so she cooperated. "Let me guess. Is it Dara? I remember hearing that she and Willow built their auditorium near there on property she inherited."

"Close but no. Tilda owned all that property surrounding Marlowe's land, so I guess Miss Myrna owns it now. I also found some more nearby land that Mr. Marlowe probably wants. It's hard for me to tell, because I don't know exactly how big a golf course needs to be."

"Are you going to tell me who owns that land, or are you going to make me guess again?"

"Guessing would be fun, but I do need to get billable, so I'll tell you. Myrna owns it outright. She didn't inherit it from Tilda."

Faye had heard Myrna say that Tilda had opposed Gilbert Marlowe's plans as much as she did. She realized that her next billable museum chore needed to wait. First, she needed to let Avery know that Tilda Armistead, and probably Myrna too, had stood between Gilbert Marlowe and the golf course that his resort probably needed to be profitable. When Faye had seen Marlowe and Myrna arguing, he had obviously been surprised that she opposed him. Before Tilda's death, he might have presumed she was the only person in his way, not knowing that her sister had more grit than he'd thought. Perhaps he had thought that, with Tilda out of the way, Dara would sell him her inheritance and Myrna would go along meekly with whatever he and her niece wanted.

Was Myrna in danger now? Faye didn't think Marlowe's obstacles fared well in this world.

Myrna was growing more frail by the day. Did her resistance matter to Gilbert Marlowe, when he knew that her heirs, Willow and Dara, would probably sell him anything he wanted after she was dead? The answer to that question depended on how long Gilbert Marlowe was willing to wait.

◇◇◇

Faye waited until the door closed behind Joe before she hissed, "How did it go?"

He walked across the room and sat on her desk. Amande sat next to him. They both leaned down to put their mouths next to Faye's ears, making it impossible for Samuel to overhear this impromptu company meeting.

"What did he say? Was he pissed that I'd flown my mostly Creek husband up here to explain that, even in the absence of Europeans, civilization can be possible?"

"You were there when he first saw me, before you disappeared into this room. He was very polite. He has some weird ideas, but he has good manners."

"Good. Because you certainly dressed to rub your not-European-ness in his face today."

Joe had made a new pair of moccasins for the occasion, and he'd stuck a feather in his braid. This was his version of formal business attire. On "Casual Fridays," he went barefoot.

Amande couldn't contain herself. "So what did he say?"

"He said the same stuff to me he's been saying to your mother, and it ain't nothing new. People have been talking about ancient dead 'moundbuilder' cultures since Columbus stepped off the boat. They didn't want to believe that the people who were here waiting for him could possibly have built awesome things like mounds and pyramids. 'Cause if they believed that, they would've had to think twice about treating them the way they did. Samuel still thinks that way. He wants our report to say that his artifacts prove that aliens came to upstate New York in ancient times."

"I think there are still plenty of aliens living here in Rosebower," Amande muttered. "And some of them are ancient, themselves."

Faye covered Amande's mouth with her hand so she would let her father talk. "What did you say to him?"

"I told him the same stuff you've been telling him. The space-man artifact is just a souvenir somebody brought home from a trip to Mexico. The Rosebower spear is made out of rock that looks local to me. His runestone is a piece of pottery. It ain't rare and it's also local."

"Did he blow you off, like he did me?"

"Not exactly. I'm supposed to come back tomorrow with proof. He wants 'authoritative' sources, which to Samuel means books. I told him I couldn't gather up all the books I needed that quick, but that I could do it if he would consider some Internet sources, too. Maybe he'll listen. Maybe our problem's solved."

Faye should have been happy that Joe had made progress with Samuel, but she was mostly pissed off. If Samuel had been willing to let her show him published proof, she could have done it a week ago. Instead, he'd spent quite a lot of money on bringing in Joe to tell him the same thing.

Joe held up his hands in surrender. "I know what you're thinking. Maybe this guy only listens to men, but hey. We're making some money off the deal."

If this statement was supposed to keep Faye from being angry, it missed the mark.

◇◇◇

Faye couldn't believe it. The pile of shabby cardboard boxes waiting to be sorted was undeniably smaller. She leaned back in her desk chair, crossed her arms, and did nothing but look at it for a moment. She was glad she'd asked Avery to wait a day for the house tour, because three people working a full eight hours could do an impressive amount of work. Joe had to go back to Florida in a week but, at this pace, Faye had no doubt that she and Amande could finish this contract on schedule.

"We're off the clock now, right? Mom?" The unnatural glow of a computer screen reflected on Amande's young skin.

"Yes. You're free to chat or web-surf or watch cat videos. You've earned the right to waste your time."

"Actually, I'm looking at aerial photos of Tilda's and Myrna's land and comparing them to a website on golf course design. I think Marlowe could squeeze a course onto their combined property, but he'd be better off if he had some of the other land around it, too."

Joe had gotten comfortable at some point in the day, so his moccasins had been kicked into the corner. He poked Faye in the calf with his bare toe. "She's as nosy as you are."

Faye poked him back without actually acknowledging his "nosy" comment. "Why don't you email those links to Avery, sweetie, then shut the computer down? I'm starving."

"Wait," Joe said. This was uncharacteristic. Nobody in their family was known for turning down food, or even delaying it slightly.

Then he walked out of the work room and checked to make sure the rest of the museum was empty. When he returned he said, "I want to talk about the golf course and the burnt house and all the things that go with them. And I want to do it here, where nobody will hear us."

Amande rose silently to check the closet. Faye heard the service door's lock slide into place. Smart girl.

"It seems to me that we learned some stuff today that changes everything. Marlowe is distracting people from the fact that he doesn't have enough land to build the development that he's trying to jam down their throats. The person who did own the land is dead, and the person who owns it now doesn't look so good. Does any of this mean anything?"

"It means that Marlowe had a motive for Tilda's death, but it doesn't give us anything to link him to the fire. Technically, it means that Myrna had a motive, since she could now sell Marlowe the property that Tilda wouldn't sell him.

"But that doesn't add up, Mom, since we heard Myrna say she'd never sell it to him."

"True. But Marlowe seemed surprised by her refusal, didn't you think? If a man killed a woman, believing that her sister would sell him what he wanted, then it would be an ugly surprise to find out that she *wouldn't* sell."

"I think I know somebody else that's surprised," Joe said. "I think the red-haired psychic was real shocked to find out she wasn't getting an inheritance. I saw how much she wanted that crystal ball this morning. Maybe she wanted the property that bad, too, so's she could sell it to Marlowe. It would be a terrible thing to kill your own mother, then find out you weren't going to inherit a fortune, after all."

"Or to kill your mother-in-law, only to find out that your wife has been disinherited," Faye said, watching Amande pout at a suggestion of Willow's guilt.

Amande responded by changing the subject. "What about the crystal ball and the lemons and nails and pennies?"

"The lemons and nails and pennies are a hex." Joe said it matter-of-factly, as if everybody knew that walking over rotten citrus fruit would give a person bad luck. "I've heard of it. I've seen it done. Never tried it myself."

Faye hoped Joe never tried to hex her. She said, "So somebody who believes in hoodoo was trying to give the Armistead sisters some bad luck."

"It looks that way to me," Joe said. "The crystal ball is different, though. I don't think it was a hex. It wasn't there nearly as long as those lemons—"

"Yuck," said Amande. "They were gross."

"—and the two of you sat in the same room with it on Monday night. It left the house right afterward, or Avery would have found it while she was searching through the ashes. I'd say that either Mrs. Armistead or her killer took it out of the house right after you left."

"Makes sense," Faye said. "But which?"

"Let's start with the set-up you told me first—the killer nailed the séance room shut, thinking she was in there, but she wasn't. She escaped from the burning house, but not before she breathed in enough smoke to die from smoke inhalation. The only way the killer comes away from that scenario with the crystal ball is by taking it before he thought Mrs. Armistead would go in the room. After that, the ball was nailed up in the room."

"That doesn't sound right," Faye said. "Tilda was so attached to her crystal ball. No one who knew her would be certain how she would behave if she opened the séance room door and saw that it was missing. Maybe she would go in to look for it, making it possible for the killer to nail the door shut behind her. But maybe she wouldn't go in. Maybe she'd start searching the house for her crystal ball. Maybe she'd even leave the house to get help finding it."

"But if Tilda suspected something," Faye said, "she might have gone in and gotten the ball before the killer even arrived. Maybe because she knew the killer wanted it?"

Amande interrupted her again but, again, her observation was astute. "Or maybe she just wanted to be sure her prized possession was safe."

"I think that's our answer," Faye said. "Tilda managed to get out of the room—but not the house— in the tiny window of time before her killer came, and she took the ball with her. The killer nailed an empty room shut and set the house on fire. Tilda escaped, but the hot smoke had already ruined her lungs. I lean toward this scenario because it explains the hiding place of the ball. Why would the killer have left it behind after going to the trouble of stealing it from Tilda's? And remember what Tilda said when she was dying? She said she tried to wake Myrna. I think she saved herself and the ball from the fire, then ran across the street to wake up her sister. The ball was heavy, so she hid it under Myrna's house."

Joe and Amande both liked this logic. Their satisfied smiles were so alike that Faye would have sworn they were blood-kin.

"But Mom, none of this explains why Tilda came to you. That's been bothering me all week. She hasn't left town in years, but she crawled behind the wheel of her car to come to you for help. Don't take this the wrong way, but she hardly knew you."

"I didn't understand it then, but five more days in this town has answered that question. Think about it. Who would Tilda have gone to for help?"

"She tried to get to Myrna and couldn't," Amande said. "I'm not sure if she trusted anybody else."

"Exactly. She wasn't on speaking terms with Willow and Dara. Samuel told me himself that they weren't close. He said she wasn't close to their neighbors, either. Sister Mama would have been no help, and I wouldn't trust Ennis as far as I could throw him. Most people would call 911, but we've seen how her sister feels about doctors. Tilda probably felt the same way about any emergency responder. Besides, who would that responder be? A call to 911 might bring someone who hated her for the way she voted at council meetings. Tilda must have felt her only choice was to turn to a friendly stranger. Of course I would help her. Why wouldn't I? More importantly, I had no reason to hurt her."

"I see what you're saying, but Mom. It's horrible. Other than Myrna, there was no one in Rosebower that Tilda could trust."

Chapter Twenty-seven

There are few things more awkward than gossiping about someone, then finding yourself face-to-face with her. Faye had just spent ten minutes dissecting Dara like a laboratory specimen. Her husband and daughter had listened while Faye dumped on her for feuding with her mother. She'd made catty comments about Dara's faux-red hair, smug in the knowledge that her own hair was still black and her grandmother's hair had stayed black until she was eighty. She'd rolled her eyes at the way the woman failed to turn off her theatrical mannerisms after the curtain had dropped. Then the three of them had walked out the museum door, only to see Dara hurrying toward them.

"I'm so glad I caught you before you went home."

Faye had done the mocking, but the other two had egged her on. The fact that Dara couldn't read their shame-faced auras spoke against any claim she might make for telepathic powers.

"I can't sleep tonight without trying to contact my mother again. She was with us this morning, but Willow ruined everything. Now I've disturbed her without giving her peace. My mother and I must reconcile, or neither of us will ever rest. Can you find it in yourselves to help me again? Tonight?"

"Now?" Faye asked, trying not to form the thought, *What a drama queen!* And failing. "Do you mean that you want all six of us at the table again, with Joe watching and Willow taking notes? Before bedtime?"

Amande butted in. "Forget before bedtime. You have a show tonight. Are you saying you want to do this tonight before curtain time? It's not possible."

"We're not doing a show tonight. Maybe not ever again. Willow and I have split. He doesn't believe in what I do. Never has. He wants me to cheat. Nags me into it, every night. He thinks I threw that bowl at his head, but it wasn't me. It was my mother. She was controlling my body."

She ran the shaking fingers of her hands through her hair. Her rings snagged on the abundant curls and she yanked both hands free, letting single orange strands fall to the ground. "*My mother.* She knew what Willow was. She told me, years ago, and still I let him come between us. If I ask her tonight, without cheating and without Willow, she will come. She will."

Faye repeated her question. "Do you need all of us? Everybody who was there this morning? I'm not sure Sister Mama is up to it." Faye wasn't sure she was up to it either. Surely Dara had noticed that none of them had said yes, not yet.

"No. We'll be four at the table. You, your daughter, me, and my aunt. I don't need an assistant. Willow made me include him so that he could knock on the walls and stir up smelly breezes. I can't tell you how glad I am to be rid of him."

Faye was thinking of a different kind of assistance. If she had been nervous enough that morning to ask Joe to stand guard, she was doubly so tonight. "Avery can help Joe stand watch. She's trained and she's armed."

It crossed Faye's mind that Dara accepted the need for guards very easily. She wasn't supposed to know that her mother's death was due to arson, but she had already commented on Avery's prolonged investigation.

"Invite Avery? Good idea. If she's still hanging onto my mother's crystal ball as evidence, instead of doing the right thing by giving it to my aunt, I'll bet I can talk her into bringing it. I'm not stupid enough to think that Avery would still be here if my mother died in a simple house fire. If she wants information, she should like the notion of this séance because, basically, we're restaging the night of the fire even more closely than we did this morning. The only difference is that I'll be sitting in my mother's chair.

"And there will be two people standing guard," Faye said.

Dara nodded. "Even the house is virtually identical. I know that Mother has things to reveal. Tonight, she'll come back to me from the other side. She will."

◇◇◇

Toni pulled the wig over her head. Her own hair, coiled on her crown, fit under it snugly. The wig was the same color as her natural hair, making it possible for her to tug out a few short locks. Teased and combed over the wig's edge, they gave a more natural-looking hairline. She held up a hand-mirror to check the result from all angles, and she saw that she'd achieved the desired look. Her head looked like it belonged to an aging man who liked to wait a little too long between haircuts.

She was the first to admit that she owned far too much makeup. Creams to change the skin tone, powders to emphasize brows, pencils to create wrinkles that she didn't have yet—she loved them the way an artist loves charcoals and pastels. Smoothing concealer over her lips, she changed them to a color that was less pink and more mannish. With the sweep of a powder-laden brush, she gave herself a five-o'clock shadow. A bit of stippling with a fine black pencil made that shadow still more believable. Contouring powder made her brow more pronounced and her jaw firmer.

After strategic application of three colors of foundation makeup, her hands now looked less soft and more sun-damaged. When she was satisfied with her manly looks, she slid the camera watch over a newly rugged hand. If Willow, Dara, or anybody at their show, recognized her tonight, then she would know that the magic had left her life for good. It would be her sign that it was time to walk away from illusion. It would be time to really retire.

But not now. Right now, Toni felt the familiar rush of pre-performance adrenaline. She was ready to do some magician's espionage and get video of two fakers in action. She was ready to have some fun.

◇◇◇

If Joe's over-analytical wife had ever said that she would someday be willing to submit to three séances in a week, he would have called her nuts. Yet here she was, doing it again.

He watched Myrna bustle around her parlor. Dara had refused to allow her enough time to brew tea, saying, "Sunset is approaching and we all know that it is the best time to reach the spirit world, other than dawn and midnight."

Joe wasn't sure he agreed with her, but he saw no need to argue. It wasn't his business to watch for spirits tonight. He intended to stand watch for three-dimensional people who might want to hurt his wife and his child and these other nice people. If any spirits happened by, he would alert the observant Spiritualist after she finished consulting her mother's crystal ball.

Deprived of her teapot, Myrna was still driven to play hostess, so she circulated through the room, handing out candy. Even before he smelled it, Joe could see by the look on his wife's face that it was licorice. He rather liked licorice, so he held out an unobtrusive hand and Faye slid her piece of candy into it with the stealth of a stage magician. He knew Amande felt the same way, so they performed an identical act of sleight-of-hand. Now he had three big pieces of licorice to keep him company while he watched for evildoers. Score!

Joe and Avery had divided their duties sensibly, based on the fact that she had a gun and he didn't. He was back in his chair in the front doorway. People in Rosebower kept their front yards manicured, so he had a good line-of-sight up and down Main and Walnut Streets. If anybody wanted to come from any of those directions to set this house on fire, they'd see Joe and they'd know he saw them. He doubted any of them would risk it. If they did, Avery and her gun were within earshot, if he should call for her.

Rosebower's back yards were less well-kept than the front lawns. Maybe they always had been, or maybe people had let that part of their yardwork go as they got older. Avery had said that she wanted to be able to prowl through those bushes, gun drawn. She wanted to make it hard for someone to slip into the undergrowth and hide. He understood her rationale for taking that job, and he agreed.

They both had cell phones, obviously, but they were also in direct audio contact, because there was no place on Myrna Armistead's small property where one of them could call out for the other without being heard. This plan was all Avery's and it was a good one.

Behind him, Dara was leading Faye, Amande, and Myrna into the tiny little room where she talked to spirits. He turned his head to watch. Through the séance room's open door, Tilda Armistead's crystal ball reflected light from her sister's parlor chandelier. It shone dimly on the faces of the four participants for a moment, then Dara shut the door.

Joe didn't understand the need to shut oneself away from the world for such things. He couldn't imagine spirits remembering that walls even existed, once they'd left this Earth. He was even less capable of imagining that spirits cared about spherical lumps of quartz.

Thrusting a hand deep into his leather bag, he came out with a lump of candy that was only slightly dirtied by its time in the bag. He bit into it and the flavor hit him like a jolt. Damn. Joe had never tasted licorice candy so good in his life. This stuff made all other licorice taste like the black jellybeans left in the bottom of a two-year-old's Easter basket.

While he chewed that first bite, he used Myrna's torch-strong porch light to take a look at the uneaten portion of his candy. The filling was jet-black and gelatinous, as he would have expected of licorice, and the coating looked like chocolate. He needed to know where she got this stuff. If he hadn't needed to know this so badly, he would never have noticed that the candy had puncture marks.

Joe had made dipped candy before. He usually made the filling, skewered it on a toothpick, then dipped it in chocolate. This method left a single puncture-like hole, and even that wasn't an irreparable problem. Artful cooks, and Joe was one of them, knew how to patch over the dipping hole with more chocolate.

He could see the patch on this piece, so it was clearly hand-dipped by someone who knew how. Sometime after the careful chef patched this hole, at least one more hole had appeared on the candy's flat bottom.

He pulled the other two pieces of licorice from his bag and laid them out on one of his big palms, belly-up. On the bottom of each, there were three small holes in the chocolate coating. They were too far apart to be the work of a fork. Besides, they were irregularly spaced, and the holes slanted at widely varying angles.

Joe took another big bite and rolled the candy around on his tongue. It was good. It was too good. Being a very fine cook and a more than passable herbalist, Joe knew of a couple of good reasons why he, like most Americans, had never had licorice candy this fine before. First of all, why should candy makers pay for authentic licorice extract when cheap anise flavoring did the trick? And second of all, what candy maker wanted to be responsible for the pernicious side effects of true licorice?

High blood pressure.

Irregular heartbeat.

Drug interactions.

Congestive heart failure.

These were not the effects people wanted from their candy.

Joe had chewed licorice root a few times, and it had tasted awesome, but the pleasure wasn't worth the risk. Oh, it wouldn't hurt a casual, healthy candy-lover. But could constant use tip a habitual user with existing cardiac problems into congestive heart failure? Yes. It certainly could. He'd heard that some manufacturers in other countries still made real licorice candy, but how many American companies would open themselves to lawsuits for giving their customers heart failure?

If Joe had to guess, he'd say that somebody was taking easily obtained anise candy and injecting it with homemade licorice extract, making it simultaneously tastier and deadlier. Faye had described Sister Mama's garden, so he had a pretty good idea as to where the licorice grew. He didn't know the citizens of Rosebower well enough to guess who was dosing Myrna with an herb that could kill an elderly heart patient, but Faye did. He slid the deadly candy back into his bag and sat still, doing nothing but looking for danger.

Watching the stars pop out of a quiet sky usually brought Joe's world into complete equilibrium. Tonight, all he could do was count the stars and wait for a private talk with Faye.

◇◇◇

Myrna had produced a quaintly ornate lamp from one of her china cabinets. It fit neatly within the stand that supported the old crystal ball, just like Tilda's lamp, so Faye assumed it was another family heirloom. Because Willow was not there to fake a spiritual visitation with rappings and odorous breezes, Dara didn't need utter darkness. The faces of Amande, Myrna, and Dara glowed in the lamp's light, but the rest of the room remained in near-utter darkness.

Dara lit no incense, nor did she smear scented oils over the ball. Away from Willow's influence, she revealed a style even more spare than her mother's. After the four of them had spent a few breaths studying the uplit ball, she instructed them to join hands. They did so, but not in the awkward hands-flat-and-pinkies-touching style that she'd required before. This time, they held hands like friends, palms together and fingers interlaced.

Then she did nothing but breathe. Faye found that it was impossible to ignore the breaths of the people around her. As she listened, the four of them slid into synchronized rhythm. Amande's soft and easy rhythm meshed with Dara's tense and shallow breaths, then Myrna labored to join them. Faye's chest hurt as she tried to breathe along with the frail woman. It was as if the two of them were dying at the same time.

Freed of everything in the world outside the dim lamplight in front of her, freed even of the need to choose the rhythm of her own breath, Faye's mind had nothing left to fight. Intuition surfaced. Faye felt that she had seen enough this week to solve the riddle of Tilda's last hour. Now, at last, she could stop fighting her subconscious and let it surface.

The first thing it told her was to listen to Myrna. She had been fine last week, almost perky. Now she sounded sick. Not old. Sick. There had to be a reason.

◇◇◇

Toni walked across the empty auditorium parking lot. She wasn't surprised to see the sign on the door saying that the evening's show was canceled—the absence of cars had told her that—but the silence around her was disconcerting.

Cancel a show? People like Dara and Willow didn't cancel. They performed with pneumonia. They hauled themselves onstage with broken arms hidden under their sleeves. They barely even paused to acknowledge death. The show must go on.

Toni knew of only one likely event that would cause Dara to turn away an audience. Something must have happened to Myrna. And even though logic told her that people in their eighties died of natural causes all the time, intuition told her that now was not Myrna's time. If Tilda's death hadn't been an accident, and Toni had never believed that it was, then nothing that had happened to Myrna this week was an accident. She *could* succumb to natural causes this week but, if she did, Toni could never be made to believe it.

Still wearing a camera on her wrist, Toni left the deserted parking lot at a dead sprint.

◇◇◇

As Dara closed the door to the séance room, Avery was completing her first circuit of Myrna's property boundaries. All was clear.

Faye's husband Joe had allowed her a brief nod as she passed, then gone back to his previous state of relaxed vigilance. She sensed that he was a good man to have around in a crisis. Not that she expected a crisis, but who could have predicted what happened to Tilda? Her sense was that a sane criminal would be put off by the mere presence of an armed law enforcement official, backed up by Joe's scary-looking impression of a security guard, but this was no reason to take the situation lightly. All criminals are not sane.

◇◇◇

At some point, Dara had begun talking. Too deep within herself to notice, Faye paid no attention to the literal words Dara was saying.

This was unusual for Faye. For her, words were serious business. They communicated, they clarified, they made sure people understood each other. Tonight, the sounds of Dara's words were striking her eardrums, but her mind wasn't interested. Her brain was busy reading between the lines.

Faye heard grief in Dara's voice, but not guilt. She heard an urgent desire for reconciliation. She heard unresolved questions festering in Dara's mind. The woman knew that her mother's death made no sense. She didn't have to be told that there was no reasonable explanation for the destruction of her girlhood home. Dara needed answers and, for a woman born in Rosebower, the way to get answers was to ask a dead person who knows.

"Mother. I know you can tell me what I need to know. I am sitting with three people who care for you. We will wait for you to come."

Faye didn't believe Dara killed her mother. She lacked proof for this belief, but so be it. If not Dara, then who?

If the motive had been political, there were too many suspects to count. Half the town had objected to Tilda's actions as town councilor. Faye set those near-strangers aside, and limited her list of potential killers to the people who would benefit directly and immediately from Tilda's death. This made the list of suspects much shorter.

Dara had presumed, wrongly, that she was her mother's sole heir, so there was a place for her on that list, but Faye had mentally drawn a line through her name already. Myrna *was* Tilda's sole heir, but Faye couldn't imagine the tender-hearted woman killing her sister. From a more cold-blooded standpoint, Myrna wasn't physically capable of nailing a door shut, hurling burning lamps at it, spreading more accelerant around to burn, and then escaping unscathed. Faye drew an imaginary line through her name, too.

Willow had possessed every reason to believe that he was married to the sole heir of a woman with property, money, and family jewels. People had murdered for far less. The fact that Tilda had owned property that Gilbert Marlowe needed only gave Willow a bigger motive. Faye knew that developers did not stick with deals that moved too slowly. Time is money, and it always has been. Willow might or might not have been willing to wait for Tilda to die to get her money and jewels, but Marlowe's project had a deadline.

A tract of land big enough—or nearly big enough—for a golf course was worth a small fortune, but only when there was a buyer handy. Tilda would never have sold it to Marlowe. Her death made it possible for her daughter and son-in-law to reap that small fortune before he moved on to a project that would turn a quicker profit. This theory was mostly supported on air, but Faye had one factual piece of evidence. She couldn't forget her glimpse of Willow riding with Marlowe in his limousine.

Marlowe himself must be on the suspect list, for many of the same reasons as Willow. He was heavily invested in developing Rosebower into a major tourist attraction, but those plans were constrained by a lack of land. Who knew what else he might build if he had Tilda's land? And Myrna's? The elder Armistead women were standing between Gilbert Marlowe and money. Faye guessed that Marlowe *already* considered the money and the land to be his. Layer a little sociopathy on top of that narcissism, and the man would absolutely be able to rationalize taking out a little old lady or two who stood in his way. After all, they were going to die soon, anyway.

Dara's voice intruded into her thoughts. "Mother, I'm sorry. I was wrong. Now that you're on the other side, I know you can see my heart so much better. Maybe there is no word for 'forgiveness' where you are. Maybe there is only understanding. On this side of the veil of death, we lack that understanding, so I ask you to forgive me. We will wait here for your answer."

As they waited, Faye allowed her mind to rest a moment with the question, "Who else would profit from Tilda's death?" Sister Mama's name flashed into her consciousness, but she was even less physically capable of murder than Myrna, and Faye knew of no motive for her.

Ennis, however…Ennis had no alibi for that night. No one who had attended the council meeting could have any doubt that Ennis and Marlowe were already in negotiations. In exchange for publicly shifting his vote and Sister Mama's, Ennis was being rewarded with a lucrative job that would take him away from his exile in Rosebower. Faye knew nothing about Ennis' character that would argue against his being a killer. This was a rather damning indictment against a human being.

"We wait." Dara had now repeated this statement several times and in several ways. She sounded firm and open, yet not demanding. This, in itself, was a gift. Even if she had no others, this gift was worth having. She breathed deeply, and the others followed suit. Myrna's breath rattled in her chest. Faye's subconscious took note.

Two women had stood in the way of Marlowe, Willow, and Ennis. One of them was dead. The other one had suffered health reverses that would have been stunning, if they hadn't been obscured by age. Why was Myrna getting sicker by the minute? And why were the people around her so happy to pump her full of mystery drugs? Yes, Sister Mama enjoyed a reputation for fine root doctoring, but she wasn't prescribing Myrna's tinctures any longer. Ennis was.

Myrna lowered her head and used her shoulder to stifle a cough. She was too much a woman of Rosebower to break the circle to raise her hand to cover her mouth. Nothing was worth breaking the circle, not if her sister might be near.

"Speak to us, Mother."

The lamp beneath Tilda's crystal ball flickered, and its weak light illuminated Dara's glowing curls. Faye knew it was silly, but part of her hoped that the dancing fire heralded the arrival of Tilda Armistead, the only person who had a prayer of telling them how she died.

Chapter Twenty-eight

Avery was approaching the most dangerous moment in a stake-out, the moment when boredom makes a watcher careless. She almost welcomed the barely audible noise in the shrubbery of Myrna Armistead's back yard.

She understood Joe's strategy of making himself plainly visible as a way to forestall trouble, but she preferred being inconspicuous. Crouched by the back doorstep, she had a decent view of most of the yard. She would have been easily visible in daylight, but a shadow cast by a nearly new moon yields all-but-complete darkness. She could only be seen by someone who already knew she was there. To anyone else, she was invisible, so long as she stayed motionless.

Her eyes flicked toward the noise. A few heartbeats later, she saw the branches of a shrub tremble, four feet to the left of the original noise. She might be tracking an intruder or she might be tracking a raccoon, but at least she knew its direction of travel. She waited.

After a breathless moment, another faint sound came. The intruder/raccoon was still moving to her left, and the massive house would soon obscure her line-of-sight. Slowly—and soundlessly, she hoped—she crept from the dark shadow of the stairs and into the slightly less dark openness.

◇◇◇

Joe heard nothing. Or, rather, he heard only the breath of a noise, so faint that it was hardly more than a vibration of air across his cheek. He forgot that Avery had said his first priority was to open the séance room door. Instinct told him that his first priority should be to keep any intruder from entering the house. He was on his feet and running before the vibration stopped.

◇◇◇

Faye's intuition had taken her this far. Someone was poisoning Myrna, using Sister Mama's herbs to do it. Someone had tried to kill Sister Mama herself, possibly with her own herbs soaked into the soporific sponge. The obvious conclusion was that Ennis was the culprit. Every day, he brought Myrna an unlabeled concoction to put in her tea. Every day she drank it. And he had total access to Sister Mama. Thus, he was the poisoner. She should feel the satisfaction of solving a riddle, like the solid clink of the last puzzle piece fitting into place, but she didn't.

What was the question left unanswered by this scenario?

The lamp and its fire drew her eye again, and it asked her the critical question. Fire had killed Tilda quickly, while Myrna was fading slowly away. Sister Mama, too. If the same killer was at work, driven by the same motive, why were the murder methods so different?

It seemed to Faye that the difference lay in access. If Ennis had shown up daily on Tilda's doorstep, carrying some weird concoction and claiming that it was a tonic straight from Sister Mama, Tilda would have downed it without question. It would have been the easiest murder in history. It made no sense for Ennis to burn down her house.

Would Tilda have taken the same tonic from Willow? No. She wouldn't have even accepted a piece of his licorice candy.

Faye tested her theory and the pieces fit, in a twisted and Rosebower-like way. Dara was innocent because Faye's intuition said so. Marlowe had no motive to commit murder himself, not when he had sycophants like Willow and Ennis to do it for him. Ennis had no need to risk arson to dispatch an old lady who was in his way, not when he could have poisoned her without attracting attention. Willow was the one who couldn't kill Tilda any other way.

Willow burned down his mother-in-law's house, with her locked inside. Faye was sure of it. There was no other way to get his hands on his wife's inheritance before Marlowe bolted, because Tilda didn't trust him enough to let him poison her.

But there was something else, some other message in the timing of Tilda's quick death and Myrna's slow failing. What was it?

A cold fact clicked into place. As of this morning, Myrna was much more of an obstacle than she had been. The resort could possibly be built without the property she had always owned, but not without the larger property that had been Tilda's and was now hers. Now that the knowledge was out that she was Tilda's heir, rather than Dara, Myrna was a direct impediment. Until today, the resort deal could proceed while Myrna died slowly, with Dara and Willow eventually selling Marlowe the less-important piece of property she'd always owned. Now, there was no deal until he held the land she'd inherited from Tilda. As of today, Myrna was vulnerable to a murder attempt that was not slow and stealthy.

◇◇◇

Misdirection and camouflage are the only real weapons in a stage magician's arsenal. Being in possession of impeccable timing doesn't hurt, either.

Willow sat motionless, shielded by the same viburnum bush that had sheltered him for hours, since just after his wife walked out on him. He wore the matte-black elasticized jumpsuit that he had often used when working as a magician's assistant in stage shows where he didn't want to be seen. He'd worn it two nights before, when he'd slipped in and out of Sister Mama's bedroom. Their current auditorium was too small for him to do invisible onstage magic, but on a properly lit flat-black stage in a large hall, this suit rendered him invisible. It made him capable of things that looked impossible from the cheap seats. Outdoors, in the shadows on a dark night, he was almost as impossible to see.

He had known Dara would come here again, looking for her mother. She was hardly out their door before he was out of the house, dressed to be unseen. Thus camouflaged, he had waited for the chance to torch another house. Anonymous hands-off murder gave the same kind of rush as a successful illusion, magnified a million times.

His wife and her aunt Myrna were the only things that stood between him and the money Marlowe was dangling for the Armistead sisters' land. Sister Mama, too, needed to go, not because she was an immediate and direct impediment but because Marlowe wanted a little more land for his golf course's clubhouse, and she had some. Ennis would sell it to Marlowe, and they would both enjoy the financial benefits of his pleasure, but Willow would be the only one holding the secret of why the three old ladies had died with such convenient timing.

Willow liked having this kind of private knowledge. There was power in secrecy. Secrets were magic.

Willow would have liked to continue dispatching Myrna and Sister Mama slowly and unobtrusively with medicinal potions and toxic candy, and he wouldn't have minded staying married to Dara, as long as she shared the proceeds of selling her inheritance. She was entertaining, she kept their home and business running, and the sex was amazing. But she'd said she was divorcing him, and Dara never failed to live up to her word. Now he had to kill her, and he had to do it quickly, before a divorce court severed his claim on her inheritance.

It would have been better to find another way to kill Dara and her aunt. A second house fire was too obvious, but he was short on time and he'd gotten away with the first one. It didn't matter if the arson inspector hiding in the shadows of Myrna's house suspected foul play, as long as she couldn't pin it on him. Next to him, hidden under an opaque black shroud, sat a stout board, a hammer, a jar of nails, a can of gasoline, and a large box of matches, all of them stolen from Myrna's own storage shed. In the darkness, the shroud would serve as his cloak of invisibility while he transported these tools into the house. Dara and Myrna would be dead in an hour, and he would be the sole heir to both their estates. Whoever else sat with them around the crystal ball would be collateral damage.

But first, he needed to dispatch the arson inspector who thought she was hiding behind the porch steps. A moment ago, he had struck the ground lightly with his hand, making a sound like an errant footfall. That must have gotten her attention. He wasn't even slightly concerned that it also gave away his position.

After giving her a moment to echo-locate him, he had reached out a long leg and shook a bush just enough for her to see it. Without moving from his original position, he had diverted her attention to a new spot. Then, to finish the illusion, he had thrown a small rock in the direction his leg was pointing. It dropped to the ground. Its impact was softened by fallen leaves, but it was still audible.

Misdirection. Human senses were so very vulnerable to its lies. Avery was now watching someone whom she believed to be moving toward the front of the house, while he remained in his original position, perfectly camouflaged. When she gave chase, he would be just behind her, waiting with a rag soaked in the tincture of many things he'd stolen from Sister Mama's garden. They would have killed Sister Mama effectively, if the Longchamp-Mantooth women had left the soporific sponge in place long enough. All he would have had to do was sneak back into her room after she was dead and pluck out the sponge.

The tincture wasn't chloroform or ether, but it would serve the same purpose equally as well. Applied to a healthy adult, it was a toss-up as to whether this tincture would sedate or kill. Either way, it would help him take Dara's inconvenient guard out of the way.

◇◇◇

Willow had planned his illusion perfectly. He could see Avery running. The excellent spatial skills that marked the true illusionist plotted her trajectory for him. She was headed for the precise spot he'd chosen. Once she passed his hiding place, she would have her back to him. She would be utterly blind to his attack, and the anesthetic he held would render her unconscious in seconds.

The flaw in his perfect plan was Faye's husband. Even though Joe had placed himself in full view of everyone passing on Walnut and Main Streets, he had done so after Willow took up residence in the bushes. Before this moment, there had been no way for Willow to know that Avery had backup. Now, Willow sank back into darkness and asked himself how to handle two adversaries, one carrying a gun and the other huge, who were both running full-tilt for a spot just a few feet away from him. In a fraction of a second, he would have to decide what to do.

In addition to excellent spatial skills, talented illusionists have remarkable coordination and razor-sharp senses. These things are also true of trained law enforcement officers and natural-born hunters. Three elements of a human explosion were gathering in a single spot at the heart of Rosebower.

◇◇◇

In the bedroom where she had slept since she was twenty-nine years old, Sister Mama lay quietly. There was no light in the room and no sound. The only sensory stimulus was the downy softness of the quilt covering her twisted limbs. In such comfort, she should have slept straight through until morning, but something troublesome brushed through her dreams. Her eyes opened suddenly, dark and wise. She studied the ceiling and wondered what kind of trouble was afoot.

◇◇◇

Only one magician's tool was on Willow's side now. It was the element of surprise.

He allowed Avery to run three steps past him, until Joe came within arm's length. With an arcing swing of his hammer, he brought the big man down.

Avery swung her weapon around in a very similar arc and tried to point it at him, but no one can take perfect aim while running and Willow was prepared for her. The hammer knocked the gun far out of her reach and his. It also broke two bones in her hand, and its impact sent her sprawling. She lay curled on the ground, cradling her hand, and her violent collision with the ground left her unable to even look up at her attacker.

A killer who sets fires and delivers poisons to helpless octogenarians is not of the same breed as the killer who beats a human

being to death by hand. Arsonists don't like knives. Poisoners
don't like guns. Neither breed is likely to strangle. They are as
evil as the hands-on murderer, but they prefer the remote exercise of that evil.

Willow needed them both out of his way while he dispatched
his wife and her aunt. He could have ensured this by bashing
Avery's brains out with his hammer, then doing the same thing
to Joe. Instead, he held the dripping cloth over their faces until
they slept almost as deeply as the dead. Perhaps they would
never wake up. Willow didn't care. He merely didn't want to be
involved in the messiness of it all.

He gathered his instruments of death and draped the dark
shroud over them. Then he mounted the rear steps of a house
where four people sat in a claustrophobic little room. He should
have been invisible as he went about this task. He thought he
was invisible. He would have been invisible, if there hadn't been
someone unexpected coming his way. A magician cannot misdirect a person when he doesn't know that person is watching.

◇◇◇

The voice wasn't Dara's. It wasn't Amande's. It didn't sound like
Myrna's, but it had to be, because Myrna's lips were moving. The
words were slurred but Faye heard power in her voice.

"The viper in the bed…broken trust…you are not safe. No
one is safe."

She shook her head back and forth, fighting for words. Faye
was not prepared for the words that came.

"Get the hell out of this house."

Amande stared, wide-eyed. Dara and Faye both instinctively
broke the circle and reached a hand out to Myrna. They had
lived long enough to know the symptoms of brain injury, and
Myrna was showing a lot of them. Her face had lost expression.
Her vocal quality had deteriorated. Raving uncontrollably in a
spiritual setting was beyond inappropriate for a woman of her
religious background. And cursing? Faye wouldn't have thought
Myrna knew how.

"Can't you people hear? I want you gone. *Get my sister out.* And my daughter. Keep her safe." Myrna's head lolled onto Dara's shoulder. "Keep her safe."

The repeated impact of a hammer striking wood reverberated. It told them that it was too late to heed Tilda's warning. An oily scent penetrated the room that was organic but not herbal, and it was unmistakable. Nothing else smells like gasoline.

"Get the door," Faye barked, and the other three women obeyed in an instant. They lunged together at the door. Even Myrna threw herself at the stout slab of wood, but it was no use. The door was nailed shut.

No one had to be told to hit the floor. They all had recent and painful memories of the things fire-hot smoke could do to a human being's lungs. Faye pressed her cheek to the time-worn oak and reached out for her daughter's hand.

Chapter Twenty-nine

The tiny oil lamp still rested on the table, casting its weak light around the room. Even from the floor, Faye could see that the crystal ball was gone. She looked at Dara, lying three feet away. She was clinging to Myrna with one arm and the crystal ball with the other.

The ball taunted Faye. Several scenarios had been proposed that attempted to explain how Tilda and her crystal ball had escaped her burning house. Faye didn't believe any of them.

She didn't believe that Tilda ever removed it from its spot in her séance room. It had sat at the heart of her house as if it must always be there.

The practical part of Faye also understood that it was heavy and awkward to carry. Moving it would have required a second stand to hold it, or something else to keep it from rolling around in its new location. When Faye pictured Tilda's actions after she and Amande and Myrna left on that fatal night, she imagined her leaving the room and closing the door with the ball still inside. Or she imagined her lingering there to spend a few more moments in spirit. She didn't picture her hauling a heavy lump of crystal out of the room for no reason.

This meant that the ball was still in the room when the killer nailed the door shut. Tilda was in one of two places, outside the room or inside the room. If she'd been outside the room, the question was, "How did she get the ball out?" And if she'd been inside the room, the question was, "How did she get the ball and *herself* out?"

Since Faye needed rather desperately to get herself, her daughter, and her friends out of an identical room, she decided to go with the second question. It implied that there was a way out of her predicament. If Tilda got herself and the ball out of an identical room in an identical situation, then Faye could do the same. This room where she was trapped had served as a site for spiritual readings for generations, and she had seen letters from one of those Spiritualists to a known faker. Everybody around Faye believed in the traditional honesty of the Armisteads, but this didn't mean that they were right. Maybe this room had secrets.

If Faye were building a room where she planned to fool people into believing in ghosts, she was pretty sure she'd build some tricks into the very structure of the room. The very first trick she'd install would be a secret exit. The mysterious escape of Tilda and the crystal ball was perfectly explainable if she'd had access to a secret door.

Faye began feeling her way across the floor, looking for escape.

◇◇◇

Avery always claimed later that Faye's voice, calling her name, was the thing that woke her. Faye denied it, because she'd been frozen silent with fear.

It takes a great deal of will to shake off a powerful sedative but, whether she was goaded to it by Faye's voice or not, Avery managed it. She rose from the spot where she had fallen, dragging herself vertical and asking her eyes to focus.

The first plumes of smoke were drifting out an open window. They were so tenuous and new that Avery thought that the arsonist couldn't possibly have had time yet to leave. If this was true, she knew where her adversary was. She crept around the house and slipped through the back door.

◇◇◇

Faye remembered Myrna saying that Tilda had assisted her father, but that Myrna herself never had. Maybe the secrets shared by father and daughter had included a way out of the room, and maybe the knowledge of that secret passage had died with Tilda, but Faye intended to use her last moments to look for it. She circled the small space, ignoring Amande's hissed orders to "Get down!"

Completing her circuit of the room, she crawled up under the slant of the staircase. Trying each stair, she found that one of the risers shook slightly. With effort, Faye was able to remove it, revealing an opening less than a foot tall. Slender Tilda could have squeezed through it, but not Myrna.

Here was the reason Tilda had been chosen as her father's assistant. The only "psychic ability" that had enabled Tilda to assist her dishonest father was her slender form. She could easily have sneaked into séances through this entry, performing "magic" in a darkened room before slipping out again. Myrna would have been too large for such things by the time she was past toddlerhood.

Tilda had been thin enough to sneak in and out of the room, faking the sounds and apparitions that her father passed off as spirits. Myrna was too large to help, so she'd been spared the knowledge of her father's dishonesty. And her sister's. On the night of her death, Tilda had performed a Houdini-like illusion. She'd been nailed into this room, but "miraculously" exited through this hidden escape hatch. And she'd brought her treasured crystal ball with her.

Tilda must have been beside herself when she couldn't rouse her sister. Even if she'd had a key to Myrna's door, it was probably inside her own burning house. Faye knew from experience that it took a ladder to reach the windows on both houses' first floors, so Tilda would never have been able to break in, not in her condition. And she wouldn't have known whom to trust. With tempers running high over the Marlowe development and all the money it represented, anybody in town could have been suspect.

An agoraphobic in her eighties who lived within walking distance of everything in her life would have needed no cell phone.

If Tilda had been thinking clearly, she could have stopped at a gas station once she left Rosebower and called for help, but by then she was dying of smoke inhalation. Coming up with a new plan would have been too much for her. She was probably only capable of continuing to carry out her original plan to chase down the only person who surely had no motive to hurt either of the Armistead sisters—their brand-new friend Faye.

The brimstone smell of another newly struck match crept into the room. Lingering near the tiny opening, Faye looked at the people in the room behind her. All three of them were hugging the floor, where the little fresh air left would be driven when the house went up in flames. Amande was dialing 911, as Faye had known she would be. They were doing all the right things, but they would be dead in minutes, unless the call to 911 brought help in time.

And where were Avery and Joe? Their absence told Faye that they were probably in trouble, too.

Faye's daughter weighed half again as much as she did. Dara's full hips were too large to fit through the gap, and Myrna's entire life had been shaped by the fact that she was too big to squeeze through this secret exit. Faye was the only one in the room small enough to escape. If she could get out without being seen by the arsonist—by Willow, she was sure—then maybe she could get help. Maybe there was an ax in Myrna's shed that she could use to break down the door.

There was time to kiss her daughter once, but then she must go.

◇◇◇

Joe held his hands in front of his face. There were four of them. He had twenty fingers total. This could not be a good thing.

There was a knot forming at the base of his skull. It promised to be the size of Tilda's crystal ball. Willow had swung wildly and been lucky enough to connect. If his aim had been good enough to strike Joe in the temple, his skull would have shattered like an egg. As it was, Willow had flattened a much bigger man with a single blow. Rolling onto his belly, Joe tried to convince his arms and legs to lift him. No luck.

The only part of his body that he could get off the ground was his aching head. He lifted it and scanned his surroundings, not such an easy trick with double vision. He could see an Avery or two climbing the back steps. This was good, because Joe thought it might be a while before he'd be able to get in the house to fetch his wife and child. Then he began to wonder whether he was suffering from some kind of bizarre mirror-double vision, because somebody was also climbing the front steps.

Focus. He needed to turn his head and focus. Who else was barging into Myrna's house? It was a slender man with graying hair.

Samuel.

Why was Samuel here? Joe didn't like it. He put his hands on the ground, palms down, and shoved himself onto his knees. Without waiting to find his equilibrium, Joe staggered to his feet and used the momentum of his falling body to propel himself toward the door where Samuel stood.

Joe had been sitting in front of the open front door while keeping watch, so it was still open. Samuel barged into Myrna's house without knocking, without even pausing. Joe's wife and child were in that house. He had to get in there, whether his body wanted to help him or not. He stumbled after Samuel as quickly as his uncooperative legs would take him.

◇◇◇

Myrna's house was huge, far too large for Avery to cross the entire first floor quickly and silently enough to reach her assailant unseen. There he stood—and she was pretty sure she was looking at a "he"—wearing a jumpsuit so tight that it looked like he had been dipped in black paint. Even his eyes were covered by heavy black netting. He was sloshing gasoline around the nailed-shut séance room door. As Avery paused to plan her next step, he slid open the box of matches in his hand. He lit one, and all her firefighter instincts kicked in.

She knew he could probably fling the match into the spreading puddle of gasoline before she got there. She knew he probably had her gun. She knew that being drugged had slowed her reflexes and that the agony of her broken hand would slow her even more. She didn't care. Her only conscious thought was, "Get that match."

As if to prove to Avery that it was still possible to be more confused, a trim man with salt-and-pepper hair stepped through the open front door. What was Gilbert Marlowe doing here?

Avery had no time to consider an answer to that question, because there was an open flame that needed to be doused. She launched herself at the unidentified killer in head-to-toe black.

◇◇◇

As Faye removed the stair riser that hid the room's secret entrance, she refused to let herself think about what would happen if she couldn't get Amande, Myrna, and Dara out. Her plan was simple. First, she had to get out of the séance room. If Willow was still in sight, she needed to dispatch him…somehow. That part of the plan was murky. Then she needed to find a tool that would get the door open. An ax. A hatchet. A crowbar. A magic wand. She didn't care what it was.

She slithered through the opening, then stopped with her feet still dangling into the séance room. Willow was not finished setting the fire that would kill them all. It would probably kill Avery, too, because the arson investigator was running past her like a linebacker hoping to sack a star quarterback. As she struggled to pass from one room into another, Faye watched a gray-haired man walk through the front door. She'd never seen him before, so she had no idea whether he had come to stop Willow or to help him kill people.

The match in Willow's hand gave off the scent of burning sulfur. It joined the odor of gasoline that rose from the wet, stained floor. Avery went after the match, leaving Willow with a free hand that he used to slam her against the wall. Faye, finally free of the tight access hole, launched herself at Willow's slim, muscular form, carrying no weapon but the stout oak board that had once masqueraded as a riser in a grand antique staircase.

Willow was at a disadvantage, caught off-guard by a law enforcement professional and a determined archaeologist wielding a stout board, but he was a trickster so he used what he had—the fuel can in his hand. He sloshed gasoline in Avery's face, a lot of it. Her trained reflexes allowed her to fling her arm over her eyes in time, but this gave Willow an opportunity to struggle free.

It also gave him an opportunity to douse Faye, too. A single spark would turn both women into walking torches. Faye and Avery locked eyes and achieved their own brand of mindreading. Silently, they agreed on the timing of the only blow they were going to have a chance to land. They tackled him, and all three went down in a puddle of gas growing ever larger as the toppled fuel can emptied itself.

Straddling Willow's torso and pinning his shoulders to the floor, Avery clapped the lit match tight between her bare hands. They were gasoline-soaked, but the fuel would not combust without oxygen. Faye knew that, in theory, Avery could snuff the match this way without going up in flames. In theory.

Faye waited for Avery to ignite. She didn't. Instead, she kept the hot match clutched between her palms and nodded. Faye responded by whamming the board down on Willow's black-sheathed head. He lay still.

Avery leapt to her feet and took charge. "The place could go up any second. We need to get that door open. Faye, there's an ax in Myrna's storage shed. Get it." She ran to study the board barring the door.

The gray-haired man ignored Avery, running for the hinged side of the nailed-shut door. Faye tried to remember what Gilbert Marlowe looked like. Was this him? The fumes seemed to be snarling Faye's mind, because she could not figure out why Marlowe would be here. When he hired killers, did he chase them around to make sure they got the job done?

Joe shoved him away, hard. "Get away from that door, Langley. My daughter's in there."

What on earth was he talking about? Had he mistaken Marlowe for their client, Samuel Langley?

Joe was clearly less worried about the man's identity than he was about Amande, because he merely shoved him to the floor and kicked the door off its hinges. Amande, Myrna, and Dara scrabbled out of the room on their hands and knees, just in time to see Willow roll over onto his belly. He was too stunned from Faye's blow to do more than raise his torso and prop himself on his elbows. His white locks, no longer sleek, were matted into the dirt and gasoline that coated the old wooden floor.

In a deadly act of sleight-of-hand, he made a match appear in his right hand. Then he struck it.

◇◇◇

Avery understood the thermodynamics of what she was seeing. The vapors rising from the puddle around Willow were highly flammable. The flame in his hand didn't need to touch the gasoline visible on the floor. The vapors, invisible but inarguably there, would be igniting immediately. They *were* igniting immediately. And Willow's hair was serving as a long and beautiful wick, drawing fuel from the puddles on the floor to feed the flame.

Avery could see Faye preparing to be heroic. Joe would have been doing the same, but he had dropped to the floor right after he kicked the door open, cradling a foot that was probably broken. Marlowe, Dara, Amande, and Myrna stood behind him, thunderstruck by the sight of a man erupting in flames.

Wrapping one arm around Faye to keep her from rushing to Willow's aid, Avery used the other arm to yank Joe to his feet. "Go, go, go...go now...go!" They were all leaving the house together, and she didn't intend for any of them to be on fire when they got out.

Her eyes were screwed shut against the fumes and rising heat, but she knew Faye and Joe were with her, because she had a solid grip on them. And she knew without looking that Amande and Dara would be right behind her, keeping Myrna safe, because that's who they were. Marlowe seemed to have a talent for taking care of himself, so she guessed he'd be with them, too.

There was no help for Willow. The laws of thermodynamics said that he was doomed, and Avery had never seen anyone successfully break them yet.

◇◇◇

The swelling roar of the fire that was consuming Myrna's home nearly drowned the sound of approaching sirens. Amande, Myrna, and Dara scrabbled out of the room on their hands and knees, just in time to see Willow roll over onto his belly and peel the black hood off his head. He was too stunned from Faye's blow to do more than raise his torso and prop himself on his elbows. His white locks, no longer sleek, fell into the dirt and gasoline that coated the old wooden floor.

Faye leaned on Joe's shoulder with both arms wrapped tight around her daughter. Myrna stroked Dara's tear-stained cheek. Avery was using her broken and burned hands as best she could, gently palpating Joe's injured foot.

As the man who was neither Marlowe nor Langley watched her work, he slid off his wig and let a shoulder-length mane of gray-streaked hair fall to his shoulders. Or, rather, to her shoulders. The freed locks framed Toni's face, still partially obscured by several layers of theatrical makeup.

She gestured at Joe's wounded foot, saying, "That wasn't necessary. I had things under control." Opening her hand, she displayed a collection of slender metal tools arrayed on her palm. "I'm a magician. Harry Houdini kept files and…other things…on him at all times, and so do I. I could have gotten the door open, and you could have spared yourself some time at the orthopedist's office."

Then the tools vanished. It is possible that they went up Toni's sleeve.

Chapter Thirty

Youth is a state of mind. If Faye had ever needed proof of that adage, she had it now. She and Amande lurked beneath a tree near the lakeshore, watching Myrna push Sister Mama's wheelchair down an uneven sidewalk and park it by a concrete bench. Myrna's head was high and she was full to the brim with energy. After setting the chair's safety brake and brushing the bench free of leaves, she solicitously helped Sister Mama stand and walk a few steps. The stricken woman looked overjoyed to sit someplace that wasn't a wheelchair. As she relaxed on the bench, she didn't look so stricken after all.

Myrna bustled around, fetching Sister Mama's coffee cup and spreading a shawl over her knees. Judging by the way she treated her friend like a treasured elder, one would think there was a huge difference between the ages of eighty-one and eighty-six. Maybe there was.

Faye was startled to see Ennis standing a stone's-throw away, watching the same scene. He met her eyes, and she could see that he'd known they were there the whole time. He walked over as if to speak to Faye and Amande, but when he got there, he paused. Silent, he watched the two women a moment more.

At last, he said, "They're doing better."

"Once Dara convinced Myrna to throw away the candy that was making her sick, she started looking stronger every day."

Ennis nodded in response to Faye, but he kept looking at the friends, sitting on a park bench and talking. "Not just Myrna. Sister Mama. She's doing better, too."

"I'm glad," Faye said. Then, though she didn't know why she said it because she didn't wholly believe it, she added, "You must have been taking good care of her."

"No. I wasn't." Tears welled in his eyes. "I was letting that bastard help me with her medicine. Miss Myrna's, too. Willow made friends with me a while back, right out of the blue. I was never sure why, but it was good to have somebody to talk to. And he knew a lot about root medicine. He told me what tinctures to give Sister Mama because I don't know shit about roots. I listened to him. And I was happy with what those tinctures did, because they made her quieter. She slept a lot. Life was easier that way. I hate myself for being happy about that."

Amande was eyeing him, but she didn't say anything.

"I want you to tell me something," he said.

Faye couldn't tell whether he was talking to her or Amande, but Amande didn't seem to be answering him. Wondering what Ennis was going to ask, she said, "Okay."

"Did Sister Mama have something Willow wanted? Do you think he might have wanted her dead, too? Like Tilda and Myrna?"

"Does she own any property?"

"Yeah, a big plot near the road coming in from Buffalo. Across the highway from Tilda's land."

Faye heard Amande take in a little gasp. Ennis gave her a sharp look.

Faye could see he already had his answer, but she told him anyway. "Marlowe wanted that land. I'd bet on it. Marlowe doesn't seem to have done anything illegal himself, but we think he told Willow to do whatever it took to make his development happen. Willow decided that the easiest tactic was to kill everybody in the way. Tilda and Myrna, for sure. Probably Sister Mama, too, because Willow had to be the one who made the soporific sponge. Avery's chemist friend found opiates on it, and she says he may kill himself with overwork because he won't rest until he figures out what else Willow put on it. In the end, he went after his own wife, along with Myrna and the two of us. Joe and Avery, too, because they got in his way. There's no way he'd have gotten away with killing us all. He must have just cracked."

"I threw away the medicines he told me to give Sister Mama a week ago, when he got arrested. Look at her now." He nodded at Sister Mama, laughing with Myrna. "She can walk a little. She's talking again. She's talking a lot, actually. I don't think there ever was a second stroke. Goddamn that man for using me to hurt her. And other people."

This time Faye was sure he was talking to her daughter.

"I threw the rock at Toni's window. It was stupid. Willow had filled my ears full of how evil Toni was. He'd looked her up on the internet and she scared him. He knew she was getting ready to expose him and Dara as fakes. I thought he was my friend, so it wasn't hard to get me all riled up against her. The only thing that makes me better than him is that he set fires to kill people he didn't like, and I threw a stupid rock. And I buried some lemons under the porches of nice ladies that never did me any harm, because I wanted to hex them into selling their property to Gilbert Marlowe. I didn't think about hurting anybody. I just didn't think."

"Are you going to stay here?" The tone in Amande's voice said she actually cared about the answer to her question. Her face gave away nothing.

"I got to. I can't leave Sister Mama to be taken care of by somebody who won't even do the piss-poor job I've done. And I got to get her to teach me about roots and herbs, while she still can. While I'm at it, I have really got to figure out what part of her business is legal. Opium poppy juice? It's a miracle the Feds haven't already come to get us. And I don't even want to think about what would happen if they found out about the home brew. Mostly, I've got to learn what Sister Mama knows, while she's still here. How'm I going to keep her work going when she's gone, if I don't understand it?"

"You'll have to start by figuring out how to keep people out of her garden," Faye said. "Willow stole licorice from you, for sure, plus all the stuff he put on that soporific sponge. God only knows what he put in the tinctures your aunt and Myrna were drinking."

"I'm looking into electric fences."

Amande laughed out loud.

"No, seriously. I am. I don't think anybody but my great-aunt understands what some of that stuff can do. She told me one thing that's gonna make both of you laugh. I know how Miss Tilda made her séances...special. All these years, Sister Mama's been a big help to her. More than either of them knew, actually."

Faye tried to picture Sister Mama slipping through the secret staircase entrance to help Tilda fake metaphysical magic. She couldn't, so she asked, "How was she a big help?"

"Sister Mama said that she steeped calming herbs in oil, and that Miss Tilda would rub them on her crystal ball and let the warm lamp underneath spread the essences around for people to breathe."

"I remember that!" Amande said.

"Sister Mama was quick to say that using her oil wasn't cheating. Tilda never cheated. She'd grown up helping her father fool people, and she hated it. Hated it. She believed she had real talent. *I* believe she did. But my aunt's herbs helped her put people in the mood, and Tilda didn't consider that cheating."

"What about the incense?" Amande asked. "Did she make that, too?"

"She did, and that's the part that'll make you laugh. Sister Mama made it out of wild lettuce sap. We were about to run out of it when Tilda died. Sister Mama was too sick to tell me how to make more, so I looked it up on the internet. And you know what? Wild lettuce sap's perfectly legal, and it's got an awful lot in common with opium juice. I *really* got to put up an electric fence."

He'd been right when he said they would laugh.

"So those things we saw during Tilda's séance weren't real?" Amande asked.

"Maybe they were and maybe they weren't, but you were flying high when you saw them. No doubt about it."

When Ennis laughed, his whole face came into focus.

"I'm not sure there's any reason Miss Myrna needs to know that," he said.

Nodding at them both, a quick agreement for Faye and something slower for Amande, he said, "I need to go now. I need to see if either of those two ladies need anything. I'm all Sister Mama's got, and Dara can use some help keeping up with Miss Myrna. Dara's got a show to run, and she'll be doing it by herself from here on out."

As he walked away, Faye gave Amande the same silent eye contact that her mother had given her long ago, when she'd been sneaking around with boys at seventeen. "Is there anything about that man you want to tell me?"

"He wanted to ask me out. I didn't encourage him, so he didn't."

Faye's continued silence asked for more of a response, so her daughter said, "He's just a boy. I'm waiting for a man to come along."

◇◇◇

Joe began closing the open books scattered over Samuel's desk. "Are you convinced?"

"Yes. It's hard to accept that my treasures aren't what I thought they were, but you laid out the facts. You walked me through those books. You showed me pictures on your computer. You showed me lab reports from rock taken from American and European quarries. I'm not stupid. You've convinced me. It's not that I thought the people in America *couldn't* have built all those pyramids and mounds on their own. It's just that I thought that they *didn't.*"

Joe let that statement rest as he placed the books, one by one, in an orderly stack. "Now I want to explain something else and I want to ask you a question."

"Of course."

"I just spent two hours walking you through a bunch of research. I enjoyed myself. I think you enjoyed it, too, but my time don't come cheap. Faye's time costs even more. It should. She's the one with a Ph.D."

"Well, yes," Samuel said. "She—"

"Hang on a minute. I'm going somewhere with this. Faye already told you everything I told you this morning, but she didn't spend two hours doing it, because that wouldn't be a responsible way to spend your money. If you want her to walk you through this project, she can do that, but it will cost you a lot. It might be cheaper to let her get her work done, hands-off. You could use that time to take some archaeology classes, since you do seem awful interested. Yeah, you can pay her to explain every last thing to you, but it would be like paying a private tutor to make a doctor out of you. Only you wouldn't get the piece of paper that says 'Ph.D.'"

This made Samuel laugh. "I don't need the piece of paper, but I just might take some classes."

Joe closed his computer, stood, and shook his client's hand. "Good. If you want me to, I'll let you know next time we're doing a dig. We can always use volunteers. But here's the question I wanted to ask you. Is it maybe possible that you listened to me today, after you ignored Faye when she told you the same thing, because she's a little tiny woman and I'm not? Because if it is, you owe my wife an apology."

Samuel had risen when Joe did, but he was still holding the Langley Object. He turned it over in his hands, studied it a bit, then spoke. "She'll get one."

"I presume that means that there will be no trouble with her bill. It will show some hours for things we've done that are beyond the original scope of work." He nodded at the pile of books cradled in the crook of his elbow. "Like, for instance, this conversation you and I just had."

"Tell her to send me a bill. There will be no trouble at all."

Joe said goodbye to his client. He thought Faye would be happy with the way he handled their accounts receivable.

◇◇◇

"Mom?"

Faye took off her reading glasses and looked up at her daughter.

"I've been reading about Elizabeth Cady Stanton," Amande said.

"It'll take you a while. She wrote the *Declaration of Sentiments* and read it at Seneca Falls. She was friends with Susan B. Anthony and Lucretia Mott and Amelia Bloomer. She raised hell for decades in favor of women's rights and the abolition of slavery. I forget how many children she raised while she was doing that. About a billion, or so it seemed when I read her biography. She was a complicated person, and I don't agree with everything she did, but she made history. Nobody can argue with that."

"I think there's something about her that you didn't notice, or you'd have said so."

Faye, being the competitive soul that she was, said, "Oh, yeah? Bet me."

"I bet you a banana split."

"You're on. What did you notice about Elizabeth Cady Stanton that I didn't?"

"She has the same last name as your great-great-grandmother, Cally Stanton. And Cally's husband, Courtney Stanton, obviously, because she took his name. What do you know about Courtney Stanton's family?"

Faye realized that she owed her daughter a banana split. "Um...nothing. When Cally was interviewed by the Federal Writers' Project for their slave narratives, she just said that Courtney and his mother were Yankees. To Cally, a Yankee might be anybody born north of Florida."

"New York is north of Florida. We should try to find out whether you're distant kin to one of your heroes."

Faye blurted out, "I don't want to know."

Why had she said that? Probably because she liked the idea of being kin to Elizabeth Cady Stanton, and she didn't want mere facts to get in the way of that feeling.

"Too late. I've already emailed your cousin Bobby, the family genealogist. He's on the case."

Faye hoped Bobby found the link Amande believed was there. If not, she hoped he hit a dead end that left the question of kinship forever unanswered. Elizabeth Cady Stanton would have fit right in with the stalwart women on Faye's family tree, and Faye wanted to always be able to imagine her among them.

Working notes for Pulling the Wool Over Our Eyes: An Unauthorized History of Spiritualism in Rosebower, New York

by Antonia Caruso

My work in Rosebower is done. I have everything I need to write the book I came here to write. I have photos of Virginia Armistead's letters, in her own handwriting, confessing to fakery. I know that Tilda Armistead was as honest as she looked, but that she was unknowingly drugging her clients with Sister Mama's psychotropic-but-legal wild lettuce sap. And I have the nasty little story of the charlatan Willow, husband of the last in the long line of Rosebower Armisteads.

Dara is so anxious to distance herself from his crimes that she has shared every detail of how they fooled their audiences. I was gratified to learn that I'd unraveled most of their tricks, but Dara is an artist of the stage. She taught me a few things I didn't know, and I was doing sleight-of-hand before she was born. I know what they say about old dogs, but this one loves learning new tricks.

I also know that, not so long ago on a summer night in Rosebower, Myrna Armistead convinced a hard-headed archaeologist and her daughter that she was channeling her sister's spirit. Faye Longchamp-Mantooth and her daughter Amande are certain that Myrna knew they were in danger before the danger presented itself. They are even more certain that she warned them in her sister's voice, not her own. In that voice, she ordered them out of the house and she begged them to save her sister and her daughter. When Myrna Armistead said those words, she had no daughter and no living sister. But Tilda Armistead did.

The physicist in me knows that Myrna was being systematically drugged. She was grief-stricken. And prolonged congestive heart failure may have starved her brain of oxygen. There is a real possibility that she was hallucinating. But the physicist in me also knows that science learns new things every day.

In other words, things that are perfectly explainable today were utter mysteries yesterday.

For this reason, although I have everything I need to write my Rosebower exposé, I'm not going to do it. I have other books to write, other trips to take, other ways to wring every last ounce of fun out of my retirement. I don't need to do it at the expense of people who don't deserve my scorn.

It is likely that I will come back to Rosebower, now and again. Dara's tired of working seven days a week, year-round, but an empty auditorium is a wasted money-making opportunity. She would never share a stage with me, because she still believes she's the real thing and I make no such claim, but she'll gladly rent me the hall. I may spend some years gadding about, returning here to perform for occasional extended runs.

I may even retire here. I'm learning that the aging process doesn't change us. It just makes us more like the people we've always been. I want to be the best old lady possible. If I went looking for role models, I could never find better ones than Myrna Armistead and Sister Mama. They're loving. Strong. Contrary, when the *situation requires it. Maybe it's not too late for me to learn to be more like them.*

My first step toward being a loving and generous person in old age will be to kill this book. Faye Longchamp-Mantooth only told me what she knew about the letters and the wild lettuce because I promised not to publish it while Myrna Armistead was alive. The world has waited this long for the truth. It can wait a few years longer. I made the same promise to Dara Armistead and, in exchange, she taught me something about magic.

Magic is what you believe it to be. So is life.

Guide for the Incurably Curious

This is the place where I usually give a little background for readers who are interested in which parts of the history Faye is investigating are really true. Teachers, homeschoolers, and book group leaders tell me that this kind of information spurs discussion, and I find that my readers tend to be like me. We are incurably curious, so we are always happy to have a few questions answered.

For this book, however, I find myself wanting to leave the magic alone. Instead of sharing with you every last historical detail about the roots of Spiritualism and the activities of the brave ladies at Seneca Falls, I think I will do things differently this time. I will point you in the direction of a couple of books I used while writing *Rituals*, then I will tell you a story about my own one-and-only brush with the metaphysical.

I have owned a copy of James Randi's *Flim-Flam! Psychics, Unicorns, and Other Delusions* for quite some time. I knew that I would someday want to draw from his exposé of metaphysical fraud, but I was waiting for the right story to come to me. Randi, also known as the magician "The Amazing Randi," has been a crusader for truth, and my "Toni the Astonisher" was in part inspired by him. If you read *Flim-Flam!*, you will learn about real-life fakers far more brazen than my fictional Dara and Willow.

In constructing my imaginary Rosebower, I visited a Florida town built by 19th-century Spiritualists called Cassadaga, where I attended a church service, experienced the laying on of hands, and received a psychic reading. I also did my usual writerly exploration of the town itself, just walking around and stopping into local businesses and checking out the public buildings. Even my imaginary places need to be rooted in the real world. This is why I like to travel to the sites of my books or, when those sites are imaginary, I like to travel to someplace nearby. If you're curious about Spiritualist towns in general, or about Cassadaga in particular, I recommend *Cassadaga: The South's Oldest Spiritualist Community* by John J. Guthrie Jr., Phillip Charles Lucas, and Gary Monroe.

I did not, however, go to western New York, and I did not go to the real-life town known as the home of Spiritualism, Lily Dale. Rosebower is only modeled on Lily Dale in the sense that they both have lovely floral names. I made the decision not to go to Lily Dale rather late in the process of preparing to write *Rituals*, and here's why. Although some of the residents of my Rosebower are wonderful people, honest and devoted to their faith, some of them are not. I felt that it would be disrespectful to the faith of real-life Spiritualists to taint their town with fakery and murder, so I wanted there to be no suggestion that I was accusing real people of such things. Instead, I created Rosebower, where I could let my fictional crooks come out to play. Now that the book is finished, I want very much to visit Lily Dale and Seneca Falls, and I expect I will do so soon.

And now I'll share my personal story of mysterious metaphysics. Like Faye, I was educated in the sciences, so it would take unassailable evidence for me to believe in anything that cannot be rationally explained. I know that there are things in this universe that we don't understand, so I leave the door open for miracles, but I set a very high bar when it comes to proof. Nevertheless, I have visited psychics from time to time, out of sheer curiosity.

In 2002, I attended a wonderful party. As part of the entertainment, the hostess had hired a psychic, and all attendees could sign up for a brief session with her. I found her to be pleasant, but her advice was fairly generic. She said nothing that would have required her to have arcane powers...until the very end of the session. Out of the blue, she said, "I hear three names. Barbara, Robert, and Sam. They will be important people for you."

Those of you who are familiar with my publishing house know that Robert Rosenwald is the publisher and Barbara Peters is the editor-in-chief. When this woman pulled their names out of the air, my first novel, *Artifacts*, had been submitted to them for possible publication. No one else at that party (or probably in the world, except for my agent and the people at Poisoned Pen Press) knew this. Shortly after that psychic reading, Poisoned Pen Press bought *Artifacts*. Or, in other words, when that woman pulled those two names out the air, two people named Robert and Barbara were poised to change my life.

Is this proof? Not really. Barbara and Robert are not the two rarest names in the world. Still, I do think that the odds are heavily stacked against that psychic being lucky enough to guess two names that were, right that minute, much on my mind.

I know what you're thinking. You're asking me: "So what about Sam?" Well, the third name she called out wasn't really Sam. I'm keeping his name to myself, and I'm watchfully waiting. If somebody named "Sam" comes along and changes my life again, then this engineer might be forced to believe in magic.

To receive a free catalog of Poisoned Pen Press titles, please contact us in one of the following ways:

Phone: 1-800-421-3976
Facsimile: 1-480-949-1707
Email: info@poisonedpenpress.com
Website: www.poisonedpenpress.com

Poisoned Pen Press
6962 E. First Ave. Ste 103
Scottsdale, AZ 85251